THE DUKE AND THE WALLFLOWER

JESSIE CLEVER

SOMEDAY LADY PUBLISHING, LLC.

ISBN-13: 978-1-7333262-7-8

Cover Design by The Killion Group

We've all been Eliza, so this book is for you.

CHAPTER 1

$\mathcal{L}$ady Eliza Darby, daughter of the sixth Duke of Ravenwood, sister to the now seventh Duke of Ravenwood, was determined not to upset her stomach in the middle of the Duchess of Sudsbury's ball.

It would just be rude.

"I'm certain Viv will be considerate in her machinations," Louisa said from Eliza's left.

Johanna scoffed to her right. "When has Viv ever been considerate of anything that affected one of us?"

Louisa frowned. "Do be kind, Jo. You know Viv is only trying to protect us."

This roused Eliza from her determination to not upset her stomach across the ballroom floor.

"Protect us?" She shook her head. "She's not so much protecting us as hoping to keep us from finding our husbands abed with an opera singer like she did."

The words came out more forcefully than she had intended, her rattled nerves driving her usual cutting wit toward unsavory sarcasm. She pressed a hand to her stomach, willing it to settle.

Jo snorted in her lemonade and peered around sheepishly as if hoping no one spied her unladylike behavior. But as was the case with all of the Duchess of Sudsbury's events, the night was a crush, and no one was paying particular attention to the forgotten Darby sisters.

"Is that really something one can prevent another person from experiencing?" Louisa posed.

"Surely not," Jo responded, having recovered from her lemonade dousing. "I think that only serves to illustrate the futility of what she is trying to do."

Louisa shrugged. "I must commend her. After all, there's nothing to compel her to help us now that Andrew is the duke. It's rather perceptive of her to think he may not want three unwed sisters underfoot when searching for a wife."

Johanna lifted her chin. "I see nothing wrong with the matter. We are family after all. Andrew's duchess should accept us."

Eliza gave her younger sister a sharp look. "Are you mad? Even I find it difficult to accept us."

She didn't miss the soft laugh Louisa attempted to hide.

Jo frowned and rolled her glass of lemonade between her hands. "Still. I see nothing wrong with the current situation."

The current situation was three unwed sisters living in the home of their unattached brother, the Duke of Ravenwood now that Father had passed the previous year. With Mother succumbing to the influenza when Johanna was only two, it had left far too many females in the hands of an absentminded father to see them safely off and into society. That was why Viv was the only one of the Darby sisters to wed, and then only because Aunt Phyllis had been alive to sponsor her. Aunt Phyllis had promptly died before the next season, leaving Eliza without proper guidance. Father had tried, of course. Each girl had gotten...well, it resembled a season at least.

But as all three were still unwed, it was obvious their father's attempt had rather lacked in ambition.

Louisa leaned around Eliza to peer at Jo. "Of course, you don't. You have no wish to wed at all."

Jo opened her mouth to retort, but oddly, no sound emerged except for a gurgled word, a shadow of what might have been intelligible speech. Eliza blinked at her sister. Jo was the strong one, always quick to speak her mind no matter the consequences. For her to stumble so was...well, Eliza didn't know because she'd never witnessed it before then.

Louisa leaned into Eliza now to get a better look at Jo. "Johanna Elizabeth, do you really wish to wed?"

The sisters, Eliza included, had always assumed Jo's independent nature would not incline her to the married state, but perhaps they had been wrong. Viv would be only too pleased.

The conversation was momentarily suspended when Lady Setterton collided with them as she attempted to drag her poor daughter closer to the dancing. Eliza eyed the young woman, pity pouring through her at the poor girl's unusually yellow complexion.

Eliza had thought she was safely on the shelf until Viv had come stampeding back through the doors of Ravenwood House, a scorned woman determined to ensure her sisters did not meet the same fate. Now here she was again, feeling just as yellow as Lady Setterton's daughter appeared.

As she had already discussed with her sisters, Eliza could not determine how this plan was at all logical. But there was no reasoning with Viv once she'd set her mind to something, so that was that.

Eliza was taken down from the shelf, dusted off, and returned to the marriage mart much to her dismay. She was no fool after all. It wasn't that she hadn't received her fair share of marriage proposals from fortune hunters. As the daughter of a duke, she had a sizable dowry to tantalize most gentlemen in need of funds into ignoring the rest of it.

The horrible truth of the matter was the fact that Eliza had had the unfortunate circumstance of inheriting her father's visage.

When people were polite, they used the word *plain* to describe her. When they were not polite, well…she would rather forget what she'd been called.

Even to think on it had her hands going together, twisting the fine silk of her gloves against her knuckles. She wasn't entirely sure she could bear any more of this. Standing on the fringes of a society that had deemed her less even while her sister searched for a match for her. For poor Eliza with the hooked nose, thin lips, and bespectacled eyes too small for the rest of her face.

She forced her hands apart and squared her shoulders. If she kept her posture, her gown didn't hang so billowy on her overly thin frame, and perhaps whoever the suitor Viv found wouldn't notice her lack of…bits.

Her eyes drifted downward to her own chest before she could stop them, but she wrenched her gaze away when the wilted bit of lace Viv had stuffed into her décolletage earlier that evening stared back at her. No, she most sincerely was not fooling anyone about her lack of bits.

The momentary interruption must have derailed Louisa's thoughts because suddenly she said, "I'm sure Viv will select a most reasonable man for you, Eliza."

"A most reasonable man?" Jo gave an unladylike snort. "That sounds like an enticing future."

Louisa frowned and swatted a hand at her sister. "You are not helping at all. I'm sure there's someone here tonight that is utterly perfect for you."

And without hesitation, Louisa popped up on her toes to

scan over the top of the crowd. The ballroom was already teeming with the best the *ton* had to offer, and still names were announced one after the other in a waterfall of earls, marquesses, and barons.

Jo placed her empty glass of lemonade on the tray of a passing footmen.

She studied Eliza briefly, some sort of understanding passing over her features, before she turned away saying, "Someone sensible," as she scanned the other side of the ballroom.

"He would enjoy reading, of course," Louisa said, coming back down on her heels.

"Of course," Jo readily agreed. "And he'd be kind to animals."

Louisa brought her hands together in glee. "Oh, I bet he'll have a beloved hound."

Eliza swallowed the sudden surge of bile in her throat. Wasn't that what every girl dreamed of when she thought of her future husband? Not that he'd be dashing and strong and handsome. Not that his kiss would make her toes curl or that his touch could—

"Books and hounds is it then?" she whispered.

Louisa's eyes pinched until a line appeared between them. "Oh, Eliza, you know—"

Louisa reached a hand toward her, but Eliza took a step back, her chest squeezing in familiar pain for things she'd never have.

Eliza did know.

Standing there between her beautiful sisters, Eliza could feel her plainness like a cloak, too heavy and suffocating. She wiggled her shoulders, ensuring they were perfectly square before lifting her chin. She had to remember her goal in all of this silliness. She couldn't let her feelings of inadequacy or society's ideas of her cloud her thinking.

Because there *was* something she wanted out of all of this, and her looks wouldn't prevent it from happening.

Because every duke needed an heir.

"Perhaps we should catalog the dukes seeking wives this season and determine who it is Viv may select for my match," she said, her practical nature coming to the fore.

Louisa, ever the one to bolster a soul, clapped her hands together and turned once more to the crush about them.

"Let's see," she began.

Jo gave her one last slow look, a hint of understanding in her deep eyes once more before joining her sister's perusal of the crowd.

"Well, there's Lyndhurst," Louisa said.

"He breeds beagles." Jo turned with a bright smile to Eliza. Beagles.

Lovely.

"Bradley," Louisa continued but quickly wrinkled her nose. "Oh, but he smells like mushrooms. I had to dance a quadrille with him once." She laid a hand on Eliza's arm. "I'm sure Viv will consider such a thing and remove him from the prospects."

"Dunderton is a fool. Cheever is a silly boy." Jo rattled off the titles of dukes like items on the list Cook took to market every week. "Matthews isn't too bad, I should think."

Isn't too bad.

That was where she had landed. Her future depended on *isn't too bad.*

She clasped her hands together, twining her fingers until knuckle rubbed knuckle, willing her unspoken desires to go away.

Her desire for more.

For more than just a good match. For a respectable gentleman to call her husband. For a good name that would bolster the title of Ravenwood.

For a family of her own.

She had to keep her focus on that. Through all of this, from society's judgements to being treated like a specimen on the block, she had to remember what she would get in the end.

A babe to hold in her arms, a child to watch grow.

Someone to love her when no one else did.

She would be lucky to be anything other than spinster, and a loveless marriage was surely no cause for concern if it meant she would finally get the child she so desired.

"Nevins is a good man. I've heard Andrew say as much," Louisa said before falling back on her heels so quickly they made a snapping nose against the marble of the ballroom floor. "Oh." The syllable was so soft she may not have spoken it at all.

"What is it?" Eliza stepped forward, blood surging through her limbs as if discovering them for the first time.

Louisa slid a glance to Jo, a small smile tugging at her lips. Jo tilted her head before going up on her toes to see where Louisa had been looking. She landed flat on her feet with a soft snort as she tried to stop a smile from forming.

"Oh indeed," she breathed.

Eliza looked between the two of them. "Whatever is the matter?"

Defeated, Louisa let the smile come to her lips. "I had heard His Grace, the Duke of Ashbourne had returned to the marriage mart."

The blood drained from Eliza's head. Surely not. No. Viv couldn't—

Jo's smile was equally as filled with silly young girl nonsense. "The Jilted Duke, back for more." She peered around the crowd as if to catch a glimpse of him again. "I'm surprised he's having another go at it. What with what happened and all."

"What happened?" The question came out stilted, and both sisters gave her a blank stare. She put her hands to her hip. "You know I am not one to stay abreast of society gossip."

Jo shook her head. "This wasn't gossip. Ashbourne's jilting occurred in the middle of a ball for all of the *ton* to witness."

"He'd arranged the ball as a formal proposal to the woman he thought he had an understanding with. Only she didn't show." Louisa's smile slipped from her face, and the line appeared between her eyes again. "It was quite sad actually. She'd run off with his best friend to Gretna Green. Or so the rumors went." Louisa peered back over her shoulder where presumably they'd spotted the duke in question. "I can't imagine wishing to find a wife after that."

"I would think the marriageable ladies of society don't feel that way." Jo's smile tilted into a smirk.

"Whatever do you mean?" Eliza was not at all enjoying where their conversation was going.

Again, her sisters blinked at her with odd expressions.

"Because he's gorgeous," Jo blurted out.

Eliza's gaze darted to Louisa, who nodded emphatically.

"It's true. He's quite handsome. Any girl would be lucky to scoop him up. Mmmm, simply remarkable." She put one hand to her hip as she seemed to consider just how delectable the Duke of Ashbourne was.

Eliza regarded both of her sisters, seemingly lost in their own imaginings of snaring the Jilted Duke for themselves.

"I've never heard you speak like this," she finally said, and she heard exactly how silly she sounded.

Louisa's gaze snapped back first. "We speak like this all the time."

"We just figured you wouldn't care for such things, so we never invited you to join in," Jo clarified.

Eliza struggled to keep her mouth closed. "Do you really think about eligible gentlemen in these terms?"

They exchanged glances.

"Of course," Louisa said while Jo shrugged. "Why not?"

Because it was far more likely for Louisa and Jo to fetch a handsome husband and thus make the discussion of a man's attractiveness a likely subject for debate. Eliza's nerves settled with a thud in the pit of her stomach.

What had she to worry over truly? Viv would find a dull, suitable match for her and that would be it. She'd be married and with child within the year. She need only remember that when her nerves returned.

The crowd parted on a wave of emerald silk, and the sister of most importance that night spilled into their small square of ballroom floor.

Viv looked neither crumpled nor frazzled from having made her way through the crowd and simply pressed a hand to an errant strand of auburn hair along her forehead, pressing it back into place as if hurtling oneself through a ball required the most modest of exertions.

"There you three are," she said, running her hands along her skirts even though the emerald silk remained pristine. "I trust you have not wasted time chattering about over here and have filled your dance cards for the evening."

Louisa raised her hand, brandishing her dance card like a cat presented a dead mouse to its master, all pride and glee. "I've filled every slot with eligible young men worthy of a connection with Ravenwood."

Viv nodded. "Very good." And turned to Jo.

Jo brandished her dance card more like a weapon. "Filled to capacity, I'm afraid."

Viv frowned. "Do try to be a little optimistic."

"I can't," Jo returned. "It might crack my face."

Viv only blinked at her sister, clearly refusing to rise to the bait.

"Now then," she said, "you must both be sure to present well and with ample conversation." She turned with a pointed finger at Jo. "But not too *much* conversation."

And by this she meant for Jo to keep her mouth shut and smile and look pretty. Eliza wondered what this must be like. For someone to worry you may attract too much attention from a man.

But even as she considered it, she did not miss the fact that Viv had not asked about her dance card. It lay empty and untouched at her wrist. Just like it always did.

She pretended not to care. She feigned disinterest in dancing and usually found a seat with the spinsters along the peripheries of the ballrooms. It was safer that way.

Louisa, however, never missed anything.

"What about Eliza's dance card?"

Viv waved a dismissive hand. "I've already arranged a partner for her for the first waltz. The rest should be taken care of after that."

"A partner?" This from Jo.

"The rest of the dances?" From Louisa.

Eliza opened her mouth, determined to ask with whom it was she was supposed to partner but no sound emerged because just at that moment the first strands of a waltz permeated the air as the crowd around them began to shift. The people moving like water cutting around the bow of a schooner as if whoever came toward them propelled people from his path.

As if his reputation proceeded him.

Eliza swallowed, but it was too late.

The Jilted Duke stepped from the crowd, his gaze directed squarely at her.

"Your Grace." Viv smiled and extended a curtsy. "May I introduce my sister, Lady Eliza Darby?"

Eliza knew she was meant to curtsy. She was meant to bow in respect. She was meant to—something, but she couldn't move, her mind absorbed with only one thought.

Louisa and Jo were right.

The Duke of Ashbourne was gorgeous.

* * *

THE RUMORS WERE CORRECT.

Lady Eliza Darby had a rather unfortunate face.

She was skinny, so much so her gown hung on her like a mill sack. Her face was dwarfed by enormous gold spectacles that sat atop a perfectly hooked nose. Her mouth was hardly there, and he suspected at any moment her hair would explode free of its pins in a riotous mass of frizzy, dull brown hair.

He had never seen anything more perfect in his life.

He bowed. "Lady Eliza, it is an honor to make your acquaintance."

When he straightened, he saw her mouth had gone slack, a strange garbled noise emanating from its depths.

Perhaps the girl was stricken by periods of muteness. Even more promising.

The Duchess of Margate stepped in. "My sister is honored you would select her as your partner for the first waltz."

He smiled but stopped when it became apparent it may cause physical harm to the plain Darby sister.

Oh, she was marvelous indeed.

He turned the smile on the duchess instead. "Yes, of course. I could not think of a better partner."

Truer words.

He held out his arm. "Shall we?"

Panic surged for but a moment when he realized she may not be well enough to take his arm. He encountered similar behavior in other debutantes overwhelmed by his presence, but the chance at a duke usually righted their senses with alacrity. While the girl did step forward and slip her hand onto his arm, her expression didn't clear.

Was that fear he saw in her eyes?

The notion unsettled him, but he couldn't allow it countenance. He very much needed a bride, one specifically suited to his needs, and it was only luck that would have returned the unfortunate Darby sister to the marriage mart that season. He didn't know why he hadn't thought of her before the duchess had approached him. She would play the part splendidly.

He turned her onto the dance floor and slipped his hand about her waist as was proper.

The gasp that escaped her lips was anything but however.

He paused, the slightest hesitation he knew no one else would have seen, but she felt it. Her eyes flew to his, and he *knew* she felt it.

What was happening here?

The sound she had made, the barest of...whimpers? As if she were so unused to being touched that the simple, chaste positioning of his hand at her waist elicited a vocal response.

A twinge pinched his chest, and he sucked in a breath, slipping them into the first step of the waltz as if physical movement would propel him from the traitorous feelings that surged through him in so innocuous and brief a moment.

How many other ladies had he swept into a waltz without similar reaction? With nothing more than the cool, focused step of a well-bred lady assuming a dance with an eligible partner?

It was several measures into the dance before he ventured conversation.

"I understand you're fond of hounds, Lady Eliza."

Her frown was swift, and he wondered how so few words could garner such a reaction.

Perhaps Lady Eliza was not what she appeared.

"I am," she said, and that was all. The first and only words he'd heard come from her lips.

"I see. I'm quite fond of them myself." He tried another smile, and this time she didn't coil in fear.

Indeed, she lifted her chin and met his gaze with uncomfortable focus.

"Just what kind of hounds are you fond of, Your Grace?"

He blinked. "I'm sorry?"

"If you're so fond of hounds, you should know which types suit you best. So please. Regal me with your knowledge of hounds."

"I…" He'd never before been so quickly cut down by a woman, and he didn't know quite what to say. "I beg your pardon. I was told you enjoyed the company of a good canine—"

"So you claim to enjoy hounds in order to pander to an apparent interest I have? How good of you, Your Grace."

If he had not been so well schooled on the required steps of a waltz, he might have floundered then. Instead he turned her neatly about the floor, perfectly synchronized with the couples about them.

Never before had a lady treated him with such…

Honesty.

"I'm afraid you've trapped me in the truth, Lady Eliza. But for what it's worth, I've never encountered a lady who would object to such pandering. It's my understanding the attention of a duke is worth the cost."

Something passed over her eyes, but he was too unfamiliar with her expressions yet to know what it was.

"If the cost is self-respect, then I'm happy to say I shan't pay the price."

He did falter then. The slightest hesitation in the turn of a foot, but their momentum carried them nicely into the next turn.

"I admit it's rather tiresome to tediously converse with young ladies schooled in the expectations of the opposite sex. I'm rather surprised to discover your candor. I should think a lady such as yourself has been well trained on what her future husband would expect."

Her eyes flashed. Even through her ghastly spectacles, he could see it.

"And are you to be my future husband?"

The question was bold, but from her, he was coming to understand it was not unexpected.

"I believe we have not been acquainted long enough for us to have reached such a conclusion."

The lady scoffed, turning her head as she bit her lower lip.

"We are both aware of my sister's machinations in this dance, and I am one to call a horse a horse if that's what it is, Your Grace."

It was unfortunate timing that the last strains of the waltz died away, leaving them suspended on the edge of the ballroom, opposite from where he'd discovered her with her sisters. As a gentleman he was required to return her, but as a man, he wasn't yet finished speaking to her. A perplexing thought, and one he didn't wish to have. Not about his prospective bride.

His prospective bride was to fit into a nice bundle he could discard when he was finished with her. Lady Eliza Darby suggested nothing was neat about her. From her riotous hair to her too large spectacles, she defied convention but it wasn't from a desire to flaunt. Rather, Lady Eliza exuded an air of indifference. She quite simply had better things to do than bow to the demands of society.

He offered her his arm to turn about the room. She didn't hesitate this time as she laid her hand atop his arm.

"I believe your sister did mention something of the sort." He nodded to an acquaintance from his club as they passed, not missing the man's raised eyebrow and quick turn to his partner, his lips already moving on a salacious whisper. Dax kept them moving.

"I should think her suggestion would be rather unnecessary. We are two eligible individuals at a ball. Isn't that what these gatherings are for?"

When she delivered it so bluntly, the ball lost a little of its glamour. Not that he thought of it in those terms to begin. Balls had been anything but glamorous since that day so many years before when he'd found himself standing in the pit of his own humiliation. Balls were nothing more than a necessary evil when his position required his attendance and a damned nuisance when he wanted nothing more than to avoid them.

"It is at that," he said.

The crowd shuffled about them as new partners matched up to begin the next dance, and he moved them expertly between passersby. He couldn't help but notice the sidelong glances and surreptitious peeks. It was quite something he was sure to see Lady Eliza Darby on the arm of the Jilted Duke.

He hadn't meant to cause such a ripple, but it wasn't to be avoided, he supposed. Lady Eliza would not have been the obvious choice for the bride to a duke, but that was exactly why she was so perfect.

He studied Lady Eliza beside him. Her chin was firm and

tilted slightly upward as if she struggled to see through her enormous spectacles. Her shoulders were wound tightly back, and from this position, her gown didn't hang so shapelessly. But her gaze was steady before them, seeming to not see their gawkers. Or if he were truly coming to understand her, she didn't care to see them.

"Do you spend most of your time in London?"

The question startled him for its practicality. Never before had a debutante, or other female acquaintance, asked such a relevant question.

"I spend a good deal of time in London, yes. The title requires my presence in Parliament for the term as you likely know."

She nodded. "Do you have a country seat you prefer?"

His glance lingered a little longer on her profile. "I have a home to the south of London on the shore. It's a lovely respite from the crowds of the city."

You would like it.

He wasn't sure where the thought came from, and it was only luck that he hadn't said it aloud. But he realized with sudden certainty that Lady Eliza Darby would do well at Ashbourne Manor perched along the cliffs as it was.

There was plenty of room for hounds.

He stopped abruptly when they were mere feet from her sisters. He'd only need take a few more steps, and his duties this night would be through. He'd made contact with his prospective bride, exchanged pleasantries, and been seen dancing with her by nearly the entire *ton.* He could hurry off to his club now and sink into the welcoming arms of a good whiskey.

And yet he stopped. Compelled to prolong this interlude with the unexpected Lady Eliza Darby.

She turned, her expression blank as she viewed him. He

wondered at that. Wondered what it would take to spark interest in her eyes.

He shouldn't be thinking of such things for they didn't matter but then he heard himself ask, "What kind of hounds are you fond of, Lady Eliza?"

She considered him, and for the first time in his life, he felt the prickling finger of scrutiny. No one scrutinized a duke, let alone a wallflower.

She seemed satisfied with whatever it was she found and said, "Landrace collies."

His arm fell away from hers. "That's a working dog."

She nodded crisply. "Of course it is. That's what makes them such fun."

Fun.

He'd never before heard a lady describe dogs as fun. Gown shopping, attending a musicale, selecting hair ribbons, most certainly. Dogs? No. A prickle of unease began at the back of his neck, but for the first time since he'd laid eyes on her, her expression softened. While she wasn't smiling, she was far warmer than she'd been for the duration of their dance.

He should have ended it there and fled. Selected a different wallflower from this year's offerings. One who elicited absolutely no response from him at all.

For Eliza Darby was eliciting far too much from him.

And it scared him.

But instead of fleeing, he did the unthinkable.

He took a step closer to her.

The ballroom was filled to capacity and then more, and no one would have cause to comment, but now he stood far too close to Lady Eliza, and her eyes went wide with the realization.

He was close enough to smell her, and she smelled like…

Soap.

Debutantes splattered themselves with all kinds of nonsense thinking to lure in a gentleman. Lavender, rose water, and lemon. But not Lady Eliza. She smelled like freshly laundered sheets and sunshine.

Dear God. He had to get out of there.

But instead he tipped forward, so close now he could have...kissed her.

Once again something flashed over her eyes, and he yearned to know what it was. Right then, standing in the middle of Lady Sudsbury's ball, he vowed to find out exactly what each and every one of her expressions meant.

"Lady Eliza," he whispered her name. Despite the deafening crush of the crowd, he was close enough now that the whisper was stark and pronounced between them. "*Why* are you so fond of dogs?"

He knew the question struck her for she hesitated, but she didn't retreat. If anything her shoulders grew more taut, her chin traveling up another degree, her gaze focused directly on his.

In the short few minutes of their dance, he had come to understand Lady Eliza was a formidable opponent. Her sharp tongue surprised him, her wit even more.

But her next words—they slayed him.

"Because it's nice to have someone who always wants to be with you."

He willed his gut to unclench as he watched her retreat through the crowd.

CHAPTER 2

"*W*e're going to end up in the gossip columns."

"Isn't that what—*umph*—you want?" Johanna fell against the window sash as they jockeyed for positions around the drawing room's front windows the next day when the Duke of Ashbourne arrived quite unexpectedly.

Viv rested her chin on her folded hand, one arm braced against the other as she peered down into the street as the Duke of Ashbourne alighted from his sleek black curricle. "I wanted all of you safely and respectfully married. Not the subject of tattling tongues."

"I'm not certain you can have one without the other," Louisa pointed out.

Eliza was glad for their conversation for it distracted her sisters from seeing her obvious discomfort. If she weren't careful, she was sure to rip her gown asunder from plying the folds of her skirt between both clenched fists. She willed herself to let go, forcing her mind to focus only on the things she knew.

Ashbourne was a skilled dancer. He was polite and respected. He had all his teeth.

If she caught a whiff of his scent just once more she would most definitely fall to her knees in surrender.

She had been so busy preparing herself for his physical nearness, she had not known to prepare herself for the alluring quality of his scent.

She glanced down at her rough collie, Henry, sitting lovingly at her feet, his head pressed to her thigh. He returned her gaze with his quiet, soulful dark eyes as if to say he understood the attractive quality of scent.

She scratched absently between his ears and felt his sigh against her leg.

Viv turned from the window.

"Come, girls. Let's prepare to receive him." She took a seat on the sofa, spreading her skirts appropriately.

Louisa followed obediently, perching on the end of a chair, her eyes glittering in the direction of the door. Johanna followed more sluggishly, choosing a chair just outside of the main seating area, keeping her back slightly to the door.

Eliza did not move at all. She stood where she'd been sorting her watercolors on top of the piano by the window where the light was good. She had hopes of completing her collection of rabbit illustrations soon and wanted to check once more that she'd captured all of the necessary scenes.

And sorting watercolors kept her mind busy enough to forget about the Duke of Ashbourne.

About the way her heart had leapt at the simple touch of his hand at her waist.

At the way his smile reached naturally across his face and how she yearned to absorb just a little of that happiness.

There was a cleft in his chin, and for whatever absurd reason, she wanted to place a single finger there as if to mark her spot. Heat burned across her cheeks instantly, and she willed herself to distraction.

Her brain skittered, recalling the events that had earned him the name of Jilted Duke.

Surely a man so scorned would not be smiling so if he had not recovered from the embarrassment.

She looked down at her rendition of a bunny hopping through ferns, pushing the thought aside.

It didn't matter what Ashbourne felt. It had no bearing on her whatsoever.

"Eliza, do come sit. You should be ready to receive your guest when Mallard presents him." Viv motioned for her to take the chair opposite and most advantageously positioned near the door.

She straightened her watercolors, reassuring herself once more that the Duke of Ashbourne was of no concern to her when the sound of a door closing down the hall shot through the stillness of the drawing room like an arrow piercing the center of its target.

Viv shot to her feet, her skirts falling about her in a rush of muslin. Louisa got to her feet with far more gentility, but Johanna not only surged to her feet but ran the few steps to stand between her sisters.

"He's gone to see Andrew."

Johanna needn't have whispered it so scandalously. Eliza's heart already threatened to pop directly out of her chest. Henry whimpered at her side, and she absently scratched his head again, her watercolors completely forgotten.

She left the sanctuary of the piano, moving toward the safety of her sisters, her eyes unable to leave the door, her ears straining to hear even the slightest noise.

"He wouldn't—" The words stuck in her throat like a chimney sweep's broom in a clogged flue. "He wouldn't be asking for my hand already. Would he?" She asked the question of Viv, the most experienced of all the sisters, but her eyes refused to leave the door.

She felt Louisa's hand touch her arm even as she couldn't look to acknowledge the comfort.

Viv shook her head. "He can very well do what he wishes. He is a duke after all." The cynicism in her voice was not missed by Eliza and likely not her sisters, but none of them commented.

Minutes passed, and none of the Darby sisters moved. The door was like a siren, and they were victims to its call.

Henry resumed his place next to Eliza, and she set a hand atop his hand, drawing comfort in the familiar roughness of his coat, the way his heat seemed to calm her nerves. Somewhere a clock ticked. Carriages rattled by on the street outside. Louisa swallowed. That's how deathly still they were. She could hear her sister swallow beside her.

Finally, somewhere in the bowels of the house, footsteps. They were so faint and yet, so unmistakably clear.

Someone was coming.

"It's Andrew." Louisa gasped.

"Quick. We mustn't act as though we've been waiting." Viv waved her hands at the seats.

"I should hardly think that's necessary." Johanna remained where she was, moving only to put her hands on her hips.

Viv frowned. "Why ever not?"

As soon as the question was asked, the door opened. It was as if a locomotive had careened into the drawing room, leaving a trail of grease all across the Aubusson rugs.

But it was only Mallard.

"Because we didn't hear Andrew's door open," Johanna said with a polite smile for the butler.

Viv slowly closed her eyes, never one to show her frustration with her younger sisters. Eliza scratched at Henry's head furiously, and he pushed at her hand with his nose. She looked down at him apologetically.

"I thought you might want for some fresh tea, Your Grace," he said with a bow to Viv.

She smiled, folding her hands in her lap. "That would be quite wonderful. Thank you, Mallard." She said nothing more but tilted her head ever so much to the right.

Mallard gave a nod and without further prompting said, "His Grace has granted an audience to the Duke of Ashbourne. He asked specifically for the duke upon his arrival."

Viv's smile broadened. "Very good, Mallard. Thank you."

The butler withdrew, and as if his existence pulled the oxygen from the room with him, Louisa let out a magnificent sigh.

"This is entirely too much." She turned to Eliza, her gaze penetrating. "Whatever did you speak of with the duke to cause such a swift reaction?"

"Hounds." The word propelled itself from her lips. The only thing she could really say.

For how was she to tell her sisters the simple touch of his hand at her waist had made her...whimper? The memory of his scent haunted her? The warm browns of his eyes reminded her of...Henry's.

She gave herself a mental shake.

He hardly reminded her of a dog. That wasn't the case. But his eyes.

God, his eyes went on forever.

She didn't know that was possible in a creature other than a dog.

She moved closer to the center of the room, skirting the chair where Johanna had resumed her roost.

"Why would it be so hard to believe I could not instill a

sense of urgency in the duke?" She hadn't meant to ask the question, and she should never have asked it so forcefully of her poor sister. Not Louisa anyway. Louisa had not a single mean bone in her entire body.

So why was Eliza suddenly so defensive?

Louisa's smile tipped to one side. "Urgency?" She took an eager step toward Eliza. "Is that what you felt with the duke? Oh, you must explain."

Viv leaned back in the sofa to peer up at her. "Urgency? What sort of urgency?"

This time Eliza shook her head for all to see, holding up her hands as if to physically stop the questions. "This is getting out of hand. I hadn't meant any urgency at all."

"Well, that's good to hear as the duke is quite urgent in his request."

All eyes flew to the door.

They had not heard the door open or Andrew enter as they had been too busy arguing, or rather not arguing, with one another.

The very air slipped from Eliza's lungs like a scared pup, and she was left with a mouth hanging half open on a sentence she could no longer remember.

Viv came to her feet. "He's asked for her hand then."

Andrew slid her a glance, but his eyes returned to Eliza without pause. "If you would excuse us, I must speak with Eliza in private."

Johanna stepped up behind her. "I think we should stay." She put her hand on Eliza's shoulder, drawing a small growl from Henry.

Eliza quickly patted his head to let him know it was all right, but it needn't matter. Andrew was adamant.

"I think not. I wish to speak to Eliza privately. For her sake."

Viv gestured to Louisa and Johanna. "Come then, ladies. We mustn't keep the duke waiting."

Louisa maintained eye contact with her brother as she dragged her feet in the direction of the door while Johanna was a little more obvious about it.

She stepped up to Andrew and poked him in the chest. "You better do what's right by Eliza, dear brother." She didn't wait for a reply and followed Louisa out the door.

Viv never moved.

Henry whined next to her, and Eliza put her hand on his head, unsure herself.

Andrew tilted his head. "Viv?"

She blinked. "Surely you don't mean to make me leave as well?"

Andrew returned his gaze to Eliza, his gaze steady, studying. "I do mean. This is Eliza's future. Not yours."

Viv squared her shoulders. "But I may offer some assistance—"

"Out." The single word was a bark, and as Andrew had never been the barking sort, Viv left without another word.

The door clicked shut. Such a simple sound to mark Eliza's fate.

She removed her hand from Henry's head, not wanting to tear out the poor dog's fur unknowingly as she heard what Andrew had to say.

"The Duke of Ashbourne has requested your hand in marriage."

That was about what she expected him to say and still— her heart sped up a bit.

She'd known since Viv had returned to Ravenwood House that her fate was unerringly being pushed in the direction of marriage, but she never believed it would happen so quickly.

And with the Jilted Duke no less.

"I see," she said because it appeared as though Andrew wished for a response.

"He offers a favorable agreement and has accepted the terms of your dowry." The way he said it made her sound as though he'd negotiated with Ashbourne over how to divvy up the parts of a prized steer.

Eliza could have done worse.

"Well, then it's all arranged, I should think." While the words slipped from her lips with ease, her mind raced, poking at the dark recesses, searching, prodding, for...something.

They were determining her future right at that very moment, and her mind was an utter blank.

All she could remember was how the Duke of Ashbourne smelled.

How he had touched her.

How he had attempted to hide a smile from her.

She knew better than to hope that one day he may love her. Men did not fall in love with women like Eliza. But perhaps one day she may find contentment. And that was far greater than anything she could have hoped for only just yesterday.

Andrew drew closer to her. He was tall as their father had been but he had their mother's coloring. Soft browns, deep eyes, and a wide smile.

In a startling flash, she realized Andrew just might be a catch for some other debutante that season. It made her smile at the thought.

But then Andrew spoke. "You know I would never agree to this without your consent, Eliza, and I must say—" He stopped as if he'd run out of words entirely.

"The Jilted Duke is an odd choice for a marriage partner?" she suggested.

Andrew frowned. "To put it plainly."

This did make her smile as Andrew was singularly the most irritated family member when it came to her wit.

"I would agree it is rather unorthodox, but aside from the business with his previous attempt at a proposal, I should say the Duke of Ashbourne is respectable, well liked in his circles, and an exemplarily member of Parliament."

Andrew cocked an eyebrow. "You know of his record in Parliament?"

She gave an aborted wave. "I've read of him in the papers, of course."

Andrew did not like his sisters reading the papers either, and this drew a deeper frown from him. It wasn't that Andrew did not think his sisters were entitled to be well informed and educated. Rather he *feared* his sisters being well informed and educated as any smart man would.

"So then you are inclined to accept his proposal?" The skepticism was not missed in his voice.

Something glided over her then, like a soft blanket tossed over a sleeping child, falling to cover its form in a silent shield of slumber. Inevitability. That was what it was. In that instance she could see her whole life spread out before her, neatly planned and determined by her simple acceptance of the Duke of Ashbourne's suit.

If it were so simple, why was her stomach twisted about itself?

Sandalwood.

He smelled of sandalwood.

But there was something else there.

For a blinding moment, it occurred to her she could very well fall in love with the Duke of Ashbourne based only on his scent.

It was a ludicrous idea but once thought it was there.

She had no business falling in love with the man. He would never love her, and it would only cause her pain.

But was the pain of being unloved worse than the pain of being utterly alone?

She looked at Henry.

Never alone. Not when she had Henry.

She raised her eyes to Andrew. "Yes. Yes, I am inclined to accept his proposal."

Andrew didn't move right away. It was as if he cataloged his thoughts as he stood there before her. He must have reached a satisfactory conclusion for he stepped back, gave a neat bow.

"I shall send Ashbourne in then to speak with you directly as is our custom."

She smiled, grateful that the Darby men considered the feelings of the women in their family when it came to matters directly affecting them.

Andrew stopped his retreat, turned back, and pulled her into an unexpected hug. While their family was close, they weren't ones to engage in physical affection, and the gesture surprised her. It was a beat before she remembered to fold her arms around him. He backed up nearly as quickly as he'd come and left.

Henry whined beside her, the noise soft and questioning. She knelt to properly scratch at his ears and nuzzle her nose against his.

"It's all right, lad," she whispered. "I'm sure he'll like you just as well as I do."

She knew that couldn't possibly be true. No one could love Henry more than she did. She straightened and brushed at her skirts, shedding the strands of dog hair that had become affixed to the muslin.

That was why she didn't see Ashbourne enter. That was why Henry's growl was unexpected.

That was why she didn't catch the dog before he launched himself at the Jilted Duke.

* * *

THE LADY DID INDEED HAVE a fondness for hounds.

This was the thought that zipped through his brain as the largest, hairiest beast he'd ever witnessed on four paws flew through the air, jaws wide, fangs glinting in the morning sun, his enormous bite ready to clench around Dax's most vulnerable parts.

But the bite never came.

Instead a piercing whistle split the air, and the command, "Touch!" rang through the room.

As none of what Dax had been about that day made any particular sense to him, this course of events fit in perfectly.

When his senses righted and he was able to take in the room again, he saw the dog had retreated at the sound of the whistle, spun about in mid-lunge, and returned to press his nose into his mistress's hand.

Dax blinked, one thought tumbling over another, but none clearer than this.

If she had the power to quell the natural instinct of a herding dog with the mere pursing of her lips, he had absolutely no hope of surviving this marriage.

That prickle of awareness surged along the back of his neck once more.

"A landrace collie, I presume?" He stood perfectly still, not wishing to incite the beast any further.

Eliza's brow creased, a study in curious bemusement. "He's never done that before." The words were spoken so softly, so proudly, he felt guilty for having heard them. But then she straightened, meeting his gaze directly as he was finding she did with regular frequency. "This is Henry. He's a Scottish collie of the rough haired variety."

"Scottish?" He tried a smile, and the dog emitted a low

growl. He dropped his face into a neutral position. "How wild."

"Scottish collies are some of the hardest working dogs and excel at agility and herding." Her words were solid, certain, and while she had not raised her voice in the slightest, he felt properly scolded.

"Henry, you say?" Another low growl.

Eliza put her hands to her hips and oddly enough, turned her attention to the dog. "Really, Henry, you've exhibited your prowess quite enough for one day. Do you have a bit of mutton or ham perhaps?"

It was a moment before he realized this last part was directed at him. He patted his pockets before he gathered the absurdity of her question.

"I seem to be completely out of either. How thoughtless of me." He gestured to her. "Do you carry around bits of meat with you?"

He was coming to understand Lady Eliza was far different than most of the debutantes he encountered, and perhaps a question such as the one he'd just posed involving meats wasn't so outlandish. A flicker of concern flared inside of him, but it was promptly extinguished when he recalled his goal. A wife who carried meat morsels in her pockets was not one with whom he would ever be in danger of falling in love.

A single eyebrow appeared above the frame of her gold spectacles. "I should hardly think that prudent, Your Grace."

His expression fell. So she thought it outlandish too. Perhaps she jested with him.

He cleared his throat. This was going to be more difficult than he had first surmised.

"Lady Eliza, I do hope you are well, and I do beg your pardon for calling so unexpectedly after so soon making your acquaintance."

"You're not sorry at all." She scratched absently at the head of her dog—what had she called him? Henry?—but her expression remained focused and attentive.

"I'm sorry?"

"Precisely." She withdrew her hand, folding them both against her stomach. "You're not at all sorry. My brother informs me that you have come here with intentions. I believe it is best if we speak of them now. There's no need to carry this on any longer than necessary."

He couldn't help but smile at her quiet practicality. He recalled only too well her forthrightness at Lady Sudsbury's ball, and that tickle of unease went through him. He dropped his gaze to the dog who lounged deceptively against her side, and her parting words rushed back to him.

What had happened to Lady Eliza that caused her to draw such comfort from a dog?

He moved his gaze to her face, unerringly finding those ever-changing eyes she hid behind those damned lenses. He shouldn't be so interested. Even more, she shouldn't stir such concern in him. Wasn't the whole intent of his plan to seek a wife who stirred nothing within him?

He cleared his throat. "I can see the wisdom in that, Lady Eliza."

She moved her chin up a notch. "Eliza."

He studied her, and he was suddenly struck with the realization that her pronouncement had taken a great deal out of her. Any number of widows and lonely wives had invited him to call them by their given names, usually when he was between their thighs, and yet this was likely the most difficult thing Lady Eliza had ever attempted, asking him to call her by her given name. He couldn't help it when his gaze dropped to the dog again.

"Eliza." He said the word like it were a token, a magical

incantation. His hands shook ever so slightly, and sweat trickled down the back of his neck.

This was to be a simple proposal of marriage. When he'd set out that morning, he had been exuberant with the idea he would soon have exactly what he needed—an unattractive wife with whom he could beget an heir without ever being in danger of falling in love with her. And now he shook from simply saying her name?

He swallowed. "Eliza—"

He took a step forward and immediately realized his mistake. Henry bristled, his jowls flapping with a growl.

"Stop." The word was clipped, and it took him a moment to realize it was directed at him. "Henry clearly perceives you as some kind of danger. Will you excuse me for one moment?"

He blinked. "You're leaving?"

She had walked to the other side of the sofa that aligned the seating area in the room, and she paused as if his question startled her.

"Do you wish to have this conversation with your dignity intact?"

He squelched the smile that came to his lips at her words. "Yes, I believe I would."

She nodded and left, the dog trailing after her.

He wasn't alone for long. Surely not long enough for him to contemplate what his turmoil of emotions meant because soon she returned with Henry bounding after her.

"You brought him back?"

She eyed him sharply. "Of course, I did. If the two of you are to live peacefully together, he must learn you're not a threat."

Delicious tension coiled in the pit of his stomach at her words, and he realized with a jolt exactly what kind of threat he was thinking of and that would not do at all.

"Live together?"

She had been making odd hand gestures to the dog who'd responded by going flat on his belly on the floor, and she turned fearful eyes to him.

"You did speak with my brother about my hand in marriage, did you not?"

"Yes, I did but—"

"Well, if you should still desire my hand, then you should know Henry is coming with me. There is no question in regards to that."

He considered the dog, now prone on the ground and staring adoringly up at his mistress.

"I can see that now, but—"

Her hands dropped, and she looked away so quickly he missed the expression on her face.

"I see then. You've changed your mind. Come, Henry. We shan't take up any more of the duke's time."

He reached for her before he realized the error of it. He had thought the dog placid at his mistress's feet but at his first reach, the dog lunged, surging to his feet and plunging toward Dax.

"Henry." Eliza did not shout. She didn't even raise her voice.

She turned ever so slightly and very slowly held out her hand. She was giving him something. He kept his eyes on Henry as he slowly reached out a hand. The dog growled, softly, menacingly, but there wasn't anything aggressive about the noise. It was more defensive, a warning to whomever might hurt his mistress.

Something slightly slimy and smelling of salt landed in his palm. He finally averted his gaze to see what it was.

Ham.

He looked up and wished he hadn't.

Unshed tears shone in Eliza's eyes, the kind that spring

up involuntarily in reaction to a palpable hurt. He'd done that. He'd put those tears there because she thought he had changed his mind.

He forgot about the dog. He forgot about the piece of ham in his hand and leaned forward.

"Eliza—"

Henry let out a warning growl, harsher and deeper this time.

He hesitated. "Eliza—"

The dog took the smallest of steps forward.

"Give him the ham." She said the words with a low urgency, but guilt gnawed at him.

He turned and thrust out his hand to the dog, which again was the wrong thing to do. The dog moved to snap at his fingers before he must have caught a sniff of the ham because the snap turned into a lick. Immediately, Henry put his butt down, head up in a perfect sit, his gaze once more peaceful.

"Here." This time Eliza thrust the piece of ham into his hand, and her fingers gently brushed his palm. That tiniest of touches sparked something within him, and he hurriedly gave the ham to Henry.

Henry licked satisfyingly at his jowls, the ham gone in an instant. He adjusted his great paws and looked up as if expecting more.

"Henry is very protective of me. He just needs to know you're a friend." Eliza's words were rushed, so unlike the calm, cunning woman he was beginning to know.

He grabbed her. He just had to stop the flow of words.

Henry whined now, but he didn't try to bite him, thank God. Instead, Eliza's expression turned to stone. Her eyes went wide behind her lenses, and her small mouth all but disappeared as she sucked her lips in.

He remembered that ghost of a whimper when he'd

touched her the night before in a way far more proper than this, and something sliced through him, hot and devouring.

"Eliza, I have not changed my mind. I simply didn't realize you had a dog at all. Henry will love Ashbourne Manor."

At the sound of his name, Henry thumped his tail against the floor as if he understood whatever that was being said of him was a positive thing.

The tears never slid their way from Eliza's eyes, and he wondered at the strength there. How many other times had she been condemned because of her appearance alone? How many other times had she been rejected? Found wanting? He could easily forget the fragility that lay beneath her sharp tongue, and he would do better not to forget it.

"You have not changed your mind."

It wasn't a question, and he wondered if she spoke aloud as to reassure herself.

"I have not." The words breathed out of him like the last puff of energy he held.

This was a far cry from the day he had imagined, but it struck him suddenly that perhaps it was better.

He held Eliza by the arms, and she stood mere inches from him so he could see the flecks of gold in her irises even behind the lenses of her spectacles. There was a small freckle by her left ear. Without thinking he let his gaze wander, and before he knew what he was about, he'd firmly imagined her wild hair loosened from its pins and blowing in the wind that swept along the cliffs of Ashbourne Manor. It suddenly wasn't frizzy at all. It was wild and thick and luxurious, he just knew it.

He swallowed. This was not good. This was not good at all.

"Then I accept," she said.

He forgot for an instant what it was she was agreeing to before he remembered he'd asked for her hand.

Later he would blame her hair and the transfixing quality it possessed, because otherwise, he couldn't think of why he did what he did.

Because he said, "Then we should seal the bargain with a kiss, shan't we?"

CHAPTER 3

$\mathcal{W}$as that how one agreed to an offer of marriage?

Viv had not warned her of such.

Eliza would have felt inadequate if she had simply not dismissed the entire subject of relationships such as these as a matter with which she would have very little interaction.

"Is that customary?" The question seemed like a reasonable one, but a smile tipped the corners of Ashbourne's mouth.

She wondered now if she might have made a misstep in inviting him to call her by her given name, but it was tedious to hear him say her moniker over and over like that when it was highly unnecessary. Except he hadn't reciprocated the gesture, and she was left feeling hollow and unsure. No matter. As long as she could keep her mouth shut and maintain a civil distance from him until they were wed, she could get this matter over quickly.

And then she would have her baby.

There was just this kissing matter to get out of the way.

"I should think when two people pledge their lives to one another a sign of mutual respect is not out of line."

She tilted her head. "This is hardly a pledge, Your Grace. You arranged the matter with my brother. I'm simply lucky to be the daughter of a forward-thinking family that allowed me to have a say on the subject."

"Dax."

She blinked. "I beg your pardon."

"You may address me by my given name."

Her eyes widened. "Your given name is Dax? I thought you had sneezed or something."

His laugh was startling, and Henry tensed beside her. She wiggled just enough in Ashbourne's grasp to scratch at the dog's head.

"The full name is Daxton Phillip Wilmington Kane, but my mother shortened it to Dax when she tired of calling out the entire thing in reprimand."

"You were a naughty boy?" It was supposed to have been a curious question, but something tightened Ashbourne's features, and he licked his lips nervously. How odd.

"Something like that."

His face was marvelous. She had been overcome by the beauty of it, but now that the novelty had passed, she could better observe his features. He had a rather square face, and for once, she understood what artists meant when someone had a chiseled face. Ashbourne looked like he may have erupted straight from granite for the hard lines of his forehead and jaw. There was the cleft in his chin she found particularly remarkable, and his eyes were so, so deep.

While his features were lovely to gaze upon, she was finding his change of mood and the way it translated on those features to be of far more interest. For example, he quite clearly was in pain now from the line that appeared between his brows, and she thought it likely it had something to do with the thought of having to kiss her.

She tried to step back, but he held her too tightly.

"It's quite all right, but I shall not hold you to the custom."

"I'm sorry?"

"The customary kiss. Do not feel obligated to perform the ritual. Our agreement on the matter suits me."

His laugh was softer this time.

"It isn't so much a custom."

She was close enough to smell a hint of coffee on his breath and something spicy, like cinnamon. She leaned in, just a little, hoping to catch that tantalizing whiff of sandalwood, but his words drew her back.

"It isn't a custom? Then why would you suggest it?"

His eyes clouded, and she wondered if she'd said something wrong.

"You're questioning why a man would want to kiss you?"

"Well, it's never happened before, so if it's not a custom, I can't think of a reason why you would want to."

Once again his eyes took on the quality so much like a dog, deep and fathomless. Something she had said had caused him to think and whatever it was, he did not seem to like where his thoughts took him.

"You've never been kissed?"

"What an absurd question. Of course, I have not."

His hands dropped away from her, and she swayed ever so slightly at the loss of his strength. Her stomach rolled at the sensation.

"What is absurd about it?" His eyes had come back to her, sharp and focused.

She gestured to her person. "Are you quite serious?"

His frown could have frozen lava.

"I see nothing amiss that would prevent a gentleman from attempting to procure a kiss."

She returned his frown. "You do not need to waste pleasantries on me, Your Grace. I know very well how plain I am. The term used is wallflower although I cannot see why. I think wallflowers are quite pretty. I understand we may choose to stand on the periphery of gatherings as wallflowers enjoy climbing walls at the edge of the garden for growth, but I still cannot ascertain its application to one's appearance." She shrugged. "Be that as it may I see no point for this kiss if it's not customary."

She may have gone and dumbfounded him now for he did not speak. He blinked several times and licked his lips again.

Finally, he spoke. "Allow me to be absolutely certain. You're saying there is no reason I should want to kiss you other than a demand of custom or ritual that calls for such an action."

"Yes, that's quite precisely what I'm saying."

He crossed his arms now. The effect was unsettling as his jacket strained against his broad shoulders, and his hands fisted like meaty lumps. God, his hands were huge. How had she not noticed before? Henry whined beside her, and she scratched his head.

"Are you always like this?"

She bit her tongue. It was a reflex from the many times her father had spoken similar words when she'd said something inappropriately witty for the occasion.

"I do beg your pardon, Your Grace." She took a small step to put herself behind Henry and allowed a slight, unassuming smile to take her lips. "I've never received a proposal before, and I apologize if my behavior was not appropriate. I promise to do better." She cast her gaze to the floor as was her habit when she'd drawn too much attention to herself because of her sharp tongue.

"Do you have any more ham?"

She had to look at him then. "Ham?"

He nodded to Henry.

She held up the hand that contained the last morsel of ham. He extended his own hand, and she dropped the piece of meat into it.

Ashbourne dipped low toward Henry, a smile coming to his face. "Henry, I hear you're a very good boy. Do you like to play fetch?"

Before she could understand what he was about, Ashbourne straightened and threw the piece of ham down the length of the drawing room. Henry bolted. He cleared the sofa in a single leap of furry tail and flinging drool. But that was all she saw because just then Daxton Kane, the Duke of Ashbourne, swept her into a kiss.

As she had never before been ravished by a duke, Eliza wasn't sure what to think or do for that matter, and there was a moment of time where she hung suspended, both in the kiss and on the periphery of it as if she were her former self looking in.

For this kiss obviously marked a place time. Forever now there would be Eliza before and Eliza after. There was no way around it. Something in her shifted with the realization, and with a start, she realized it was something cold and sad. Almost like this kiss marked the end of wallflower Eliza, and that would be terrible because Eliza rather liked herself as a wallflower.

But surely that didn't make sense. One kiss from a duke didn't change matters, but was this really just a kiss?

Because Ashbourne's hands were like vises, pulling her in until she was pressed against the entire length of his body. Her knees knocked against his legs, her stomach his torso, her lips…

This was no ordinary kiss. It couldn't be. If she were to kiss someone like this every day she would evaporate.

41

Finally, she had conscious of mind to touch him. It was only to quietly lay her hands on his towering shoulders, but at least, she had an anchor should he release her suddenly, which she would not mark as impossible because she had not been expecting this kind of kiss in the slightest, and surely he could end it just as abruptly.

But then he shifted. It was so subtle she thought she might have missed it, but no. He held her tighter, the hand against her back—did he just fist the back of her gown into his palm to pull her closer?

That was when she became aware of her own emotions as a thrill shot through her so violently she was forced to tighten her grip on Ashbourne's shoulders. Her stomach clenched, and she had to remember to breathe through her nose lest she faint because—

Oh God, this kiss was marvelous.

It was more than she'd ever dreamed kissing could be. His lips were so soft against hers, gentle and coaxing. She tasted the coffee now, but her senses were overwhelmed with the tantalizing lure of sandalwood she had discovered upon their first meeting.

The kiss was not in the least fixed as she had thought kisses would be. She had always pictured lips coming together and parting, but this was not that. Ashbourne's lips never stilled against hers. He caressed and nibbled, and her stomach clenched against a roll of sensation so acute a whimper escaped her.

She had hoped he wouldn't have noticed it, but he must have because he gave a responding groan and—yes, he was holding onto her gown, and yes, he was pulling her even closer. She came up on her tiptoes, no longer able to hold herself up on her own, and she clutched at his shoulders as he plundered her mouth, all gentleness gone.

And she reveled in it.

Pure light coiled deep within her, spreading through her limb by limb. Heat rose, easing its way through muscle and sinew until she had no choice but to push back against him, fight this clawing sensation to be even closer to him. His groan turned into a growl as he pressed her against the drawing room door, his knee sliding between her legs as he lifted her just off her feet.

She scrambled to gain a hold on his shoulders, but it needn't matter because he held her so exquisitely. Suddenly, she knew she was safe there in Ashbourne's arms. He would never let her go.

The thought sent a spark of pain through her as she remembered countless days of never feeling another's touch, the long dark nights when she knew, just knew this would never happen. This kiss. This man. This future.

Her whimper was about more now than just the physical ecstasy of his kiss, and he must have sensed it because suddenly he broke away. It was gentle, and he made sure to set her properly back on her feet before stepping back, but he might as well have ripped her asunder for all the good the gentleness did.

The loss of him struck a new spark within her, and the pain crescendoed, her thoughts tumbling one after another.

Would he ever kiss her like that again?

Would he ever kiss at all?

Or was that to be the one and only kiss she would ever receive in this lifetime?

Quickly she tried to remember every detail, imprint it in her memory so in the future of long, dark, lonely nights she could recall it and draw whatever comfort she could from knowing it had happened.

It was several seconds before she could force herself to open her eyes and look at him. Fear of embarrassment, guilt, and inadequacy surged through her, but it would be so much worse if she didn't open her eyes.

He stood in front of her, breathing heavily as she had expected, but his expression—

It looked as if he had lost something.

Doubt coursed through her, and she pressed a hand to her stomach.

She wanted to assure he needn't ever do that again, that he must never be forced to endure such intimate contact with her unless necessary to beget an heir.

But the words stopped in her throat, colliding into one another like a tower of children's blocks crumpling down, one atop the other.

Ashbourne swallowed, the movement harsh and pronounced, and the pain flared within her.

"I shall make the necessary arrangements then." He spoke to the door behind her, and guilt and sorrow rampaged through her.

She wanted to assure him he need never know she was even there. She had been tutored by a superb governess who had taught her everything she must know to be the perfect duchess. He'd need never worry.

He'd never look upon her again unless absolutely necessary.

She would make sure of that.

But before she could say anything, he bid her goodbye and slipped out the door without once looking at her again.

* * *

HE CLIMBED into his curricle and picked up the reins, sending the matched pair of bays into a steady trot.

He didn't know where he was going. He just knew he needed air, lots and lots of precious air.

He was several blocks away from Ravenwood House before he could think clearly, and the first thing he did was adjust his trousers.

Dear God, what had he done?

He'd nearly climbed Eliza right there against her drawing room door. Never before had he reacted to a woman in such a way. It was so pure, so instinctual. He hadn't even realized what he'd done until she'd made that final whimper.

The sound had been so full of pain, anguish, longing, and denial. He had drowned in it, overwhelmed by the despair and loneliness he had tasted in her kiss.

For the first time, he began to see the flaws in his plan.

He wanted to be callous. He wanted to be hard-hearted when it came to her burden as a wallflower in a society that demanded perfection. But he wasn't like that. He could never be blind to another's pain and not attempt to do something about it.

He felt the foundation of his plan quiver, and he tightened his grip on the reins.

The way she had ducked her head, stepped ever so slightly behind that defending beast of hers when he'd questioned her behavior—God, it still stabbed him in the gut. Who had done that to her? Who had made her so wary of even herself?

Who had valued her so little she could not see what she was worth?

The bays flicked their heads and whinnied, and he loosened his grip on the reins.

He'd made it to the park without knowing, and the most fashionable of the *ton* streamed through its gates, vibrating with the possibilities an afternoon's outing would entail. Feathered hats and parasols bobbed alongside top hats, but he didn't see any of it. He only saw Eliza's face right before he kissed her.

Hurt.

Confusion.

Wariness.

Loneliness.

Her hand on that damn dog.

He turned the bays before he could change his mind and headed in the direction of his club. He couldn't afford to let her get to him, not like this. Only one other person had ever gotten under his skin, and he wouldn't think of her. Not again. Not ever.

He had to remain objective. He would marry Eliza and give her a home with sprawling fields she could fill with all of the dogs of her choosing. Hell, he'd build her a paddock just for her dogs if that suited her. But what he would not do was fall in love with her.

He handed off his curricle to the man at the club and bounded up the steps two at a time. It was an unusual time of day for him to be there, but Mandricks gave a nod as soon as he'd entered and by the time he'd settled into his favorite chair in his favorite retreating room, a whiskey, neat, appeared in his hand.

It was a warm day for a fire, but he sat before it anyway, staring into the flames as if to lose himself.

Too quickly memories of that day reared up in his mind. He could smell the crush of the ball around him, hear the butler announcing the names of guests as they spilled into the already full room, the muted hush that fell over the crowd as each name called was not the one for which everyone waited.

Bethany.

Damn her.

A hand to his shoulder startled him from his reverie, and he looked up to find Sebastian Fielding, the Duke of Waverly.

"Sebastian." Dax indicated the seat opposite him. "Rather

unusual to see you here."

"I could say the same to you." Fielding took the seat indicated. "I normally lunch with my mother on Tuesdays, but she was invited to a quilting tea. What is your excuse?"

Dax made a grumbling noise in his whiskey.

"Is that so?" Sebastian said, leaning back in his chair and propping an ankle on the opposite knee.

Dax eyed Fielding. The Duke of Waverly was a respected member of society. Dax had witnessed his attentiveness during the Parliament session and knew from various sources that the Fielding coffers were quite flush and his estates well maintained. Fielding was an analytical sort, and Dax knew him to be perceived as rude at times, but it wasn't that the man was being hurtful. Fielding simply did not mince words. The most interesting fact about the man was that he was the closest thing Dax had to a best friend.

"I'm in search of a bride," Dax decided to say.

Fielding merely raised an eyebrow. "It is the obligation of the title. I assume you are finding it difficult."

"Something like that." Dax took a swallow of whiskey. "Have you given thought to your duty in that regard?"

"Of course, I have. One shouldn't leave such a matter to chance."

This boded well for Dax's own thinking.

"And what parameters have you set on the matter?"

Dax expected the usual quips of making a match that added valuable connections to a family, perhaps bringing with it valuable land and natural resources.

Instead, Sebastian said, "She must have broad hips."

"I beg your pardon?" Dax nearly choked on his whiskey.

"Hips. I expect her to have a body well built for breeding. I must ensure the continuation of the line after all, and what better way than to acquire a wife with good hips for birthing."

Dax cleared his throat, feeling Sebastian's criteria fall too closely to his own. After all, Dax sought a wife with plain features. What more was it to require one with hips adequate for birthing babies?

But hearing the words from Sebastian brought a sour taste to Dax's mouth.

He shook his head. "I suppose adequate hips is a sensible choice."

Sebastian made a noise of agreement. "Of course, it is. I would choose a filly for her bloodlines. Why would I not choose a woman with the biological make up in favor of healthy birthing?"

"You're comparing the future Duchess of Waverly to a stud horse?"

"The mare actually," Sebastian corrected. "But yes, I can see the analogy."

Dax studied his friend for several seconds. They had been at Eton together, and their fathers had passed at nearly the same time so they entered Parliament sessions nearly together. Sebastian had always been rather dry and calculating, but since his father's death...well, he'd grown cold somehow. Again, Dax recalled how people often found him rude and crass, but it wasn't that at all. Unfortunately, it was something far more complicated.

Dax took a sip of his whiskey. "Have you found any of this season's debutantes to your liking?"

"I must say it's been a rather disappointing year."

Mandricks appeared then with a glass for Sebastian and fresh whiskey for Dax. Both men nodded their thanks and waited for Mandricks to retreat before speaking.

"I take it you have not found anyone suitable," Sebastian said after taking a sip of his own drink.

Dax wondered briefly how much to tell Sebastian. He studied his friend. Sebastian hadn't been there the night of

Dax's humiliation. The previous Duke of Waverly had passed away suddenly, and there were several months where Dax had lost contact with his school chum. He wondered what had happened to his friend in those dark months, and all too clearly, he recalled the boy who had raced the ball fields with him at Eton.

Sebastian watched him carefully, his face impassive, and Dax suddenly realized Sebastian would likely be the very person to understand his plan.

"I'm seeking a plain wife," Dax said.

Sebastian tapped a finger against his glass. "A plain wife? You mean one of unfortunate visage?"

Dax gave a sharp nod, and the guilt of betrayal whispered through him.

Sebastian seemed to consider this for a moment as his gaze drifted upwards.

"I can see how such an attribute in a wife could be advantageous. You'd need never be concerned about being cuckolded."

Dax winced at the word.

"Ah," Sebastian said. "Attempting to avoid a repeat of the past, I see."

Dax gave a short nod, and Sebastian dropped his foot to the ground and leaned forward.

"You believe by selecting a plain wife you can avoid the public embarrassment you received at the hands of Lady Bethany Walpole?"

"The Marchioness of Isley, you mean."

Sebastian's laugh was dry. "Marchioness. I suppose she is now."

Dax studied the fire, but he could feel his friend's stare. He wondered if he could speak the truth. He was perfectly fine with his desires privately, but somehow speaking them aloud made them dangerous. But Sebastian would not think him cruel. Of all people, Sebastian would be the most likely to understand.

"I seek a plain wife so as to avoid emotional entanglement."

"You don't want to be in danger of falling in love with your wife."

Dax turned sharply to study his friend. Sebastian's words carried the same meaning but with it, a cutting sting as well.

"Yes," Dax answered simply.

Sebastian straightened. "And you think by marrying a woman of unfortunate visage you will not be tempted to love her?"

"Exactly."

Sebastian scoffed, and Dax started at the noise, sloshing whiskey in his glass. He stared at his friend who was shaking his head.

"You believe emotions are tied to a person's physical appearance?"

Dax's mind traveled immediately to an image of Bethany with her long, luscious golden curls, her bright eyes, and wide smile, the way her hips perfectly filled his hands, the exquisite curve of bosom and bottom.

He blinked, destroying the image.

"Yes, I would say love is most acutely tied to one's physical attraction to another person."

Sebastian knocked back the last of his whiskey and set the glass down on the table between the chairs.

"One has absolutely nothing to do with the other." He pointed a finger so as to articulate his point. "Emotions are biological nonsense. You can't trust how you will feel from one moment to the next based on mere physical appearance. Beauty is fleeting whereas personality lasts forever."

The muscles along the back of Dax's neck tightened with a trickle of dread.

"Personality?"

Sebastian stood, adjusting the cuffs of his shirt under his jacket.

"Yes, personality. Personality is predictable." He gestured to Dax. "I supposed I'm the only person to whom you have spoken your desire to marry an unfortunate looking woman."

Dax stood. He wasn't about to have this conversation while seated.

"You are. How do you figure that?"

Sebastian shrugged carelessly. "You obviously assumed I would agree with such a heartless plan, because I'm—what does society call me? The Beastly Duke?" Again the careless shrug. "I am not pretending to be otherwise, but in this matter, you've simply made a grievous miscalculation."

Dax pulled on his own cuffs, irritation making him agitated.

"And what miscalculation is that?"

Sebastian leaned in. "If you wish to avoid falling in love with your wife, you must marry someone with a deplorable personality." His smile was cold as he straightened. "As always, it's interesting running into you, Dax. Do give my regards to your mother."

Dax raised a hand in acknowledgment as Sebastian retreated back through the smoky rooms of the club toward the front entry.

He sat heavily then, his eyes unable to focus on anything but the two empty glasses on the table before him. The ghost of Eliza's hesitant, unschooled kiss passed over his lips like a caress, and his stomach flipped.

Eliza's unexpected wit.

Her uncompromising loyalty to her dog.

Her perplexing and vacillating nature.

Dear God, he was in a great deal of danger.

CHAPTER 4

*E*liza was aware of the mating process of dogs. This, however, did not prepare her for her sister's unexpected arrival in her rooms the morning of her wedding to discuss with Eliza exactly what would be expected of her that evening.

Eliza held up a hand when Viv's lips thinned and her eyes took on a motherly softness.

"I'm quite informed when it comes to what will be expected of me this evening as the wife of the Duke of Ashbourne."

Viv let out a breath. "Oh thank heavens, because I was not looking forward to explaining it." She cocked an eyebrow. "How is it that you know?"

Henry took the opportunity to make his presence known with a whine at Viv for her neglectfulness in not bringing him a bit of morsel from the kitchens.

"Oh, I see," Viv murmured. She straightened her skirts and sat on the bench at the end of Eliza's bed.

Viv looked tired. She'd looked tired a lot lately with faint bruises under her eyes and a wilting about her lips. Eliza wondered if she were still not sleeping well. It had been nearly two months since she had appeared on Andrew's doorstep, trunks and maid in tow, declaring her intent to see her sisters properly wed. And not to some blackguard like she'd unfortunately married.

The Duke of Margate had seemed like a nice enough gentleman the few times Eliza had met him when he'd wed her sister nearly eighteen months prior. He carried butterscotches with him, and he always asked about her watercolors.

Such a shame he'd been caught abed with an opera singer from Covent Garden.

Eliza placed the last of her brushes in her painting kit and snapped it tightly shut for her maid, Lucy, to add to her things to be taken over to Ashbourne House that morning. She brushed at the skirts of her new gown, a periwinkle muslin Viv had insisted on. Eliza didn't see what was wrong with any of her other muslin gowns, but apparently she needed something new for her wedding day.

Her stomach flipped at the thought, and she wrestled down her anxiety. Only a few more hours and she would be safely wed. Only a few more hours and her dream of starting a family could actually come to fruition.

It didn't help. Her mind invariably strayed to that kiss. The way Ashbourne had held her with such ferocity as if he needed her to live, which was absurd because no one needed her. His kiss, so soft, so alluring, as if he knew not to frighten her.

But more than anything she could not forget the smell of sandalwood. She'd never been close enough to a man to understand the tantalizing qualities of his scent. The Duke of Ashbourne smelled wonderful. Oh drat, this was not at all helping to calm her nerves.

She settled on the bench next to Viv and took her sisters hands into her own.

"Have you heard from him, Viv?"

Her sister's eyes went glassy and vacant, and Eliza squeezed her hands to bring her back.

"No." The word was almost inaudible. Viv shook her head as if rousing herself. "No, I have not heard from him."

"I'm sure it's simply because he doesn't know what to say."

Viv's eyes flashed. "Begging for forgiveness would be a good start."

Eliza looked down at their hands. "I know I'm not experienced with marriage." She looked up, met her sister's gaze, and smiled awkwardly. "At least not yet. But I know some married couples have an understanding between them."

Eliza didn't say more for she didn't need to.

"Ryder and I never discussed it," Viv said softly. She seemed to hesitate, and it was strange for Eliza to see her older sister so unsure of herself.

Viv always seemed to arrive three meters ahead of herself, her confidence and vitality far preceding her. Now she twisted her wedding band around and around endlessly on her finger. She seemed to realize she was doing it and pressed her hands against her thigh.

"I realize it may have been foolish for me to assume fidelity from my husband. I can't say it's entirely common."

Eliza's mouth opened without a word coming forth as her sister's comment sank in. She'd never considered if Ashbourne planned to be faithful. Her own loyalty was not in question as it was painfully obvious she would not be sought after for assignations.

But Ashbourne...Ashbourne would seek such comfort out. Of course, he would. Pain tightened her chest, and she rubbed a hand absently along her collarbone. It didn't matter.

It was probably for the best if he were happy and his needs fulfilled. Surely, other women would be capable—no, skilled at such things.

Eliza swallowed. "No, I'm afraid you're right. But perhaps, he didn't realize your expectations. A lot can be misunderstood between two people."

Viv's smile was just a touch watery. "When did my little sister get to be so wise?"

"At the same time you were getting to be so strong." Eliza squeezed her sister's hand and stood. "I think I'd best finish up here if we are to leave for the church on time."

Viv rearranged her skirts as she stood. "Yes, I suppose. I'm rather surprised Ashbourne wished to wed by license."

Eliza paused in placing her watercolors in the remaining trunk.

"He wishes to return to his summer home soon. Apparently, he doesn't enjoy London in the summer."

Viv watched her carefully. "I can't say that I blame him. London can be dreadfully hot in the summer." She cocked her head. "Still, a week is awfully short notice to wed. I'm surprised he hasn't returned to the house in that time to meet with Andrew."

Eliza swallowed, remembering her only meeting with Andrew to discuss the terms of her marriage. She hadn't seen Ashbourne since that day in the drawing room. Embarrassment and guilt surged within her, and she tamped it down as best she could.

That kiss.

She'd nearly ruined everything with that kiss. He couldn't even bear to look at her after it was through, and yet it had kept her awake every night since.

She forced the pain away as she was so good at doing.

"He sent his instructions along with his solicitor. Andrew

assures me everything is in order." She allowed a smile then to soothe her sister's curiosity.

Viv returned her smile with one of her own and a softening of her gaze. She closed the distance between them and gave her a meaningful if slightly awkward hug. Eliza could not fathom why all the members of her family suddenly felt compelled to hug her.

Viv's eyes were moist when she pulled back, and with a slight nod, she turned and left, softly closing the door behind her.

Eliza was once more alone with her trunks, her life packed into neat boxes ready for the next part of it. Her gaze inevitably drifted to Henry, perched on the sofa she'd had placed by the fire, so he'd have somewhere to lounge. She would need to make such arrangements in her new home, and with a jolt, she realized she'd never seen her new home. She wondered if any bride ever saw her future home before her wedding day.

She squeezed in on the sofa with Henry, who obligingly lifted his head to make room. He lolled against her hip and rested his head in her lap, so it really was no compromise. She scratched at his supple fur.

"My dear, Henry, what are we about to embark on?"

She felt the stirrings of fear and apprehension. After all, what she was about to do she'd never done before. She wasn't a debutante like Viv had been. Viv had had scores of men interested in her. Eliza had spotted more than one surreptitious slip onto balconies and into hidden alcoves. Viv must have had a world of experience more than Eliza did at this very moment.

Even Louisa attracted her far amount of attention.

She scratched behind Henry's ear.

"It needn't matter, old friend. Soon we'll be a family again."

She pushed to her feet, determined to resume her packing. They were to stay in London for a few days at Ashbourne House before heading to the shore and Ashbourne Manor. She'd need to keep a trunk of the things she would require while the rest would be sent on to Glenhaven and Ashbourne Manor as the servants had been notified to open up the house.

She was glad to have something to occupy her hands, and the footmen came to collect her trunks in what hardly seemed like any time at all. She slipped Henry into his leather lead, and they headed down to the foyer to meet the rest of her family.

Andrew was already waiting, and she heard the distinct sound of the carriage pulling up as she and Henry came down into the foyer.

Her brother turned and stopped, shifting from one foot to the other.

"You needn't be so nervous, brother. I'm only getting married."

Andrew's mouth tightened, but she saw a flash of mirth in his eyes.

The ride to the chapel where Ashbourne requested the ceremony take place was uneventful. Louisa and Jo both insisted on sitting next to her, which left Henry between Andrew and Viv, which Eliza believed no one enjoyed, most of all Henry.

They arrived without incident, however, and her sisters poured from the carriage, already jabbering to one another that there had better be some nice flowers arranged. Even if it was decided a smaller ceremony would be better given the timing at the last gasp of the season, it should at least appear noble.

Eliza really couldn't have cared. Her mind kept drifting to where Ashbourne had said they were going for the summer.

Ashbourne Manor was nestled in a village just to the east of Brighton. They'd be spending the summer on the shore. She'd never spent a summer on the shore. She gathered up Henry's lead so Andrew could slip past the dog. He paused though and turned a soft smile in her direction.

She reached out a hand and placed it on his arm.

"You needn't worry so, brother. I'm going to be just fine."

"But I must worry. It's my job to do so now." His tone was neutral, but she heard the underlying cadence of steel, and it reassured her. Andrew would never allow anything to happen to his sisters.

Soon she was alone in the carriage, and she tugged on Henry's lead to tell him it was time to leave. But suddenly an unexpected tug of apprehension gripped her. Sitting there alone in the carriage, her sisters jarring voices pattering on just beyond the open door. Andrew's more muffled voice as he greeted—

He was speaking to Ashbourne.

The apprehension grew until she feared she'd not be able to move. Her chest heaved, and her skin prickled. In her mind, her plan was sterile and objective. Here it was not so much. Here it was very real, and it involved her marrying a duke.

Then Ashbourne appeared in the open doorway, and she forgot entirely how to breathe.

He wore a jacket of deep blue, a simple waistcoat and cravat, that cut a dashing line. He could have stepped from a novel, and Eliza's breathing constricted even more.

Until Ashbourne smiled.

It wasn't a seductive smile. Not that she would have thought he'd be inclined to such a thing when it came to her. No, this was a mischievous smile.

He reached into a pocket and withdraw a folded handkerchief from which he withdrew—

A piece of ham.

Henry whined.

"My good man, Henry," Ashbourne said. "Are you ready to be married?"

* * *

THE CEREMONY FELT UNUSUALLY STILTED, but as he'd avoided any wedding he possibly could in the past seven years, he wasn't entirely sure what a wedding ceremony was like.

Eliza seemed content. He wasn't sure she was the type of person to exude enthusiasm for a wedding ceremony. Perhaps if he handed her a puppy, she'd be elated, but he just felt wedding ceremonies were not to her liking. Henry sat obediently by her side, which had caused a great deal of whispering among the guests, which he'd enjoyed immensely.

If he were to be forced to wed, at least he would get some kind of enjoyment out of it.

The wedding breakfast was an even greater trial as members of the *ton* deemed necessary to invite as guests paraded past he and his new wife to express their well wishes. The entire affair was interminable, and he found himself longing for the ride to Glenhaven where at least he would find some peace and quiet to at least examine his own thoughts.

Sebastian's words continued to trip through his mind, and no matter how he tried to push them from his thoughts, he simply couldn't. He found himself studying Eliza through the entire ceremony and wedding breakfast, determined to find something to refute his friend's advice. Surely it was simply a matter of physical attraction that could keep an appropriate distance between them.

But as he stood next to her, he couldn't help but notice

how she smelled of lilacs and wondered if she had acquired a new soap for her toilette for he was sure Eliza was not the type to dally in perfumes or colognes. She was, however, wearing a new gown. He could tell by the lack of staining along the cuffs, which he was coming to understand was from the dog drool she acquired when working with Henry. The dog deposited a great deal of moisture on the giver's hand and wrist when given a treat he was coming to discover from the few times he had rewarded the dog with a morsel.

When they were finally seated for the meal, Eliza leaned into him, and he tried not to think about lilacs.

"Your Grace, I don't mean to intrude, but I noticed your family is not in attendance."

"Dax," he whispered in reply.

She straightened ever so slightly as if the intimacy of his given name were enough to upset her.

"Dax." She said his name as if testing out a foreign word, and he drew far too much pleasure from it.

"My mother largely keeps to her ancestral home on the Isle of Skye. She sends her blessing and hopes to one day make your acquaintance."

She stiffened beside him. "Is your relationship with your mother...strained?"

"Not at all." He nodded at an earl he only dimly recollected seeing in the chambers of Parliament. "My mother is a daft, flighty old bird who prefers stalking to the ballrooms of London." He turned his smile on her. "I quite enjoy her company."

His wife blinked, her mouth relaxed as she seemed to contemplate this.

"And the rest of your family?"

He gave a shrug. "I have cousins here and yon, but we're not particularly close. We all grew up at rather different times. It, unfortunately, prevented a true bond from forming."

"That's so sad." Her words were soft, and he looked at her to ensure he'd heard her correctly. She licked her lips and added, "It's just that family can be so important. It's good to have someone always there to rely on."

Since his father's death some six years previously, Dax had largely been alone in the world. He hadn't really noticed as the reach of a duke was powerful, and he'd had little cause to rely on anyone else.

"But wouldn't you agree sometimes one's family is not the greatest source of comfort?"

Her eyes narrowed, and a line appeared along her brow. He'd upset her when he truly hadn't meant to. He didn't realize how important family was to her, but he supposed he should have figured as she had an overabundance of siblings.

He reached beneath the table to find her hand and drew it into his. She gave a sharp inhalation, but had he not been sitting so close, he wouldn't have noticed. But he did notice, and her reaction to his touch had his gut clenching. Her hand was small and delicate in his, and he wished nothing more than to remove her glove and feel her soft skin against his.

Later, he realized. Later he could remove her glove and so much more.

He gave her hand a final squeeze and let it go as if it were about to ignite him in a ball of flames.

Damn Sebastian and his nonsense.

It seemed an age before the last of the guests bid them their goodbyes. He hadn't tasted the food, he'd drunk far too much of the wine, and he couldn't have named a single guest at the affair if someone had threatened the life of his horse. It seemed his entire plan was falling to pieces around him as he couldn't stop thinking about his wife.

Wife.

Her smile, her endearing expressions, her wit, her charm.

He hadn't factored into his plan the need for a woman prepared for the demands the title of duchess brought with it, but he'd found much to his delight Eliza had no qualms on the matter. Likely because she was the daughter of a duchess herself.

She moved smoothly from guest to guest, earls and countesses to marquesses and marchionesses. She nodded politely, said all the right things, and made all the correct comments. He heard nothing but commendable remarks regarding his wife and the guests had filtered out with contented smiles and valuable promises of invitations.

Only he noticed the stiffness about her. While she was well trained, she didn't take to it naturally. Henry stayed by her side, and he saw her hand slip to the dog more than once as if she drew comfort from him. He recalled what she had said that first night he met her. He wondered suddenly if dogs were the only creatures from which she'd drawn comfort.

God, he was in for it now. Why had he not considered the virginal state of his wife before this? Hadn't she said she'd never been kissed before on that fateful day in the Ravenwood drawing room?

A wash of worry swept over him. He was used to widows and unhappy wives. He was not used to virgins, especially ones that tugged at his heartstrings like she did. He was in very real danger here. Perhaps Sebastian had been right.

Soon the halls of Ashbourne House quieted, and they were left standing in the foyer bidding goodbye to her family.

Or rather, he stood by as her sisters prodded and poked her.

One toyed with a curl of her hair that had escaped a pin, informing her of the importance of a good curling rod.

Another examined her gown informing her how it could be altered to be reworn now that so many had seen her wearing it at her wedding. And the third, well, this one hung back, petting the dog and assuring Henry he would be well treated and if he weren't, there was no sin in a corrective bite.

He swallowed.

"I assure you Eliza is nothing like her sisters."

Ashbourne turned at the voice to find the Duke of Ravenwood standing mere inches away.

"I suppose you mean that in a positive way," Ashbourne said.

Ravenwood's expression was closed, but he gave a sidelong glance.

"My sister is a good woman despite what society may think of her. You will never find fault in her character."

Ashbourne's chest tightened. That was precisely of what he was afraid.

"I am beginning to understand that." He watched Eliza attempt to extract herself from her sisters and herd them to the door.

Ravenwood said nothing more and stepped aside as his sister approached. Eliza gave a final farewell to each of her sisters, tangling Henry between their legs. He stepped back to give her more room and allow the dog to find his perch by his mistress's side. He still had some morsels rolled in the handkerchief in his pocket, which he hoped would help acclimate the poor dog to his new home.

He wasn't sure why he felt a sudden pang for the collie, but he had likely known only one home his whole life and now everything would be upset.

Ravenwood stepped up and kissed his sister goodbye, making his own attempt to herd his sisters to the door. Dax was focused on Henry so when someone grabbed his arm, he started. He expected to see Ravenwood but was surprised instead to find it was one of his bride's sisters. It was the one who had encouraged Henry to take up biting. He thought her name was Johanna, but he was honestly having trouble telling them apart.

She smiled rapturously and leaned in close to whisper, "If you do anything to hurt her, I will have your ballocks."

She stepped away before he had a chance to respond and waved enthusiastically with the rest of her sisters. He swallowed and, not quite meeting her eyes, raised a hand in farewell. Eliza gave one final call before the door shut, leaving him utterly alone with his wife.

The resulting silence drummed in his ears like a stampede of wild boar.

He cleared his throat, "Eh, that was…"

"Awful." She spoke the word with such grave enormity he couldn't help but laugh.

She looked at him sharply, a stamp of wariness on her features before she realized he'd thought her funny. Her face relaxed and she bent to remove Henry's lead. The dog stood and turned to face him, nuzzling at his hand.

"Do you have more of that ham in your pockets?" Eliza asked.

He eyed her. "He can smell it?"

She frowned every so delicately. "He is a dog. Of course, he can smell it."

Henry raised a single paw as if requesting a morsel.

Dax withdraw the handkerchief and gave the dog the last of the ham. This seemed to satisfy him as he sat and whined softly at his mistress.

Then they stood there.

His plan hadn't exactly included what was to happen after he secured a wife. He had expected to be so disinterested in her person as to not require her presence further, but terribly enough, he found he didn't want the day to end for then he would have no cause to be in Eliza's company.

"Would—" He didn't have an end to that sentence as he scrambled to find a reason to keep Eliza next to him.

"Henry will need to do business," she said, thankfully cutting him off. "Would you be so kind as to direct me to the gardens?"

It took him a moment to interpret what she meant by Henry needing to do business, and his hesitation cost him.

Carver, the Ashbourne butler, had been standing by after seeing the last of the guests out, and at Eliza's question he stepped forward.

"I should be happy to show you the gardens, Your Grace." Carver gave a bow. "And if you are not too tired, the servants would very much enjoy making your acquaintance."

He opened his mouth to interject, but Eliza spoke over him.

"Thank you…" She waited to allow Carver to give an introduction.

"Carver, Your Grace. I am the butler here at Ashbourne House. Should you require anything, I am here to serve you."

Eliza showered Carver with one of her soft smiles. "Thank you, Carver. I should be happy with both of your suggestions. Come, Henry."

Before he could think of something to say, he was already alone in the foyer, his hardly married wife having deserted him.

But that was not what bothered him most. What bothered him was how much it hurt to see her go.

CHAPTER 5

*A*shbourne had had a sofa installed in her bedchamber.

It was clear the piece did not belong as it did not match the other Queen Anne furniture in the room. The sofa was a solid piece with boxy legs, which suggested it had been recently purchased. Henry deemed it acceptable as he immediately pounced upon it when the housekeeper, Mrs. Fitzhugh, had shown her to her rooms.

Henry had spent a good hour roaming the grounds of Ashbourne House and found quite a few suitable spots to do his business. She'd played a few games with him to expend his energy as well. Hiding bits of chicken Cook had procured for her so Henry could find them and tossed his favorite toy, a stuffed rabbit she'd sewn for him, so he could chase it about the lawn. When he'd returned to her, tongue lolling out of his mouth, she knew he'd relax comfortably in the strange environs of their new home.

And strange it was turning out to be.

She was glad the servants had taken to her immediately for she feared she'd be wandering the halls of Ashbourne

House like a lost puppy. Ashbourne could not have been quicker to dismiss her after the guests and her family had departed, and she could not blame him.

She wouldn't spend another thought on the subject for it needn't matter. She knew her place, and she knew what it would get her.

Tonight.

Even tonight she might conceive a baby, and it would have all been worth it. For surely, Ashbourne planned to consummate their marriage as was appropriate. Even he could not refute what was necessary in a marriage even if he could not stand to be in her presence.

Her chest tightened at the thought, and a headache pushed at the backs of her eyes. She pressed a hand to her forehead, refusing to allow tears she knew would do no good. She shouldn't upset herself over his treatment of her for it was to be expected. Better to move on to practical matters.

She tentatively opened the doors to an expansive armoire to find her things had already been aired, pressed, and hung up. There were neat drawers for her stockings and tidy shelves for her unmentionables. Her hairbrush and pins had been deposited on her dressing table and her shoes carefully laid out. She was only to stay at Ashbourne House for a few days, and she preferred this less formal arrangement. Had she a dressing room and such, she wouldn't have known what to do with it all.

She eyed Henry. "I think this will suit. How do you feel about it?"

He'd already fallen asleep, and hearing his soft snores bolstered her courage.

Her maid, Lucy, arrived within minutes to help her off with her gown. Eliza dismissed her for the evening thereafter, wishing to be alone for a few moments before

Ashbourne arrived. He'd advised her to call him by his given name several times, but for some reason, the intimacy of it stopped the word from pouring from her lips.

With the exception of her brother, she'd never called any gentleman by his given name and had never thought to be so close to someone so as to use his given name. It felt unnatural, and more, it frightened her. She had set an expectation that the familiar relations of marriage would forever be unknown to her, and to suddenly be wed was cause for consternation.

More, she realized she would need to guard her heart from disappointment. There's was not a love match, and she thought it worse that she should be alone in a marriage rather than just alone. At least when she was just alone, there was no one who held the power to hurt her so acutely, and Ashbourne most certainly held such power.

When he'd stood in the foyer and said nothing to her suggestion of seeing the gardens. When he'd been unable to look at her after their one shared kiss.

But then he'd had bits of ham at the ready for Henry and now this sofa. He continued to confuse and perplex her, and it did nothing to soothe her nerves.

She brushed out her hair and plaited it but once it was finished regretted it. Perhaps she should wear her hair loose. Would he care for it loose? It was so frizzy and wild, so unlike the beautiful golden coils she saw on the debutantes this season. He'd likely find it repulsive if she wore it down. She tied it off and stood, no longer wishing to see her reflection.

The bedchamber was spacious, and she drifted over to the draped windows to peer outside. Night had fallen with earnest, and she could just make out the shape of a passing carriage below. They weren't overly far from Ravenwood, and she wondered what her sisters were doing. She would have been already abed at this hour, Henry asleep on his sofa, snoring while she forced her eyes to remain open to read just a little longer.

Her gaze drifted to the table beside the opulent bed to find it bare. Her books were in her carpetbag, which she'd brought herself and asked Lucy not to unpack. She'd placed her most recent watercolors within it and didn't want them misplaced.

While she studied the empty table though, her eyes found the candle her maid had left burning there. She shifted her attention to the rest of the room. Lanterns were lit, scattered here and there, and the room was lit as though it were daylight.

She peered down at herself, at the snowy folds of her plain white gown and how gloriously it displayed her lack of womanly attributes. She looked about as appealing as a fence post. One by one she extinguished the lanterns about the room so only the candle beside her bed remained lit. That would do nicely. He couldn't find her repulsive if he couldn't see her.

The connecting door drew her attention, but all remained silent on the other side. She wondered where he was or what he was about, but she pushed the thoughts aside quickly. It needn't matter. What Ashbourne did was of little concern to her. She was only here as his wife, and she would do her duty in that regard. She wouldn't plague him with any of her attentions.

Her feet grew cold in the night air, and she slipped between the covers of the bed, propping herself against the headrest. Was this where maidenly brides usually awaited their husbands? Was she to stand somewhere else perhaps? Would he startle Henry when he entered, and would he find the situation vexing enough to leave without so much as touching her?

She swallowed, hard.

She'd forgotten about the rest of it. She was so consumed with whether or not he would even show, her mind had let slip the very real fact that tonight the Duke of Ashbourne would touch her. Intimately. Knowingly.

She closed her eyes, shutting out the image of Ashbourne's hands on her body. He would find every knobby joint, every flat surface. What would that be like to him? She wasn't so naive as to believe he had been celibate as a bachelor, and she wasn't so hopeful as to believe he would be faithful to her now. She understood exactly what she lacked, and she would never wish to deny him the carnal pleasure of a truly enticing woman.

A knock sounded on the connecting door so squarely and sharp it might as well have been a pistol firing at dawn. She straightened, coming away from the pillows with a gasp of air.

"Come in." Her voice hardly shook, and she was glad of at least that.

The door opened slowly, and she squared her shoulders. Belatedly, she thought to take off her spectacles, and before he could get the door fully open, she pulled them from her face. The connecting door became slightly blurred, but she could still make out the shape of him entering.

He wore a dressing gown, but even from this distance without her lenses, she could see he still wore trousers and a shirt beneath it. Her heart did an odd thing in her chest, and the familiar pain of longing blossomed. She had to stay focused. The point of all of this was to make her a mother, to give her a child to love and nurture.

"Good evening, mate," Ashbourne said, and it was a moment for her to realize he spoke to Henry. He bent over the sofa where Henry had lifted his head. The dog sniffed, and she realized Ashbourne had brought a morsel with him.

Rather clever of him. Henry accepted the bit and promptly returned his head to his pillow with a deep snore.

Then Ashbourne turned and his attention was fully directed at her.

He was close enough now that she could see his face, and what she saw there had her throat closing.

His lips were slightly parted, his eyes wide as he studied her. She clutched the bed covers to her chest, but it did little to hide her. She was exposed, vulnerable, and he had the power to slay her.

Which he did when he said, "You mustn't do this if you're not ready."

She swallowed the hurt, forcing her voice to work. "You need not worry for my sake, Your Grace. I can extinguish the light if that should make it easier for you."

Before he could say anything, she leaned over and blew out the last candle. The room dipped into darkness, but a streak of moonlight still spilled across the carpeted floor where the drapes just barely didn't meet. She could see him, illuminated by the wash of light, and his features had hardened now in the darkness. Determination set his jaw, and she steeled herself against feeling.

Without another word for she could not muster a single one, she lay back, tucking herself carefully under the covers and stared at the ceiling. She heard rustling, and she realized he undressed in the darkness somewhere before her. She wondered what he looked like and closed her eyes tightly. She shouldn't have such thoughts. They would only cause her more pain.

The bed dipped before she expected it to, and her stomach roiled. She hadn't eaten since the wedding breakfast, and she regretted it now. Perhaps some tea and toast would have been better to settle her nerves. The protection of the bed covers lifted slightly as he must have slipped between them, and she swallowed hard.

She forced her eyes open when he made no move to touch her. "Do not hesitate, Your Grace. I understand the mechanics of the process. I'm not afraid."

She could hear him swallow. "Eliza, I think—"

He didn't finish the sentence though. He made a noise somewhere between a groan and growl, and finally he moved. He came atop her with a gracefulness she didn't expect. Her legs parted for him, and he settled between them. There was no fumbling, no searching in the dark. He lifted the hem of her nightgown as if he were used to such matters.

Tears sprang to her eyes, and she forced them closed. She wouldn't think of what that meant. She wouldn't think of how many women he had lain atop. She wouldn't think how she would never have been one of them had he not wed her.

"There is often some pain the first time, but I am told it gets better."

She nodded, still unable to open her eyes.

He grunted, and she couldn't help but hear the note of frustration in it. With a surge of panic, she wondered if she were making this worse. Was there something she was supposed to do? Could she do something to make it better?

Her eyes flew opened, and she realized just how close he was. Even in the darkness, she could see him so clearly. The hard planes of his forehead and cheeks, the cleft in his chin. He was so utterly beautiful, and she was so utterly inadequate. The tears pushed against her eyes, and she distracted herself by raising her hands to grip his shoulders.

Too late she realized he was unclothed, and her hands touched bare skin. He was hot beneath her fingertips. Hot and so very strong, she pulled her hands away as if burned.

This time when he groaned, he whispered her name like an oath. "Eliza."

"I'm so very sorry," she rushed to apologize. "I'm sorry. I'm trying not to make this worse for you than it is. I swear it."

His eyes met hers for the first time, and she wanted nothing more than to look away. She couldn't though, no matter how she tried. Something pulsed between them, an unseen force holding them together, suspended in that moment in time.

"Make it worse?" His voice was strained, and she cringed.

"Yes, I'm so sorry. If you tell me what it is I'm doing wrong, I promise to try to do better."

"Do better?" This was even more strained.

"Yes, of course. Perhaps it would help if I—" She adjusted her hips, pressing upright until again too late she realized if he were atop her, their intimate…bits would be aligned. Something hard pressed into the softness of her thigh, and a startled cry flew to her lips.

Her eyes locked on his, and the strain she saw there was unbearable.

"I'm so sorry." She whispered it now, and there was nothing she could do to disguise the tears in her voice.

"Eliza." The way he said her name was like a warm bath, soothing and comforting, but then he bent, placing his elbows on the mattress on either side of her as he cupped her head within the palms of his large hands. Heat surged through her, and something else, something strong and precious.

For just a moment, she felt wanted.

The way he cradled her, the way he refused to let go of her gaze, the way he spoke her name as if it were the only thing he could say.

When she thought it was too much to bear, he bent his head and kissed her. It was just a brush of his lips to hers, the movement soft and alluring. Her head tried to come up off the pillow, following the fleeting taste of him, but his hands held her in place.

Desire spiraled through her.

It was so unexpected, she gasped against his lips. He groaned and shifted, deepening the kiss as she'd wanted him to do. Her hands came back up, and this time she was ready for the heat that seared her skin. She gripped him, pulling him closer. She wanted to feel him, all of him, pressed against her.

Now he groaned her name against her lips. "Eliza."

It wasn't enough. Her body reacted instinctively, her hips pressing up off the mattress, her thighs spreading and lifting, wrapping her body around his eyes.

"God, no." He ripped his mouth from hers, and the rejection pierced the fleeting bubble of desire that had gripped her.

No.

Pain lanced through her, sharp and lethal. She couldn't control the tears any longer, and they slipped from the sides of her eyes, disappearing into her hair before they could be seen. She blinked, trying to clear her eyes as she sucked in a steadying breath. She lay perfectly still, her hands once more flat on the mattress, her legs stiff and straight. If she could sink any farther into the mattress, she would.

He pressed his forehead to hers, his breath ragged. "Eliza."

This time she said nothing. She couldn't even summon the words to apologize again.

He shifted, coming up on one arm as he moved his other between them. His hardness pressed into her now, and she flinched involuntarily.

"Are you all right?" he whispered.

She could only nod, wishing this humiliation would end.

He pressed into her, and her body stretched, not uncomfortably so as she seemed to understand how to accommodate him. She thought he was fully seated inside of her, and the tension eased from her shoulders the smallest degrees until he asked, "Are you ready for me to push forward?"

She didn't know what he meant, so she only nodded.

He pushed the last bit into her, and she felt a sharp stab of pain. It quickly ebbed, and she bit her lower lip to keep from making any noise. Surely now it would soon be over.

He began to move inside of her, and she tried very hard to keep still. She couldn't upset him anymore or he may never do this again, and she would never have her baby. She closed her eyes, praying for a miracle. Perhaps tonight would be enough. He moved faster, the mattress dipping, her head bending awkwardly against the pillows, and then with a final groan, he stilled. She felt a slight dampness between her legs, but in all truth, she couldn't tell if anything had happened.

Had he been successful? If she were to beget an heir tonight, she would never need to suffer such embarrassment again, and he would never suffer her touch.

He rolled off of her. Surreptitiously, she moved her hands against her exposed thighs, feeling the place where he had just been. Her fingertips found the dampness she had felt, and it was sticky against her skin, but other than that there was nothing to suggest anything had happened at all. She closed her eyes, fervently sending a prayer of hope into the darkness.

It was several minutes before he rolled from the bed without a word, gathered his garments, and slipped through the connecting door. She lay still until she was sure he would not return before slipping from the bed and padding across the carpet. She quietly approached the connecting door and ever so carefully turned the lock. Only when she was assured of her privacy did she let the tears come.

* * *

SEBASTIAN WAS ONLY able to sneak up on him at the Devonshire ball three nights after his disastrous wedding night because Dax had taken to surviving by existing in a sort of catatonic state.

In the hollow recesses of his mind, he heard the turn of the bolt ringing in the darkness as his wife locked him out of her bedchamber.

God, he was a right ass.

He'd mucked up the entire thing. He knew from the moment he'd stepped into her bedchamber and seen she'd removed those damned spectacles he was lost. Her face glowed in the candlelight, and he'd wanted nothing more than to cup her face in his hands and press a kiss to her lips. Only when he'd finally gotten the chance, he'd been so damn hard he couldn't withstand the torment her reaction to his kiss had caused.

And he said the absolutely worst thing he could have said.

He'd told her no.

She had wrapped herself around him, pressed herself against him, and he'd lost all control. He felt himself slipping, and he said the first thing that had come to his mind because he didn't want it to end, and he was so close to the edge after that first, brief kiss.

He hadn't seen her other than at meals in the three days since. She kept to her rooms, coming out only to exercise Henry in the gardens. He tiptoed around his own home, worried he might upset her. He took any excuse to leave the house, rushing out when his solicitor dropped him a note about some investing affairs that required his attention. He'd even attended a lecture on the proper rotation of legumes when sowing crop fields. He didn't even harvest legumes on his estates.

It needn't matter. He simply could not bear the silence. At every meal, she drifted into the room, took her place at the table and bid him a greeting appropriate to the time of day. She was not sullen or downcast. Far worse, she was properly dignified. Sitting primly in her chair, back straight, shoulders square, and answered every question he posed to her with grace. Only her answers lacked the wit he had come to expect—no, cherish—and often they were monosyllabic.

He wanted the Eliza he had met on the ballroom floor. The one who demanded the truth from him. The one who had made his heart squeeze and his stomach churn. This Eliza was a mere ghost of the woman he had married.

It shouldn't have concerned him. He hadn't planned to enjoy the company of his bride. It wasn't part of his plan after all. He shouldn't be worried about her. He shouldn't miss her sharp comments and bold honesty.

And he didn't.

He *ached* for it.

If he knew how to fix it, how to undo the damage he had done, he would do it. But he didn't know how to tell her how much he desired her, how much he enjoyed touching her, how much he savored the taste of her.

He couldn't tell her because he was afraid of admitting it to himself.

"I understand congratulations are in order."

He started at Sebastian's voice but recovered to turn a scowl on his best friend.

"Come out of your cave, have you?"

Sebastian had the decency to appear sheepish. "Duty requires my attention and all that."

"Duty? Is that your excuse for not attending your friend's wedding?"

Sebastian had sent his regrets when Dax had informed him of his impending nuptials, and not for the first time, did he wonder what had happened to Sebastian when his father died. Even now in the glowing light of a packed ballroom, shadows found their way to Sebastian's face, speckling the surface in secrets and doubts.

His friend only gave that sheepish smile again. "Something like that." He gestured to the room around them. "Where is the bride in question?"

Dax followed the gesture, but it was useless. The room was overfull, and bodies were pressed in like sheep going to the shearing.

"She was absconded by her sisters as soon as we were announced."

He was glad of it, honestly. Perhaps her sisters would bolster her, help to soothe some of the pain he had caused.

"Ah, yes, I had heard rumors of the Darby sisters. I understand they are a formidable bunch."

Dax turned a wary eye on Sebastian. "That was rather mild for you."

"Would you rather I call your relations harpies?" Sebastian returned his stare.

"I suppose not."

His friend inclined his head. "Very well. I do try to maintain some level of decorum. At least when it comes to friends."

Dax doubted Sebastian had many friends left, not after the way he had secluded himself. Still, it was a worthy gesture.

"So how is the married life, old friend?"

Dax's chest tightened at his friend's innocent question. He must have hesitated too long because Sebastian made a noise of sympathy.

"I take it my advice has too soundly found its mark."

Dax frowned, refusing to meet Sebastian's gaze. "Something like that."

Sebastian gave a soft laugh that was more attributed to cynicism than humor. "I'm sorry for that. Although I can't say it's entirely bad. I would think it would be better to be wed to someone with whom one can converse than with someone with the intelligence of a doorknob."

Dax considered this, but it did nothing to unwind the trepidation that turned his stomach.

"I think I may have made a blunder." Even admitting it had a lightness spreading through him.

"How so?"

Finally, he turned to consider his friend. "I may have given her reason to feel inadequate in a certain, intimate aspect of our marriage."

"Did you tell her she is plain? That's rather callous even for me." Sebastian's voice was dry with scorn.

Dax waved away his accusation. "No, I'm afraid it's far worse than that."

Sebastian only raised an eyebrow.

Dax surveyed the members of the *ton* that clustered about him, ensuring they were rather alone in their conversation. Just to be safe, he took a step closer to Sebastian.

"I became somewhat over eager on our wedding night, and I gave the indication that I may not have been enjoying myself."

Sebastian's laugh was full of humor now. "You told the poor girl to stop, didn't you?"

"Something like that," Dax muttered.

"And a woman already condemned as a wallflower took this at its worst possible meaning."

Dax could only nod.

Sebastian drew a deep breath. "You've gone and done it now. Isn't that what they say?"

Dax shuffled his feet. "I suppose it is."

"I can't say I did not warn you." Sebastian studied him, and Dax grew uncomfortable under his friend's stare.

"I hadn't realized what a fatal flaw there was in my plan."

Sebastian turned away, feigning disinterest as a few people shuffled too close as someone pressed through the crowd. When the space around them emptied the slightest bit, Sebastian turned back to him.

"And what have you done to correct this misunderstanding?"

"Nothing."

Sebastian's glance was sharp and fast.

Dax frowned. "I wasn't sure how to go about it without making it worse."

"You could start by explaining why it is you said what you did. The girl is unskilled in this matter." He stopped short and peered at Dax directly. "The girl is unskilled, yes?"

"Did you just insinuate that my wife was not a virgin upon our marriage?"

"I don't see why such a matter may be one of assumed conclusion. Who am I to say what kind of activities your wife engages in?"

"Please stop suggesting my wife is a woman of immoral fiber."

Sebastian scoffed. "Your wife is hardly of immoral fiber. I've never seen a woman with more solid values and an intrinsic sense of good."

Dax was left momentarily speechless by his friend's words as he'd never heard Sebastian pay anyone such a compliment.

"I'll keep that in mind," he finally said. "That doesn't help the current situation I find myself in."

"You should be honest with her. Tell her how you feel."

"Tell her how I feel?" Dax had to struggle to keep his voice down. "The entire point of this farce was to marry a woman so ugly I would never be in danger of falling in love with her."

He sucked in a breath to calm himself and turned his gaze

on Sebastian. Only Sebastian was no longer looking at him. Instead, his attention was fixed just over Dax's shoulder.

Cold dread seeped through him.

He turned, following the line of Sebastian's gaze to find his wife standing just behind him, her arm slightly raised as if she had just been about to touch his arm to gain his attention.

"Eliza." The word rushed from him like an oath on the last bit of air he could successfully pull into his lungs.

His mind melted, one thought colliding into another.

How much had she heard?

Her lips were parted, and her eyes were wide. Her chest heaved with stilted breaths.

She'd heard everything.

She'd heard him call her ugly. She'd heard him call their marriage a farce.

She'd heard him say he could never fall in love with her.

He wanted to touch her. If he could only grab hold of her, he could keep her from falling apart in the middle of a packed ballroom at the feet of a society so critical it would take pleasure in tearing her limb from limb at her weakest moment.

But he couldn't touch her. He couldn't make himself draw air, let alone move his body. He could speak to her. He could reassure her that she'd misheard him.

Except she hadn't misheard. He'd said plainly exactly what his cold, heartless plan had been.

Only it wasn't anything like that.

What had Sebastian just said? Tell her the truth.

"Eliza, please let me explain."

She didn't move. He didn't know if she had even blinked in the seconds he'd stood before her. Her arm still hung suspended between them, her small hand reaching.

"Eliza—"

"No."

The word was so soft he almost missed it. One single word that weakened his knees, that dropped his stomach to his toes, that rendered his heart useless.

She dropped her hand, and it was like a guillotine coming down on his neck. One final blow to end him.

She shook her head, the movement gentle and with a painful grace.

"No," she repeated, louder this time and with an edge of defiance.

Then she gathered her skirts. He watched her do it, each pulse of her arms, each curl of fists, registering with painful exactness.

"No." This final word was direct, and it hit its mark solidly in his chest.

She met his gaze directly. Her lips had firmed, her jaw tightened. Her eyes—God, her eyes were like daggers, piercing right through his useless heart.

She didn't say another word. She turned and disappeared into the crowd.

CHAPTER 6

*U*gly.
  Farce.
Never be in danger of falling in love.

The words played over and over in a sick loop in her head as she wedged herself between bodies, pushing ever farther into the crowd. Each person she put between herself and her husband was a weight lifted from her lungs. She sucked in air as if there were no more to be had, and she was some kind of guilty thief.

She tumbled from the throng when she reached the periphery. She'd ended up along the refreshment tables, and a few matrons loitered about, sipping at lemonade and commenting on how their slippers pinched their feet. The chaperones should be along here somewhere.

Jo and Louisa had pulled her aside as soon as she'd entered the ballroom, and she couldn't have been more grateful for them. They'd distracted her from her unending torment and pulled the tension from her shoulders when she had thought it would live there permanently.

But now she needed more than Jo and Louisa. She needed

a savior. Someone who could get her out of here, away from this man who had so soundly shredded what little confidence she had.

Her eyes were dry, but her hands shook, her skirts rustling as she pressed once more into the crowd, thrusting herself in the direction where the chaperones must be. Once more she broke free into a lighter space where matrons milled about a line of chairs, exchanging bits of gossip.

There was Viv, resplendent in a gown of sapphire silk that set her hair alight with shots of fire. Eliza rushed forward, heedless of the stares and gawks. She grasped her sister's arm, and when she turned, Eliza needed to say only one thing.

"Viv."

She poured all of her earnestness into saying her sister's name. All of the hurt. All of her anger. All of her despair.

Viv didn't ask any questions. She didn't even return her sister's greeting. She took Eliza's arm and stormed into the crowd. The crowd always parted for the Duchess of Margate. People fell away to the side either because of the woman's status or because of the expression of utter domination on her face.

Hell hath no fury after all.

Viv understood what Eliza had poured into her name without having to ask. Viv had felt it, Eliza knew, because Viv had lived it. And Viv would seek revenge for any woman who had endured the humiliation only a husband could wrought.

Unerringly, she found Andrew ensconced in a group of men earnestly discussing the mining situation in Wales and again, she needn't say anything. Andrew saw the look on her face, and his gaze pivoted, capturing Eliza's.

Andrew had always been kind to her, a fierce and loyal brother, but she had never seen the hard look that overcame him then. It stilled Eliza's hands and a full breath of air cascaded into her lungs.

Andrew excused himself and stepped in front of Viv, parting the crowd even more effectively than the Duchess of Margate had. It was only seconds until they spilled into the cool air outside, trickling along the line of carriages still emptying people onto the front steps of the Devonshire estate.

A footman scurried down the pavement to fetch the Ravenwood carriage, and Eliza watched him go, mesmerized by his hurried movements as air, precious air seeped back into her lungs, revived her senses, and started to clear away the jumble of her mind.

"What's happened?" Andrew's tone was icy and unyielding.

"Andrew, not here." Viv kept her hand on Eliza's arm.

It needn't matter what they said. She still couldn't speak. Ashbourne's words played out over and over again in her head.

Ugly.

Farce.

Never be in danger of falling in love.

Without warning, the tears came, hot and relentless, pouring down her face in ugly streams. The sobs came next, wracking her body until she was bent over, only Viv's arms holding her up. Andrew entered her line of vision as she hurtled toward the pavement on a vicious sob. Viv said something, but she couldn't understand. Her body was overcome with so much emotion, it ripped her physically apart.

Only one sound had the power to stop it, and it cut through the night like a whip.

Ashbourne's voice as he yelled her name. "Eliza!"

Viv turned behind her. Eliza could feel her sister's body turn against her back, likely to peer up at the steps where'd they just come, where Ashbourne likely stood. Andrew moved out of her line of sight, a sharp march to the left. But Eliza couldn't turn and look. She didn't want to see him. She couldn't see him. It might just kill her.

Carriage wheels rolled to a stop in front of her. She recognized the colors, the crest, and she yearned toward their familiarity. Viv's arms tightened, and Eliza gave a strangled sound. It must have drawn Viv's attention because her arms loosened, allowing Eliza to spill toward the now open door of the Ravenwood carriage.

But before she made it, the sound of footsteps ringing on pavement met her ears, but it was cut off by the sound of her brother's voice.

It sent an icy cold finger scraping down her spine. She'd never heard her brother sound so menacing.

"Stay away from her, Ashbourne, or I'll be forced to call you out."

Viv hustled her into the carriage, but Eliza was suddenly hit with the need to turn, to find Ashbourne.

He stood on the steps of the Devonshire estate, his hand raised in her direction as if he were reaching out for her, his face a mask of contorted pain. The man he had been speaking to in the ballroom rushed down the stairs behind him, his hands reaching for Ashbourne as if to hold him back. Her gaze skittered, searching.

Ah, Andrew. Ashbourne wasn't paying attention to her brother and at any moment the two men would collide if Ashbourne wasn't stopped.

But Ashbourne was only looking at her.

The anguish on his face sliced through her despair, and she faltered on the step of the carriage. Only Viv was there to press her forward, to push her to the bench where she could finally collapse. Andrew sprang into the carriage, and they were underway before Eliza could speak.

"Tosser," Andrew muttered as soon as the door snapped shut.

"Andrew." Viv's tone was scolding.

"Well, he obviously is one." He must have gestured at Eliza, but she wasn't paying attention.

She had her face pressed to the cool glass of the window as she tried to calm her nerves, steady her breathing.

Viv's hand on her shoulder had her starting.

"Eliza, darling, whatever happened?" Her voice was so soothing, more tears came to Eliza's eyes.

She shook her head, not yet ready to speak.

The ride to Ravenwood House was tense and awkward, but she didn't care. She didn't know whether she wanted to upset her stomach or crawl into bed and never come out.

She couldn't do either of those things, she knew. As soon as she had recovered herself, she must return to Ashbourne House for Henry. She couldn't leave him there, but right now, she couldn't have set foot outside of the carriage if her very life depended on it.

When they arrived at Ravenwood, Viv alighted first and pulled Eliza down with her. It wasn't until they were safely in the house that Eliza realized Andrew wasn't behind them.

She gave Viv a questioning look.

"He's gone back for Louisa and Jo. God knows what they'll do if they hear of what happened before Andrew can collect them."

Eliza didn't respond. She just allowed herself to be trundled into the drawing room where only a week before she'd experienced her first kiss.

A kiss shared with a man who thought her so ugly he would be incapable of falling in love with her.

She winced as the words traveled through her head yet again. She should have known. It was too much to believe a duke would actually wish to marry her. She'd thought their union had promise if Ashbourne hadn't sought her hand for her money. That was at least something.

But this...

He had called it a farce.

Viv pressed a glass into her hands and forced her to sip. The brandy was hot and vile, but she choked it down until warmth spread through her stomach. Viv took the glass back.

"What happened?" she asked again.

"Did you see the man standing behind Ashbourne on the Devonshire steps?"

Viv nodded. "Sebastian Fielding, the Duke of Waverly." A line appeared between her eyes. "Did he do something to you?"

Eliza shook her head so quickly the room swam.

"No, no, it's not that. Ashbourne was speaking to him when I went to find him." She swallowed, pain capturing her voice as she tried to relay what she had overheard. "Ashbourne told this man he'd had a plan for his—" Her voice trembled and stopped at the word *farce*.

Her marriage was a farce?

It was one thing for Ashbourne to not desire her. It was another to think her entire marriage, the one thing she dreamed of and expected never to happen, was a lark to her husband.

She swallowed and closed her eyes, forcing the words out. "Ashbourne said the entire point of his farce of a marriage was to marry someone so ugly he wouldn't be in danger of falling in love with her."

She winced at Viv's sharp intake of breath, and the tears came again. She tried to suck them back in with a hiccupy sob, but once begun, she couldn't stop. Viv's arms were around her in a moment, her hand pressed to the back of

Eliza's neck until she was fully cocooned in her sister's embrace.

Viv made shushing noises and said something about men being arseholes, but Eliza couldn't really make it out over her own cries. Finally, the tears seemed to drain out of her, and there was nothing left but a hiccup or two. Viv eased her back onto the sofa, and Eliza carefully met her gaze.

She'd expected Viv to show concern, but instead her features were riddled with confusion.

"What is it?" Eliza asked, her voice soupy with shed tears.

Viv shook her head. "It just doesn't make sense."

Eliza frowned and gestured to herself. "Of course, it makes sense. I am not so naive as to believe any man would find me appealing."

Viv's own frown was quick. "I wasn't speaking of your looks, Eliza. Ashbourne's actions do not match his words."

"What do you mean?"

Viv pushed to her feet, pacing away down the length of the drawing room.

"Ashbourne called your marriage a farce. He said he planned to marry someone so ugly he would not find her appealing enough to fall in love with her." She paused to eye Eliza. "Those were his exact words?"

Eliza nodded. "Yes, that's what he told that man, Waverly."

Viv put her hands to her hips. "Eliza, why would a man who felt incapable of falling in love with you chase after you through a crowded society ball when he thought he'd hurt your feelings?" She came back to Eliza and perched on the sofa beside her. "A man doesn't chase after a woman he doesn't care about."

There was something deep in Viv's eyes, and Eliza realized her sister spoke of herself. When Viv had left, Margate had not come after her. A new kind of sadness clutched Eliza, and she took her sister's hand into her own.

"But what about what he said?"

"Did he specifically say you were ugly?"

"No." Eliza spoke the word carefully, trying hard to push the memory of her wedding night from her mind. "But wouldn't he have selected me because I fit whatever criteria he had in mind?"

Viv seemed to dismiss this. "Has Ashbourne done anything else to demonstrate how he might feel about you?"

Her wedding night sprang to the fore almost immediately, but she paused, her mind tripping over another memory.

"He purchased a sofa to be placed in my rooms at Ashbourne House for Henry."

Viv sat back. "He bought a sofa for your dog?"

Eliza nodded.

Viv pursed her lips before speaking. "Eliza, you once told me there should be an understanding between a husband and wife. For better or worse, you are wed to this man. Have you told Ashbourne what you want from your marriage?"

She opened her mouth to say she didn't want anything, but that wasn't true. She wanted a baby. She wanted a family. She wanted children to love and cherish and nurture. She wanted to share her life with someone.

"No." A calm she had not felt in days washed through her at the single word.

"Then I think you need to tell him." Viv squeezed her hand, and Eliza felt a surge of strength.

She would tell Ashbourne. She would tell Ashbourne exactly what she wanted. He could have his farce of a marriage, but she was going to get something in return.

* * *

IT WASN'T until he was three glasses into what he hoped

would be mind-numbing drunkenness that Dax realized he'd nearly ended up in a duel with his wife's brother.

"He said what?"

Dax looked over at Sebastian who seemed unaffected by alcohol at all.

"He said he was going to be forced to challenge you if you came near his sister." Sebastian said it with such neutrality, one may have thought he was discussing the weather.

"Challenge me? What for?"

Sebastian eyed him.

It was enough for him to recall the sound of Eliza's cries echoing through the chilled night air in front of the Devonshire estate. It had done something to him he swore a woman would never have the power to do to him again.

She'd cut him, deeply, with her anguish, and it was so much worse because he had been the cause of it.

He had chased after her. There was no choice in the matter. He couldn't let her go thinking what she must have thought of what she'd overheard. Sebastian was right. He had to tell her the truth. But would she believe him now?

He hadn't caught up to her in the crush of the ballroom, but he'd seen the parting of the crowd the Duchess of Margate had caused and knew Eliza had to be with her. He followed as quickly as the crowd had allowed, but he was too late. He saw the Ravenwood carriage approaching, the Duchess of Margate all but holding Eliza up, and Ravenwood. Damn Ravenwood had stood there like a mythical sentry, standing between him and his wife.

He'd called out to her. It was the only thing left to him, and he thought for a moment she would listen to him. But when she'd turned, he'd seen the tears on her cheeks, the way a sob wracked her mouth, and everything inside of him stopped.

If Sebastian hadn't caught him just at that moment, he

would likely have tumbled directly down the Devonshire stairs. He stared after his retreating bride, swept away by the bolstering familiarity and comfort of family.

He let her go.

The pain had been one thing. He understood pain, but there had been something else on Eliza's face, something with which he was far too familiar. He saw rejection. In an instant, he was a naive twenty-three year old sapling standing in the middle of a ballroom waiting for the woman he loved who never came. There in the twist of her lips, the anguish of her eyes, Dax had seen it reflected in his own wife's face, and it had rendered him dead.

"Dax, hold fast, mate."

It was only Sebastian calling him by a name his friend had not used since Eton that Dax had been able to stop himself from hurtling down those stairs, from lying prostrate at her feet and begging her to listen.

Sebastian wasn't stopping him from getting Eliza he realized now. He was preventing him from getting murdered by an irate brother. Sebastian had hustled him into his own carriage and had the driver take them immediately to the club where Mandricks began applying a steady stream of alcohol.

"I owe you a great deal then, Sebastian. Name your price." Dax drained the last of his glass.

"Leave me out of this affair." The words were said with a degree of sarcasm that made Dax laugh.

"I'm not sure I meant to get you involved in it."

Sebastian was quiet, uncomfortably so, and Dax stole a glance at him. They occupied the same chairs they had hardly a week previously when Sebastian had advised him that it was one's personality which lent itself to love. His friend had once again crossed an ankle over the opposite knee, but while he had been engaging a week ago, now his friend merely sat and pondered the fire.

Dax considered his now empty glass. "I'm afraid I've made a terrible mistake."

Sebastian moved only his eyes to him. "Made a mistake? By marrying someone you find witty and engaging? I wouldn't call that a mistake."

"It wasn't a part of the plan though."

He hated that word suddenly. Why he had thought he could be objective about any of this was preposterous. It needn't matter how formal the arrangement. The pairing of two people inherently involved emotional tensions, and he'd picked a woman far more complicated than he'd anticipated. He should have picked one of those silly debutantes that fluttered about him. Not one with an observant eye and a truthful tongue.

"Perhaps making a plan at all was your error. Learning of it seems to have upset your bride."

"You're being rather generous."

Sebastian tapped his glass against his knee. "Discovering one is playing a role in another's machinations can often be upsetting."

His friend's tone was sharp, almost as if he spoke from some old pain. Dax slid him a glance.

"I suppose you're right."

"I am right."

Dax shifted in his chair. He looked about for the footman who had been refilling his glass to find the decanter had been set on the table next to him.

"What time is it?" he was compelled to ask.

"It's gone a little past two."

Dax nearly dropped the decanter. "In the morning?"

"That would be correct."

He managed to get a few fingers of whiskey in his glass

and replaced the topper on the decanter without spilling too much before sinking back in his chair. He swallowed more of the fiery spirit than he meant to and coughed.

"Do you plan to spend the entire night here getting sloshed?"

The question was direct, the words choice.

"What if I were?"

"I would tell you you're a damned fool."

He peered at his friend over his glass. "Do you know what people say about you?"

Sebastian's smile was a little proud. "I know precisely what they say of me."

"I don't believe them in the slightest on principle, but then you go and say something to make me doubt my resolve." Dax shook his head.

"Perhaps society is right. I am the Beastly Duke after all." He met Dax's gaze. "I simply find you less irritating then most members of the *ton*."

"That's comforting."

They sat in silence for several seconds, the crackling of the fire and the tick of a clock somewhere the only sounds in the room. The club was quiet at this hour of the night but not entirely empty. Society was very much still awake as balls and soirees would just be getting into full swing. In an hour or so these rooms would be filled with gentlemen who had tipped out of a ball and needed somewhere to land when they hadn't acquired a warm bed with a willing widow or lonely wife.

But right now, Dax drew comfort from its quietness and plethora of whiskey.

"You should go get her."

The words were spoken so softly, Dax almost missed them.

"Eliza? Go after her?"

Sebastian nodded. "You should tell her the truth."

"She won't believe me now." Dax stared into his drink.

"But does the probability of her belief determine whether or not you should tell the truth at all?"

Those were heavy words for a man as drunk as him, and he waded through them carefully.

"You're saying I should tell her anyway? Despite the fact I said the worst thing imaginable to her?"

Sebastian dropped his foot to the ground. "You didn't say the words to her. You said them to me. And it wasn't the worst thing you could have said to her."

Dax straightened at this, feeling suddenly rather sober. "What would have been the worst thing?"

Sebastian's eyes were hard in the firelight. "You could have told her she mattered not to you."

Again, Sebastian's voice had a quality of knowing, and it sent a chill through Dax. One day he would make his friend tell him what had happened in those empty years but not tonight.

"Do you speak of indifference?"

Sebastian turned his gaze upon Dax. "Precisely. There's nothing worse than knowing a person cares so little for you your actions do not affect them in the slightest."

Dax studied the fire. "That they would leave you all alone standing in the middle of a ball thrown in your honor."

Sebastian said nothing, and he needn't have. They were both thinking of their own demons.

Somewhere the hour chimed, but neither of them moved. At some point the decanter was replaced with a full one, but no one disturbed them. It was nearly four o'clock when Sebastian stood.

"The balls have spit out the losers of the evening, it seems."

Dax roused himself from his study of the flames. He was

quite convinced they looked like marigolds in a quadrille. He became aware of the hushed conversations about him and the sudden odor of cigars.

"It would seem so." Dax attempted to turn about and take in the commotion behind him, but his hand slipped on the arm of his chair. He steadied himself and peered at his glass, which seemed to be empty again. Next he eyed the decanter, but his vision blurred, and he couldn't quite make it out.

"I think you've reached saturation." Sebastian stood and plucked the glass from his hand. "If you won't go retrieve your wife and explain yourself, you should at least go home and sober up."

Sobering up seemed like a terrible idea.

He scoffed. "I think I'll go home and find the good whiskey my father used to keep in the study."

Without ceremony, Sebastian grasped him by the front of his jacket and hauled him to his feet. He tipped dangerously, but Sebastian righted him with little trouble. For a moment, Dax was unusually afraid of his friend and was all too worried the gossips were right. Just how beastly had Sebastian grown?

"I realize you may not have the faculties to listen to me just now, but I'm hoping at some point these words sink in. Eliza is now your bloody wife whether you like it or not. You should at least make peace with that and come to some sort of understanding. You are wed after all. You could both gain advantages from the union and live some kind of contented life."

Sebastian let go, and Dax stumbled against the chair he had just vacated. He watched as Sebastian adjusted the cuffs of his jacket.

"I'll see you home."

He didn't wait for Dax to agree. Once again, his friend picked him up bodily and bundled him out of his club.

CHAPTER 7

When dawn began to lighten the sky, she decided to come to terms with the fact that Ashbourne may not be returning that night.

Once she'd considered this, she allowed her mind to orchestrate an endless list of heart wrenching scenarios.

He was even now abed with an opera singer. This was a familial favorite.

He was at his club, enjoying a rousing hand of cards, a good whiskey, and bawdy banter with friends.

He was frequenting a house of ill repute.

This made her loins clench, and she said a small prayer she hadn't caught something from him if he were so inclined to such activities. She'd heard the maids of Ravenwood titter about such things and wished nothing to do with it.

The list had the potential to be endless, and with her imagination, it certainly could have been.

She was saved, however, from such torture by the sound of the front door opening. She stirred from her place by the fire in the drawing room of Ashbourne House where Mrs.

Fitzhugh had sent a footman to build up the fire and brought in some tea while Eliza had waited for her husband to return.

The housekeeper was good at her position as she asked no questions when Eliza had returned in the Ravenwood carriage without her husband.

Henry had been waiting for Eliza and was glad to have a short romp in the gardens to do his business before curling up in front of the fire in the drawing room to wait for something he knew not.

Eliza had shed the gown she'd worn to the ball as the fabric began to crawl on her skin. She'd unpinned her hair and plaited it for the night, surprised Ashbourne hadn't returned while she'd attended her toilette. She'd planned to confront him in his rooms, but when he didn't return, she'd wandered into the drawing room.

It was several hours later now, and there was still no sign of him. She'd sent the servants to bed. She could tend the fire, and what was left of the tea had grown cold, not that she'd touched much of it.

She grew tired, but her body buzzed with an energy she had not felt before. Strength bristled within her, and confidence brimmed at the surface. Suddenly her marriage was no longer about her. It was about something more, something greater.

She could state her demands because they truly didn't involve her. The dukedom needed an heir. It was as simple as that. She would demand Ashbourne fulfill his duties until an heir and a spare were born. If she were lucky, she may get several girls in the process as well. She may get an entire brood of children if she were fortunate enough. A small smile came to her lips at the thought.

The clatter of the front door opening had her resolve faltering, and she stood, drawing a deep, fortifying breath. She ran her palms down her dressing gown to stop her hands from shaking. Compulsively, she ensured the collar of her plain white nightdress was secured firmly about her throat and the sash of her dressing gown tightly secured.

When she expected to hear his footsteps in the corridor, she was surprised to hear two sets of footsteps. Her stomach lurched, and her hand went to her throat.

Drat. What if he'd brought home the opera singer?

She looked about her as if to find a place to hide. Would he bring her into this room? Would he see her like this? His ugly wife hoping for a mere glimpse of him? How pitiful.

The footsteps became more distinct, and she realized they were too heavy to be a man and a woman but perhaps more likely two men. Henry lifted his head from his spot by the fire in question. She was not one for indecision, and she plunged toward the door and wrenched it open just as the footsteps reached it.

On the other side of the door was indeed her husband with the man he had been speaking to at the ball.

"Your Grace," Eliza said to the other man. Viv had said he was Sebastian Fielding, the Duke of Waverly.

He gave a startled smile as if he hadn't expected to find her there, which indeed she hadn't expected to see him either.

"Your Grace," he said in return with a nod of his head, and then he slid his gaze to the man he held under his arm.

Eliza followed his gaze to find her husband pinned beneath the other duke's arm, wavering unsteadily on his feet.

"Is he drunk?"

"Extremely," Waverly said. "Shall I?" He nodded to the interior, and she stepped back to allow him entrance.

Waverly managed to get Ashbourne to the nearest sofa before the man brought him to his knees.

"Is that my wife?" Ashbourne mumbled. "I don't want to see my wife."

Waverly shot her a nervous smile. "It is your wife, mate, and you should probably not say anything more until you have your senses about you again."

Eliza pressed her hands to the queasiness that erupted in her stomach. Ashbourne didn't wish to speak to her? Well, that was fine. He needn't speak at all. He had only to listen to her demands.

Ashbourne made another mumbling noise, but she couldn't decipher it. Waverly stood, adjusting his jacket.

"Sebastian Fielding," he said with a small bow. "I apologize for the odd introduction."

Mrs. Fitzhugh had lit several candles earlier, and now Eliza could just make out the Duke of Waverly's features. He was tall for one and possessed a quiet strength. He was not overly broad, but he'd managed to get Ashbourne up a flight of stairs and into the drawing room, which was no easy feat. His eyes, though, were haunted, and it saddened her.

"Your Grace." She returned his bow with an awkward curtsy as her dressing gown clung to her legs.

"Sebastian, please," he said with the same nervous smile. He seemed to think something over and upon making a decision stepped closer to her. "I am not prone to dabble in others' private lives. To be frank, it is none of my concern." He cast a thoughtful gaze on Ashbourne's prone body then. "But I feel compelled to speak now. As you likely know, Ashbourne suffered a great humiliation once, and it's caused him to behave oddly in matters of emotional import." He searched her face as if looking for understanding. She nodded, and he continued. "I would not listen to a thing the tosser has to say tonight."

She raised her eyebrows at the profanity, but Sebastian seemed to have no concern for speaking so in front of her.

"I see," she said, her eyes drifting to her husband who had begun to snore.

"However." She swung her gaze back to Sebastian. "If there is anything you should like to discuss with him, I would do it this evening while he lacks the ability to say no." Sebastian gave her a sarcastic smile and a bow. "Good day, Your Grace."

He spun about on his heel and left with precise steps, the door clicking soundly behind him.

Without wasting a moment, Eliza went over to her husband and poked him. He did not so much as interrupt a snore.

She shook him harder.

"Ashbourne." She'd never raised her voice before except in those rare instances when Henry had gotten into things which could have made him ill had she not stopped him with a startling noise. She tried to make it more forceful. "Ashbourne."

Nothing.

She straightened, squaring her shoulders.

She must wake him. She was not about to let this linger until the next day.

Or rather today as it were.

She looked about her, hoping to find something to wake him with when her eyes set on the abandoned tea service. She marched over and snapped up the teapot, leaving its lid on the cart. She returned to Ashbourne and shook him once more. There was no helping it. She turned over the teapot directly on his head.

He woke with a splutter and a curse she found far too satisfying. He shook tea from his head and scrubbed it from his face.

"What is this?" he muttered through the stream of cold tea down his face.

Pleased to see him awake, she sat on the low table in front of the sofa so she could face him directly.

"Ashbourne," She said sternly enough to have him focusing. "It seems there's been a misunderstanding in regards to the terms of our marriage. I was not informed that you required an ugly wife with whom you would not be in danger of falling in love to carry out your farce." She said the words as cruelly as she'd overheard them earlier that night.

Ashbourne winced and raised a hand as if to defend himself. He opened his mouth, but she did not have the fortitude to withstand an apology. Not tonight and not one to be laced with placating falsehoods as she was sure his would be.

"It needn't matter what role I am to play in this farce." She took pleasure in repeating the terrible word. "I've had worse accusations thrown at me. Being deemed ugly is hardly the worst of them. But if I am to play a role in this marriage, I should ask that you play one as well."

He blinked at her, and she knew she had his attention.

"It is my duty as the duchess to beget an heir for the continuation of the title, and I will not allow your inability to couple with someone as ugly as myself to prevent me from doing my duty."

He raised his eyebrows at the word *couple*, and she could only imagine what he thought of her. She pressed on.

"As I require your assistance in such matters, I will expect you to visit my bedchamber every evening as is suitable until an heir and a spare are produced. Do I have your word on this matter?"

Ashbourne continued to blink.

"Visit your bedchamber?"

She swallowed. How could a man so well respected be so utterly obtuse when it came to personal matters?

"I require you as a partner in sexual congress so we may create a child who may one day inherit the Ashbourne title."

He blanched, and she worried for a moment he would upset his stomach. She wasn't sure how much spirits he had consumed, but it was likely a great deal to require assistance in obtaining his home.

"Ashbourne, do you understand the terms of the agreement?"

"I'm to visit your bedchamber every evening."

"Every evening that is acceptable. I shall inform you of the evenings when I am not able to receive you, and you will be relieved of your duty for that evening. Once the heir and spare are secured, you will be released from your requirements. You need never visit my bedchamber again."

She had until that very moment kept a firm hold on her emotions, but when she realized at some point Ashbourne would no longer visit her, a coldness passed through her. The awful truth of it was she enjoyed his company. He was easy to converse with and possessed an intelligent demeanor. She had thought she had done remarkably well when it came to the match until she'd learned she was only a pawn in his terrible plan.

She cradled the empty teapot in her lap, wrapping both of her hands around the pottery and squeezing it to stay focused. She was nearly there.

A look passed over his features then, so fleeting she almost missed it. Had she not known better she would have thought him sad that she would be reduced to such an arrangement if only to get the baby she so badly wanted, but Ashbourne didn't think of her in those terms. She filled a purpose for him. He would fill a purpose for her, no matter how her heart might yearn for more.

Ashbourne nodded, his eyelids slipping.

"I require a verbal affirmation." She grabbed his arm to keep him from falling back into unconsciousness.

He pitched forward, and she feared he would tumble from the sofa.

"I will gladly visit your bedchamber every evening, Your Grace." His lips turned up in gleeful smirk before he fell backwards on the sofa with a rapturous snore.

She studied him for several seconds, her emotions in free fall as she thought of the smirk he'd given her, almost as if he looked forward to his nightly visits. It was absolute nonsense.

She pushed to her feet and whistled for Henry even as her gaze remained on her unconscious husband.

But even as she told herself it was rubbish, she couldn't help but remember what Viv had said.

Men didn't chase after women for whom they did not care.

* * *

HE AWOKE QUESTIONING several things at once.

Why was he asleep on his drawing room sofa?

Why did he smell of tea?

And most importantly, why was the sofa and his person so damp?

He struggled to a sitting position and regretted it immediately. The room swam about him like a strange theater show at Covent Garden. He shut his eyes, putting a hand to his forehead to see if he could physically stop the spinning. When he was fully upright and had stabilized himself against the sofa cushions, he attempted to open his eyes again. Just mere slits at first, he worked his way until they were completely open.

He was most definitely in the drawing room of Ashbourne House. He reeked of tea and whiskey, an odd combination of which he had no memory in terms of how it had come about.

He got his feet under him and pushed upward, but it didn't take. He collapsed back against the sofa just as the door opened. Carver entered with a silver tray. The aroma of strong coffee assailed him, and his stomach threatened to turn over. The butler deposited the tray in front of him.

"Your Grace," he said with a small bow.

The tray contained an urn of coffee and a plate of plain toast. Bile bubbled in his throat at the sight of it, but he knew if he were to gain his feet this morning, he must consume it. He started with the coffee.

"The house is readying for your departure, Your Grace, and you and the duchess shall be underway as planned."

He squinted at the butler. "Underway?"

Carver straightened. "Yes, Your Grace. You wished to leave for Ashbourne Manor today. Have your plans been altered? I will alert the staff immediately if so."

He waved a hand. They were leaving today? How was it here already? He could hardly remember the night before. Where had they been? A ball of some sort, he surmised if his wrinkled attire were any suggestion.

"Carver." His voice sounded as though it had been mangled by various forms of farm machinery. "Carver, where is the duchess?"

"She is breaking her fast presently in the morning room."

Dax had almost managed to get his fingers around the steaming cup of pitch black coffee when something in Carver's voice stopped him. The butler had been with Ashbourne House since before Dax held the title and never had he heard the butler's pitch fluctuate. But just then, Dax swore he heard the smallest of inflections.

He squinted up at the man. "She's breaking her fast. That's superb."

Carver would not meet his gaze.

"Carver." Dax struggled to clear his throat. "I appear to be suffering the effects of ingesting dangerous levels of alcohol. May I have committed some act during my state of drunkenness that I may regret?"

Carver's lips firmed, but man of honor that he was, he did not flinch.

"Your Grace, may I speak boldly?"

Dear God, what had he done? "Yes, you may."

"The servants and myself and Mrs. Fitzhugh have heard only the rumors that pass so quickly below stairs, Your Grace, and the actions of yourself and the duchess from which to draw our conclusions. I would not think to make assumptions which would impugn your honor."

"Drat, man, spit it out." Dax had the cup of coffee in his hand now and attempted a sip. The liquid was hot and rich, and it flooded every sense he hadn't shredded with alcohol. He could feel each inch of him coming back to life with every sip, and the fog began to lift from his mind.

"Your Grace, something occurred at the Devonshire ball last eve which resulted in the duchess returning to Ashbourne House alone and awaiting your arrival here in the drawing room until nearly dawn."

Carver needn't say anything more because just at that moment the previous night came careening back to Dax, and his stomach did give up then. The cup rattled on the tray as he plunked it down before dropping it.

"Carver, I've done something unforgivable."

The night before materialized in sick snatches of memory. Speaking with Sebastian about Eliza. Eliza overhearing what he'd planned for his marriage. He'd chased after her. He remembered at least that, but Sebastian had stopped him. He couldn't remember why Sebastian had stopped him, but after that, he only had cloudy pieces of memory that involved whiskey and his club.

This time when he got to his feet they held under him.

"I must speak with the duchess."

Carver took two neat steps backward. "Yes, of course, Your Grace."

Dax was fully alert by the time he made the corridor, and he raced down the stairs. The breakfast room was just off the main corridor, and he was there within seconds.

Eliza sat with her back to the front windows, and she was illuminated in morning sunshine. Her riotous hair was neatly pinned, and her gown was of an unmentionable blue. Henry was nowhere to be seen.

He stepped into the room, clearing his throat to bid his wife good morning, when he took in the rest of her visage. There were dark bruises beneath her eyes, and a puffiness to her cheeks that was not normally there. He recalled what Carver had said. She'd waited up for his return. She was likely dead on her feet, sleep deprived, and—

With cutting clarity, the sound of her sobs rushed into his memory.

He'd made her cry.

No, it was more than that. The sounds she had been making could only come from someone who had had their soul wrenched from their body.

She looked up as if sensing him, her teacup braced almost to her lips. The breath froze in his lungs, and it was a physical thing to force himself forward. He collapsed in the chair closest to her, forgetting any sense of propriety.

"Eliza, I must beg your forgiveness."

Her lips had been slightly parted as if she'd meant to say something, but at his outburst, she set down her cup with a precise thud.

"Whatever are you going on about?" Her frown caused a line to form between her eyes. "Carver was to take you some coffee and toast. Did you not receive it? I should hate to think your frivolity of last night will have undue repercussions this morning."

He blinked. Undue repercussions?

She gestured with a nod to the sideboard. "Eggs always seemed to help Andrew when he sowed his wild oats in his youth. Cook makes the most remarkable eggs. Would you like me to prepare you a plate?"

She was offering to get him some eggs?

"Eliza, last night—"

"Oh, yes, I'm glad you should bring up last night. I had cause for concern that you might not recall some of what occurred while you were under the effects of the drink."

He licked his lips. God, he could drink the entire Thames right then. "Yes, I must admit I can't recall everything, but I do remember the important parts, and I must beg your forgiveness. I can explain what it is you overheard. I didn't—"

She waved a hand at him, a smile coming to her lips. "Oh, you needn't bother about all of that. We came to an understanding when you returned early this morning. There is nothing to apologize for."

He blinked, studying her face. She was like a porcelain figurine with over-large eyes and caricature features. But it was her eyes which gave her away. Her smile never reached them, and the lines about her mouth marked a certain fragility. He hated himself then. He hated himself for his carelessness, for…everything.

"Eliza, there is. You must know—"

Again, she stopped him. "Ashbourne, please. You mustn't go on like this." She pushed to her feet, setting her napkin beside her untouched plate. She drifted over to the sideboard and loaded a plate with eggs and toast. When she returned to the table, she placed the plate in front of him and reached for the teapot. "Is tea all right? I had Carver bring up the only urn of coffee to you this morning. Cook is attempting to ready the kitchens for our departure, so there isn't any more to be had, I'm afraid." She poured a neat cup of tea for him.

He could do nothing but watch this soulless pantomime. Eliza was doing everything she could to show him she was all right. That she was unfazed by what she had overheard the previous night. He had suspected deep within her was a steel forged of the disparaging remarks and cutting actions directed at her by those members of the *ton*, but he couldn't have guessed she was this determined.

She resumed her seat. "Now then. While you break your fast, I will go over the arrangement you agreed to last evening upon your return."

"Arrangement?"

Now her smile held a degree of something else, something calculating. "Yes, arrangement. I did have to wake you from your stupor. I do apologize for that."

"You doused me with cold tea." He didn't know how he knew that, but suddenly, he understood why he was still damp.

She had the audacity to appear chagrinned. "Yes, there was that. I do apologize. However, I think we were able to come to a wonderful arrangement. Don't you agree?"

Whatever this arrangement was, it seemed to placate her somehow, so he nodded along. "Yes, a wonderful arrangement."

Now her face broke into a real smile, and he realized he'd just again agreed to whatever it was she had in mind.

"Splendid." She got to her feet again. "I must finish packing, and there's Henry to see to. One of the footman has taken him into the gardens for a romp. I must say the staff are rather enamored of him. I do hope the servants of Ashbourne Manor will feel the same."

She was almost to the door before he remembered to stop her.

"Eliza, what arrangement have we come to?"

She turned quietly, her hands held calmly before her.

"You've agreed to do your part in producing an heir for the title."

What little blood was left in his head drained immediately out of his body.

"I bed your pardon."

She straightened, facing him fully, her head canted just enough to show she was enjoying this.

"You've agreed to visit my room every night until an heir and a spare to the Ashbourne title have been created at which time your duties are fulfilled, and you must never visit my room again." She gave a shrug with a smile so tinged with sadness, it wrenched his heart. "It's a wonderful arrangement, don't you agree?"

He thought if he were to stand and go to her, wrap his arms around her and kiss her the way he had that day in the Ravenwood drawing room, she would dissolve directly under his touch. She was so carefully holding herself at that moment, he couldn't bear to torture her any longer.

"Yes, I do agree." He kept his tone low, and he could see understanding in her eyes. She knew he understood just how much this was costing her.

He wanted to say more. He wanted to get her to agree to more. He wanted her to know he was going to do his damndest to make her understand how much he wanted to be with her, how much he enjoyed being with her. But he knew right now was not the time for such truths. It would take time for her to heal from what she had heard, for her to trust him again if she had ever trusted him at all.

He used the chair to help him stand. "I should like to begin tonight when we arrive at Ashbourne Manor."

She blinked, and he realized he'd startled her. So she hadn't been quite convinced of his earnestness. A spark of something dark and instinctual burned low within him. He was going to enjoy this little arrangement as long as he kept his wits about him and didn't do something foolhardy like fall in love with his wife.

"Tonight would be most agreeable."

"Then we're agreed."

"Yes, agreed."

If either of them used the word *agree* once more, they would be hauled to Bedlam.

She nodded. "I'll leave you to your breakfast."

He was pleased to see she stumbled the slightest bit as she left the room.

CHAPTER 8

*S*he sat on the forward-facing bench, Henry perched at her side, and she settled her features into a mask of neutrality, prepared for Ashbourne to join her in the carriage.

It was hardly past noon, and the footmen had loaded the last of their trunks some moments before. She'd kept her carpetbag with her watercolors and travel writing desk in the compartment with her in hopes they'd distract her during the journey. She wasn't sure how far Glenhaven and the Ashbourne seat were from London, but she was prepared to ignore absolutely everyone and everything for the duration.

She was still shaken by their encounter in the morning room earlier. While she had prepared herself for their first true interaction after learning of his hurtful plan, she wasn't at all ready for his emotion-filled apology. She'd almost believed him.

However, she couldn't quite believe he was sorry for what he had said. He was more likely he was sorry he had been overheard. It needn't matter. She had no whimsical ideas of herself. She knew just how plain and unworthy she was. It was best that they didn't flit around the subject. A straightforward marriage predicated by structure was much more to her liking.

She pressed a hand to her chest and blinked out the window.

Yes, a marriage of arrangements was just fine.

The door snapped open, and she couldn't stop her gaze from flying to it, heart tripping at the expectation of seeing her husband again.

But it wasn't Ashbourne. It was the coachman.

"Beggin' your pardon, Your Grace. Are you ready to depart?"

She blinked at the empty seat opposite her. "Yes, but where is the duke?"

The coachman pulled on the brim of his hat. "Gone ahead, Your Grace. He prefers to ride atop his steed for this journey."

"Yes, of course," she said quickly to get the coachman to close the door.

He did with stunning speed, and the carriage rocked with the force of it.

Blissfully, she was alone, and the tears came of their own accord.

She swatted at them, hating herself for having any left to give.

He didn't wish to ride with her. Well, that was all well and good. She would enjoy the privacy for a bit anyway. With her sisters always about in her younger years, she'd grown used to them prattling on with constant frivolity. She may even enjoy the quiet around her for a bit.

Henry whined, sensing her distress, and she scratched his head.

"It's all right, old boy. It's just you and me as it always is."

She pulled her carpetbag up on the bench and unlatched it long enough to tuck her spectacles carefully inside. Her fingers deftly undid the bow of her bonnet and relief swamped her as she pulled it from her head. Last, she kicked off her slippers, propping her feet on the opposite cushion.

"See?" she said to Henry. "Just divine."

She leaned her head back, and Henry settled on the bench beside her, his head in her lap. She had not slept at all the previous night. When she'd left Ashbourne in the drawing room, she'd returned to her rooms prepared to let sleep take her, but it had refused her, her mind awash with possibilities of what was to come.

She had always seen her future as a spinster. It was an obvious enough occurrence. She'd never seen herself trapped in a marriage of such coldhearted regard though. Absently, she stroked Henry's fur. There was nothing to be done about it. She'd just have to make the best of it.

Her other hand settled on her stomach. When children came, it would be different surely. She would be consumed in the raising of them. Ensuring they had proper tutors and governesses. Teaching them the things her sisters and she had done. There were so many adventures to be had when one was a child. She smiled for the first time in days at the memory of her escapades with her sisters when they were but children.

She closed her eyes, the smile still lingering on her lips.

She wasn't sure how long she'd slept, but as she'd been utterly exhausted, she wasn't surprised the rocking of the carriage did not wake her. She woke when the cadence of the wheels changed, and she found them turning.

Sitting up, she rubbed sleep from her eyes and scrambled to pull her spectacles from her carpetbag. Shoving them on her face, she peered out the window.

The sun was a fading light in the distance, sparking bursts

of orange and yellow through the perfectly straight line of trees that bordered the road.

No, they were on a drive. This must be Ashbourne Manor.

In the distance, she could just make out the delineation between land and what must have been ocean. The sun was fading, but surely that expanse of darkness just beyond her line of sight was water.

"We'll need to explore it in the morning," she whispered to Henry, belatedly realizing he was no longer next to her.

She searched the small confines of the carriage to find him sprawled on the opposite bench, blinking lazily at her. She smiled and returned her attention to the window.

The carriage slowed even more, and she heard the distinct sound of gravel crunching beneath the wheels of the carriage as they must have entered the proper drive of the manor house. Finally, they turned, and the manor house itself rose up before her. The sun struck it at an angle, casting its features in varied spaces of light and dark. She was surprised to find the house rather Palladian in style with a sweeping arch in the center of the main house flanked by two wings on either side disappearing into the fading light.

She pushed her feet into her slippers while her hand went for her spectacles and hastily tied her bonnet in place. Finally, she wrapped Henry's leash comfortingly around her hand as the carriage rolled to a stop, and the door snapped open with the precision of a well-trained servant. She pushed to the door, steeling herself to see Ashbourne as surely he would have arrived before her, only to find the jowly, stern face of what could only be the butler.

"Your Grace," he said with a small bow of his head.

It took her a moment to realize he referred to her. It was going to take an age to get used to her new title.

"Allow me to welcome you to Ashbourne Manor. We

wish you much happiness and congratulations on your union, and we look forward to serving you." The words were spoken with a deep timbre of sobriety and polish. He straightened. "I am Stephens. It is my honor to introduce you to the rest of the staff."

She moved her gaze from the butler to see the line of servants spilling down the front stoop, all perfectly ironed and standing at attention. There were several footmen and maids, perhaps a cook and a stable lad, and at the very top, a smallish woman who was likely the housekeeper. The light had nearly gone now, and the line of servants were mostly undefined blobs of black, and a wave of uneasiness overcame her at such unfamiliarity.

She swallowed it down and attempted a pleasant smile. "Thank you all," she said as loudly as she could as the housekeeper was quite some distance away.

Henry gave a bark then, startling some of the maids in the line, and Eliza quickly stepped down so they could see he was harmless. She ignored the butler's proffered hand. If her new husband was not there to help her alight, she required no assistance at all. Henry dropped down beside her, eliciting a giggle from one of the maids.

Eliza stepped back. "Henry, say hello."

Henry dropped to the ground in a regal sit before raising his front paws to wave at the line of servants. More giggles erupted.

"Henry, say thank you."

Henry dropped his front paws and dipped into a low bow. The giggles turned to laughter, and she didn't miss the butler attempting to hide a smile.

The trepidation of unfamiliarity eased somewhat with the hope that she'd made a good first impression. She allowed her gaze to drift, taking in the rest of her surroundings, but she didn't see Ashbourne anywhere.

She could ask Stephens if he'd arrived, but she didn't wish to appear eager. Instead she allowed Stephens to bring her up the line of servants, introducing her and Henry as they went. When she arrived at the housekeeper, a Mrs. Donnelly, the exhaustion of travel and unfit sleep overcame her.

She smiled tenderly at the woman. "Mrs. Donnelly, it has been an excessively long day. I wonder if I could have a bath brought up to my rooms. I'll take my evening meal there as well."

Mrs. Donnelly nodded quickly. "Of course, Your Grace. I'll have the footmen set it up immediately."

Eliza turned to Stephens. "Stephens, Henry is in need of a good run. As I'm not familiar with Ashbourne Manor, and it's growing dark, could you please advise on the best place where I may take him?"

Stephens showed her the way as the servants disassembled to begin unloading the trunks. She was brought to a large expanse of open green to the west of the manor house, and she unclipped Henry's lead.

"Have at it, boy," she said, scratching his head.

He took off the instant he realized he was free, streaking out across the green lawn. He circled her several times until he fell at her feet panting. Stephens brought him a dish of water that he lapped up immediately.

"Thank you, Stephens," she said.

The air whipped at her as she stood there, and her eyes drifted toward the blackness she'd seen from the carriage.

"Is that the ocean over there?" she asked the butler.

"Indeed, it is, Your Grace." He seemed not at all perplexed by her question.

"I've never seen the ocean," she nearly whispered, her eyes mesmerized by the darkness, hoping to form some sort of shape out of its inky blackness.

Stephens said nothing, and she called to Henry to follow her.

Ashbourne Manor was not at all what she'd expected. She'd heard rumors that houses located along the shore were fraught with mold and moisture, but Ashbourne Manor was resplendent in marbles and gilded metals. Sconces were lit along the length of the vestibule, illuminating the vast expense of the central staircase that swept up to the balcony of the upper floor. Rooms dissolved to her left and right, and the corridors disappeared into darkness.

There was no sign of Ashbourne.

She turned to Mrs. Donnelly who stood waiting to take her things.

"I should like a tour in the morning," she said.

Mrs. Donnelly hesitated the barest of degrees, and had Eliza not been looking directly at her, she may have missed it.

"Yes, of course, Your Grace," the small woman said.

Ashbourne should have been the one to guide his wife about the estate, and he should also have been the one to introduce her to his servants. It needn't matter. She was looking forward to a long soak and a good meal.

Henry trotted along beside her as Mrs. Donnelly took her up to her rooms.

"These are not typically the duchess's rooms, but His Grace said to give you a suite facing the ocean," Mrs. Donnelly explained.

Eliza started at the mention of Ashbourne, but Mrs. Donnelly was already opening a door and disappearing inside.

Eliza stepped in behind her to find herself ensconced in luxury. The floors were covered with thick colorful rugs, the walls hung with a delicate cream paper, and opposite the door, the wall was alive with windows. They were dark now and most had their drapes drawn, but she knew what she would find come daylight.

She paused just inside the door to take it in, anticipation tingling at her fingertips. The light here would be resplendent, and there was a beautiful desk pressed just under the windows in one corner. She could set up her watercolors there. A sofa was already positioned in front of the fire, and Henry sniffed it out dubiously before deeming it acceptable and scampering up onto it.

"Excuse us, Your Grace."

She jumped at the voice behind her and tripped aside as a parade of footmen carried in a great copper tub and steaming buckets of water. Mrs. Donnelly placed a stool and some fluffy towels beside the fire to warm, just within reach of the copper tub.

"I shall return momentarily with your supper," she said as she followed the footmen out.

The door closed softly, and finally, Eliza was alone again.

She sighed in relief, reaching up to tug at her bonnet's bow. She was shed of her clothes within minutes and gingerly tested the bath water with a single toe. Finding it more than comfortable, she slipped inside the great tub, allowing it to swallow her up. She laid her head back, closing her eyes against the exhaustion.

She soaked for some minutes before turning to scoop up the pad of soap Mrs. Donnelly had left. Carefully, she tugged at the remaining ribbon in her hair, letting the mass dip into her bath water as she began scrubbing the road dust from her person.

When the sharp knock came minutes later, she didn't hesitate, anticipating what delicious food Mrs. Donnelly had hopefully brought.

"Enter," she called, passing the pad of soap up her arms and inhaling the scent of roses.

"I do hope you're hungry. Mrs. Donnelly has sent up a reputable feast."

She shrieked and dropped the soap at her husband's voice. She scrambled to both sink in the water and cover herself at the same time.

Henry bounded off the sofa at her scream and trotted over to Ashbourne with a soft growl.

"Ah, yes, Sir Henry. I had concern you had not been fed as well." Ashbourne ignored her completely, scooping up a rounded pottery dish from the tray and placing it on the floor. "The stable lad assures me this is the best combination for a healthy hound. I do believe there's even a duck bill in there, old boy."

Henry pounced on the bowl of food before Ashbourne had it set fully on the floor.

Finally, he straightened and turned, bestowing her with an innocent smile.

"Shall I help you finish your bath before we sup?"

* * *

HE HAD every intention of making this as enjoyable for her as possible, but the moment he saw her in the tub, soap clinging to her bare shoulders, her waves of lush hair loose about her, he realized he'd made a grave mistake.

He turned to the tray of supper he'd brought up for them, hoping to distract himself.

"I believe Cook has prepared an entire hen for us. Her gravy is remarkable. I really have had nothing like it." He kept his voice as even as possible, though the last thing he was thinking of was gravy.

He wondered how soft Eliza's skin must be. What it would be like to trail the soap along that same bare shoulder, take in the deep scent of her as he washed her hair. He straightened away from the table.

There was no reason why he shouldn't after all.

He went to rolling up his sleeves and made his way over to where she sat frozen in the tub. He'd discarded his outer garments upon his arrival. He was lucky he'd made it there so far ahead of her and the carriage. He'd had time to instruct Cook on what to prepare for their supper and to have the footmen carry up the sofa from the sewing room below. It was the most generous sofa in the house, and he hoped Henry enjoyed it.

He bent beside the tub, fisting his hands along the side when all he wished to do was wrest her from the tub and carry her to bed.

Her eyes were wide, and small rivulets of water made their way down either side of her face.

He reached up, unable to help himself, and pushed back a lock of hair. He didn't miss her nearly imperceptible flinch.

He paused for a moment and then carefully extracted his hand.

"Are you able to see or would you like me to fetch your spectacles?"

He thought the question would soothe her, but she reared back in the tub.

"I can see. It's things far away that are out of focus."

He studied her face. He hadn't been this close to her in the light, and he enjoyed being able to drink her in. Her eyes were just a touch too small for her face, and her nose came to a gentle hook. Her lips were overly thin, but he recalled all too clearly how they tasted.

He reached behind him for the pitcher Mrs. Donnelly had likely left.

"Shall I help you rinse your hair?"

She shook her head so violently sprays of water shot from her head.

"No, you mustn't."

He paused. "But did you not request I visit your rooms every evening? It was part of the arrangement." He kept his tone light. It wasn't confrontation he sought. There was something about this agreement she had made that was important to her, and he wanted to fulfill every expectation she had until he could figure out what it was she truly wanted.

Her hands fluttered in the water as if she wanted to pluck the pitcher from his hands, but then she must have realized how exposed it left her and scrambled to get her hands back in place.

He regretted the loss of the glimpse but tried to keep his eyes on her face.

"I did, but this is not what I had in mind."

He smiled gently. "I see. What is it you wish me to do?"

The question was unfair, but he couldn't help it.

She paled, and he set aside the pitcher to stand.

"How about this?" he asked as he positioned himself behind her. "You've had a long day of travel, and you must be starving. If I help you to rinse your hair, we can enjoy the meal Cook has prepared that much more quickly. That seems practical, doesn't it?"

She hesitated, but she'd turned her head just the slightest to follow him about her.

"Yes, it does," she replied.

He picked up the pitcher from his new position. "Tip your head back."

She did as he asked, and carefully, he poured the warm water from the pitcher, moving slowly so each part of her hair was rinsed clear of soap. He tried not to think about how it felt to have her long locks fall through his fingers or how it made him want to coil a fistful of it in his hand as she writhed beneath him.

He finished quickly after that thought sprang through his mind and stood, pacing away from the tub.

"Are you able to reach the towels?" he asked, politely looking away.

"Yes, thank you."

He heard splashing behind him but kept his gaze on the small table where he'd lain the food tray. He pulled the metal domes from the plates and steam wafted up. He set them aside and drew out the napkins and cutlery, setting the table with exquisite care. Because as long as he focused, he wouldn't think of his wife behind him, the towel caressing her naked body, finding all the hidden places he wanted to find.

With his tongue.

He coughed and reached for one of the wine glasses on the tray, quickly filling it before downing a swallow.

The noise of the towel was replaced by rustling, and he knew she must have donned her nightdress.

"You may turn about," she finally said, and of course, he spun about as quickly as would seem normal.

She'd not only donned her nightdress, but her dressing gown wrapped so tightly around her he worried it would cut off blood to her head.

He gestured to the table behind him.

"Let us eat then."

She eyed the table as if it were a monster of fairy tale origins ready to gobble her up. He sat, pulling a napkin onto his lap and reaching to fill her glass. Eventually, she made her way over, taking the seat opposite him.

They ate in silence for several seconds before he realized she wasn't eating at all. She merely pushed her food around on her plate.

"Are you not hungry?" Concern surged through him. Had the journey made her ill? Had something else happened to upset her?

Her fork clattered against the plate at his question, but she recovered it quickly.

"No. I mean yes." She shook her head. "I am hungry." But she didn't take a bite of food.

"Then what is it?" He reached across the table to place his hand over hers, but she snatched her hand away before he could touch it.

He looked up, and her gaze had him straightening. Her eyes were ferocious. Her jaw taut. He prepared himself for the retribution he so rightly deserved for what he had said.

But no words of scorn and admonishment came. Instead, she asked him something far worse, so cutting his heart clenched in his chest.

"Why are you being so nice to me?" The words were guttural with emotion, and they stopped him dead.

His lips parted, but no sound emerged as he couldn't break his gaze away from hers. There was no sadness in the question, no pity. She wasn't trying to play his emotions with theatrics. She was utterly serious, which meant she asked the question from experience.

She wasn't used to people being nice to her, and when someone demonstrated such attention, she found it fearful.

His hand still lay on the table where he had reached for her, and he carefully drew it back to rest in his lap. He toyed with his napkin as he gathered his thoughts.

"Eliza, I am sure you know what they call me in society." He paused to look back up at her. She hadn't moved, her eyes as piercing as they had been. She sat so still, like a rabbit sure she'd been spotted by a predator. He pressed on. "I earned the moniker the Jilted Duke because I was foolish enough once to believe myself in love with a woman who betrayed me. When it came time to see to the duty of the title, I created a plan that would save me from the embarrassment I had suffered previously." Now he did lift his gaze and met hers full on. "I sought a wife of unfortunate appearance, so I would not be in danger of falling in love with her."

She didn't so much as blink as he repeated the words she'd accidentally overheard the previous night. He waited, giving her the opportunity to speak, but she did not. He thought her lip trembled ever so slightly, but it firmed again, and he wondered if it had only been a trick of the candlelight.

He went to speak again but stopped. For a moment that night so many years ago came back to him, and he thought he could not tell her everything. How could he risk being so vulnerable again?

"Go on." The words were soft, the Eliza he knew seeping through once more.

It bolstered him, and he made the decision quickly. "I was wrong in selecting you, Eliza. I had not accounted for your wit and charm. I find both immensely enjoyable."

He had hoped his words would soothe her, but she didn't move. She might have turned to stone for all he could tell.

"I find how you treat the staff commendable and surprising. Not many members of the *ton* treat servants with such respect." He thought of waking to Carver's timid tray of coffee and toast that morning. "You seem to have won over the staff of Ashbourne House rather quickly. I believe those here won't take long to fall under your spell either."

Silence fell again as they studied one another.

Finally, she said the words he dreaded.

"I don't believe you."

They cut as he'd expected they would, but he accepted them for the truth they were.

"I didn't expect you to." He wasn't about to stop being

honest with her now. "I had hoped you would give me time to regain your trust."

She watched him, but she didn't speak again.

"I want to show you the ocean, Eliza. I want to teach you how to swim. I want to take you into the village and show you the sweets shop I visited when I was a boy and where the shopkeeper would sneak me lemon drops when my mother wasn't looking." Was there a softening about her jaw? He couldn't believe it, but he desperately wanted to. "I don't deserve a second chance from you. I didn't deserve a first chance. But I'm begging you now. Please take pity on me and give me one more chance."

He couldn't begin to understand what might be going through her mind just then. From birth, he had been revered as the future duke, and then once assuming the title, he'd been showered with praise and opportunity. Eliza, meanwhile, had been fed a steady stream of disapproval. Why should she believe him now?

"I must understand something first. Our agreement will still hold, yes?"

He studied her face, delved into her gaze. Why was it so important that he get her with child? She was adamant about it, and yet, he couldn't quite grasp why.

"Yes, of course," he answered quickly. "I shall never go back on my word."

She continued to watch him, warily now, and practicality took over for emotion. He nudged her plate.

"I know you did not sleep well last night, and you need sustenance. Please eat. Cook really is a master at gravies."

She reached up a tentative hand to grasp her fork again, and this time she speared a piece of hen and brought it to her mouth. She made no sign she enjoyed it, but she took another bite and another. Carefully, he picked up his own fork and resumed eating.

Henry's snores filled the silence between them as the dog had collapsed next to his empty dish, rolled on his back to stick his paws happily in the air.

Next he looked up she had cleared her plate and was replacing her napkin in her lap. She met his gaze directly.

"Thank you," she said.

He raised an eyebrow.

"For bringing up the tray. That was considerate of you."

He realized a truce hung between them. A shaky, fragile one it might be, but it was still a truce, and he would do everything he could to make the most of it.

The clock on the mantel chimed the hour.

"It's quite late," he said, and the sentence hung between them.

He was really asking if she wanted him to stay.

God, he wanted to stay. He wanted a chance to right the wrongs he had committed on their wedding night. He wanted the chance to show her how desirable she was. To prove to her she was worthy.

Worthy of what though?

He swallowed, realizing he'd come so close to admitting he was falling in love with her.

"It is." She pushed back her chair, set her napkin aside. She looked directly at him. "Will you help me extinguish the candles?"

Her lips were soft, and her gaze knowing. She was asking him to stay.

"Yes, of course," he said and got to his feet.

CHAPTER 9

$\mathcal{S}$he had promised to give him a second chance, but just because her mind agreed to something did not mean her body listened to it. She shed her dressing gown and slipped between the covers of the opulent bed while his back was turned, extinguishing the last of the candles along the mantel.

The fire still crackled, and it cast a yellow glow about the room, softening edges and muting colors.

"Oh." She hadn't meant to make a noise, but she suddenly sank in the divine heaven of the mattress.

Ashbourne whirled as if she'd startled him, but a smile soon came to his lips.

"The mattresses are made here. They're quite luxurious, are they not?"

For the first time, she realized she was in danger of immediately falling asleep. Her body ached from the journey, and the large meal and warm bath had only helped increase her sense of fatigue. But she couldn't fall asleep. They had an agreement, and she expected them both to comply.

Safely under the bedclothes, she could look her fill of her

husband and his undressed state as much as she pleased for she was fairly certain he couldn't make out her features in the near darkness now.

He had entered her room in nothing but trousers and a shirt. Even his feet were bare. She could see his toes, and she'd never found toes so enticing. He gave Henry a scratch before heading in her direction, and the dog did nothing more than fumble a snore.

"What is it that you fed him?"

He stopped short of the bed at her question.

"The stable lad's father keeps the hounds for the Earl of Dobbin across the way. He swears by feeding the hounds the purest of food, so only meat straight from a fresh kill." He pointed at Henry's sleeping form. "The dog, I fear, ate better than we did this evening."

"You mean it's given to them uncooked?"

He perched on the bed still fully clothed. "It is. I can't say I would enjoy it, but Henry didn't seem to mind."

"Fascinating. Do you think perhaps I could meet the stable boy's father?"

Ashbourne laughed softly, but it was a warm sound, not a teasing one, as if he'd found her delightful. "I can see to that if you'd like."

"I would enjoy that very much."

The crackle of the fire was the only sound for several seconds, and then she felt Ashbourne's gaze on her. She moved her attention from Henry to her husband.

He studied her carefully, and she wanted to squirm under his attention.

While he'd explained what he had meant when speaking with the Duke of Waverly the previous night, it still did not assuage her fears. She had been speaking the truth when she said she didn't believe him. How could she when what she had overheard was precisely what she'd been hearing from so many of the *ton* for so long?

Except he'd been honest with her when the laws of marriage required he needn't be. That coupled with everything else he had done for her left her wondering.

"Our agreement suggests there should be far fewer clothes between us."

His voice had turned deep and coaxing, and unbidden, a heat coiled low in her stomach.

"Yes, of course." She swallowed. "I can close my eyes to give you privacy until you are beneath the bedclothes."

She had nearly shut her eyes when his words stopped her.

"You don't want to watch?"

She was watching now but not because of any sort of conscious effort.

"Watch?"

His smile was warm, teasing. "I've heard some women enjoy such things."

She thought of his toes and licked her lips.

"I don't think that will be necessary." Except she didn't close her eyes.

"Are you certain?" His fingers began to undo the buttons of his shirt, one solitary button at time.

She watched his fingers, mesmerized.

"Yes, yes, I'm quite certain."

With each button he revealed an inch of warm, enticing skin. Before long the smoothness of his collarbones was replaced with a dark mat of hair she had not anticipated. She may have lain with this man once before, but she remembered hardly any of it. It had been so brief and disappointing.

But now she watched as each button slipped free, revealing her husband in his entirety. She had expected broad shoulders, but she hadn't expected the scar that ran the length of his right one. She'd expected sculpted muscle as she'd felt it beneath the contour of his jacket when they danced, but she hadn't expected the way his hips would taper and narrow until they slipped into the confines of his trousers.

His fingers went there now, deftly undoing the buttons, and she must have whimpered or made a sound because he stopped and met her gaze. She snapped her eyes shut but not because he'd caught her looking, but because she feared she couldn't take anymore.

She waited for the telltale dip of the bed, the rustle of bedclothes, but it never came.

When sound finally emerged it was his voice, and it was all too close.

"Eliza." He breathed her name, and her eyes flew open.

He'd moved to the side of the bed where she huddled, the bedclothes clutched at her chest. He leaned over her, large and looming, but he didn't touch her anywhere. Yet she could feel his heat, anticipate what it was like to feel his weight atop her.

He sat carefully on the bed as if he were afraid of hurting her, and when he leaned forward, he captured her between his arms as he rested against the bed on his outstretched arms.

"Eliza, I want to make this better for you, but I need you to tell me what you like and what you find unpleasant. Can you do that?"

She nodded because she couldn't speak. She was overwhelmed by a feeling of safety when he leaned over her like that, as if she were cocooned and protected within his arms.

He shifted on to one hand, drawing his other up to run a single finger down her cheek.

"Now I seem to recall you enjoyed kissing. Is that true?"

Again, she nodded, transfixed by the darkness of his eyes.

His finger stopped just under her chin, and he tilted her

head up just a little before he captured her lips in a gentle, coaxing kiss. Her head came off the pillow following the taste of him, and he laughed softly against her lips.

"I guess you do enjoy that," he said, never breaking the kiss.

She didn't know what to do with her hands, but she very much wanted to touch him. She wrenched away instead, gasping for air.

"I'd like to touch you." She hadn't meant to say that, but, well... "The last time I touched you, you appeared not to like it. Can you tell me what I did wrong so I may try to be better?"

His eyes clouded over at her words, and she feared she'd made another mistake.

"I'm sorry. Please. You mustn't. I can just lie here and be quiet." She rushed the words one after the other should he have time to regret fulfilling their bargain.

Her grip on the bedclothes became lethal, and she tried to sink back into the pillows as far as they'd let her.

He released a sigh and leaning forward, gently set his forehead against hers.

She'd done something wrong again.

She dared not breathe let alone move, and she waited for him to get up and leave. Fear rattled her more than humiliation. She couldn't be the reason she remained childless. She just couldn't.

"Dax." She said his name as if it might be the last thing she ever spoke.

He stilled above her, and she swore she could feel his heartbeat vibrating through her. The tension was palpable between them, and her chest tightened in despair.

Please don't leave.

"We're going to try something else." He stood so quickly the bed bounced, and she scrambled to keep herself together.

A pillow fell on her head, and she shoved it away. The bed moved again, and this time her husband had slipped between the covers. She expected him to stop on the opposite side of the bed as he had done previously, but this time he didn't. He slid directly over to her and without stopping, gathered her into his arms. Her cheek met the solid wall of muscle that was his chest as his arms closed around her. One hand kept her firmly pressed against him while the other speared her hair, drawing her even closer.

And it felt magnificent.

She'd never been held this way by anyone, never cradled so completely. She could almost believe he didn't mind holding her so. His heart beat beneath her cheek, and the rise and fall of his chest was hypnotic. She slipped one hand out, unable to resist touching him, and found his skin hot to the touch.

"Eliza, I think it would be best if you understood it would take a great deal of effort on your part to do something wrong in this situation."

His fingers massaged the back of her head, and once more, sleep threatened her.

"It would?" she whispered.

Absently, her fingers began to explore, traipsing through the mat of chest hair to find each individual rib.

"It would." His voice wasn't so certain now, and she lifted her head to peer at his profile.

He was just as gorgeous from this angle as any other. She ran her hand lower, found the dip of his stomach and the bones of his hips until her fingers collided with the waist of his trousers.

"You're still clothed." She didn't know why this bothered her, but it did.

"So are you," he returned.

That was the truth.

"Should I not be?" She'd never before been this bold in her life, but curiosity appeared to outweigh her insecurities.

He groaned. "No, you should not, but I won't make you do anything you're not ready for."

She pulled away from him and before she could think of it further wriggled out of her nightdress. Her back was to him as she tossed the garment aside, so it wasn't as if he saw anything but her bare back and even then, her long hair tumbled down the length of it.

Her arms automatically went to cover herself, but she wanted to take in his expression. Before she could finish turning, he sat up, gripping her shoulders, and holding her in place.

"Don't."

Just one word, spoken so deeply, so gutturally, it arrested her completely.

Her hands lay folded against her chest, and she stared at the glowing outline of the fire as his hands traced her shoulders, the line of her back. Her body tightened in places she didn't know were possible, and she bit her lip to keep back a whimper.

"Oh God, Eliza." He said each word with reverence. "I've thought of this for so long."

She blinked, her attention coming into sharp focus.

He'd thought of this? He thought of...her...like this?

His hands were in her hair again, lifting it from her shoulder to replace it with his lips. Now she did whimper as he seared kisses along the curve of her shoulder, the expanse of her neck.

"Dax."

The tension coiled hotter within her, and she knew something must be happening. Something *must* happen.

He shifted against her, one arm coming up, his hand exploring. She cowered, realizing he'd discover just how inadequate she was. But when his hand closed over her breast, he buried a deep groan into the side of her neck.

Her lady parts clenched.

Heavens, what was he doing to her?

She looked down at his hand, mesmerized by the way it toyed with her nipple, rolling it so expertly between his fingers. She moaned, grabbing Dax's hand and pinning it against her.

"Dax, I feel—"

But she couldn't finish the sentence. She didn't know what she felt, only that it was growing, and soon it would be unbearable.

"I know," he growled and turned her, capturing her lips in a kiss that sent fire through her belly.

Oh God, she was going to explode. She lost his hand somewhere as he spun her back on the mattress, his weight deliciously crushing her into the mattress. Her nipples tensed at the friction his chest hair caused as he moved along her body, and she bucked, arching her chest into him for more.

"Dax." It was the only word she could manage because she didn't know how to tell him…tell him that she liked…this.

His mouth burned a line of kisses along her jaw, down her throat, nipping at her collarbone. She bucked again, her hips driving into him, and she felt…everything. He was hard against her, and a thrill shot through her, knowing she had done that to him.

He continued his journey down her body, kissing, licking, biting, until she couldn't bear it anymore. She fisted her hands in his hair, trying to hold him in place, but he only laughed against the softness of her belly, moving ever lower.

He was almost to that spot that ached, and she tried to close her legs, embarrassment flooding back. But he soothed her with a soft shushing noise and coaxed her legs back open with soft kisses along the inside of her thighs.

He teased and tortured, and once her hips came up off the mattress in response, she recoiled in humiliation. She'd put her lady parts so dangerously close to his—

Without hesitation, he grabbed her hips, positioning her just as he seemed to want her.

"Oh God, Eliza." The tone of his voice had her struggling to sit up to see what it was he was looking at.

But he was looking at her. He was looking…there.

What could be so marvelous about there that he would—

But then he lowered his head, and she forgot about everything.

The pleasure bordered on pain, and she came up completely off the mattress, driving herself into his mouth. He groaned and took a firmer grip on her hips, pulling her toward him as she grasped at what was left of the bedclothes.

The tension built with every lick, with every suckle of his lips. She squirmed and tried to get away, but his hands held her firmly until she knew she could endure no more.

"Dax, please," she begged, but he wouldn't listen to her. He wouldn't stop. She couldn't take this any longer.

He shifted suddenly, and with one final caress, she exploded against his tongue, her body convulsing on a wave of pure energy that buzzed through each and every one of her limbs. Her scream was strangled as she tried to recover her senses, and when she thought she was lost to sensation, Dax gathered her into his arms, holding her more tightly than he ever had before.

Her heart rate slowed, her breathing evened out. Her arms remained weak, and there was a different kind of dampness between her legs.

"What…" But she couldn't finish the question.

He pressed his lips softly to her forehead before tucking her head under his chin.

"That was pleasure," he whispered, tightening his arms about her.

"I didn't know," she mumbled, her eyes drifting shut.

Another soft kiss flitted across her forehead.

"I know," he said. "Now go to sleep."

It was only as she let slumber take her that she remembered he still wore his trousers.

* * *

HE HAD NEVER HAD a problem acquiring the attentions of a good woman, and as he lay in the near dark, holding his satiated, sleeping wife in his arms, Dax knew he had never known pleasure like this before regardless of the number of women he'd had.

It frightened him.

It was true Eliza was not at all what society deemed acceptable, what a man would deem appealing, but to him, she was utterly perfect. Her breasts were small but pert and perfectly filled his palm. Her skin was the creamy paleness he thought only existed in the works of Renaissance masters. Every line, every curve, every dip of muscle and bone begged for his kiss, and he knew he would spend this summer discovering every inch of her body.

That was what frightened him most.

In the exploration, could he keep his heart immune to her charm? Could he keep his mind focused on the task at hand?

His plan had seemed so simple, so safe, but he hadn't taken into account the possibility of actually enjoying his wife's company. He had witnessed any number of societal marriages where the couple were little more than acquaintances who sometimes shared a bed when necessity dictated it. Such an existence was entirely delectable to his way of thinking, that was until he'd met Eliza.

He'd meant what he said. He did enjoy her company. Her wit and charm undid him. He'd laughed more in the week since meeting her than he had in nearly seven years.

Sebastian was right. It wasn't his wife's appearance that would be the threat. It would be her relentless personality. Eliza had a way with honesty that was refreshing and unburdening. He hadn't expected that.

He swallowed and tightened his arms about her as he willed his body to calm. She was exhausted and needed her rest, but that didn't stop him from remembering the way her body had reacted to him. The deep, involuntarily sounds she'd made as he'd tasted her skin, the way her legs had opened for him, how she'd responded to his touch, pressing into him as if she couldn't get enough.

He closed his eyes. He had to stop thinking about it, or he'd never sleep.

Carefully, he eased himself out from around her and slipped from the bed. He padded over to the remnants of his dinner, and in a single gulp, finished the last of the wine. Henry continued to snore from where he'd fallen asleep beside the fire after his luxurious dinner, and the hearth crackled merrily behind the dog.

Finishing the wine, he returned the glass to the table and cast one last look back at Eliza, soundly asleep in the bed. The firelight reached just far enough to caress her in a soft glow of orange and yellow, illuminating her in the way he found so appealing. As if she were something not of this world, and he was unworthy of her presence.

He forced himself to turn away, and painfully, his gaze fell on the connecting door. He should leave her be. Retreat to his own rooms and relieve himself of the pressure in his trousers. He had no business spending the night with his duchess. After all, that was not at all a part of the plan.

But as he stood there contemplating that cold, unyielding connecting door, he realized he didn't want to walk through it. All he wanted was to spend the night next to Eliza. He needn't touch her. He needn't wake her. He just wanted to be with her.

He expelled a harsh breath and raked his hand through his hair.

God, he was in danger. He was in very real danger.

He took a step toward the door, but he couldn't make himself go farther.

Without thought, he spun and made his way back to the bed. Quietly, he shed his trousers and naked, slipped back beneath the covers of the bed.

He settled on the edge of the mattress, so far from his wife he might have fallen completely from the bed, but it was as if he were making a bargain with himself. He could stay the night, but he must do so with an insurmountable space between them.

It was a right proper plan until Eliza turned in her sleep, a single hand moving across the sheets toward him.

"Dax."

His name, so sleepily, slipped between her lips, and for one unutterable moment, he hung suspended on a precipice. He knew this was a moment of decision even as he didn't know. It was only his wife, reaching for him in her sleep only—

Her eyes opened with a soft flutter, and she blinked, as if taking in her surroundings and trying to recall where she was.

He moved, no longer able to help himself.

"Shhh," he whispered, sliding back into his place beside

her as he gathered her into his arms. "Go back to sleep. You've had a long day and need your rest."

He expected her to drift back off, but instead, a mischievous smile came to her lips. She lifted her hand and placed a single finger in the cleft of his chin.

"I'm not sleepy," she murmured.

He couldn't stop his own smile nor the surge of lust that swept over him as she touched him. It happened every time she laid a hand on him, but unlike the timid caresses she'd given him before, now her hand was sure, confident. It slipped from his chin and began to explore, and it was all he could do not to roll on top of her and finish what he'd started. Her hand slipped lower, tracing the line of his jaw, the curve of his neck.

"I've always wondered what that felt like."

He sucked in a breath. "What what felt like?"

"A man's beard. I'd always wondered. All the wallflowers used to speak of it."

He swallowed. "Oh?"

She nodded, her hair tickling the underside of his chin. "When you know you'll never have something, it's hard not to think of it. Every wallflower imagines what it would be like. To have someone. To not be so alone."

He didn't want to keep having this conversation. He didn't want to hear about the life Eliza imagined. He didn't want to hear the echoes of her loneliness. He didn't want to fall that much more in love with her.

"What did you imagine?" The question was hardly a whisper, escaping his lips before he could stop it.

Again, she shook her head. "I didn't. I couldn't bear to think about what I would never have."

He captured her wandering hand and turned, pivoting until he was atop her, and he had her hand pinned above her head. Her eyes opened fully, and what he saw there ended him.

Longing. Disbelief. Acceptance. And the worst of all, hope.

"Eliza." Her name was an oath just before he bent his head and kissed her.

It wasn't like any of the kisses they'd shared before. That had just been physical. This was so much more. He poured everything he had into the kiss, everything he could give her and everything he was afraid to.

She struggled against his grip, and he let her go. Her arms came around him with a ferocity that tightened his chest, and he pulled her even closer. He savored her, worshiped her, deepening the kiss until she moaned against his lips.

He hadn't meant for anything more, but then she entwined her legs with his, running a heel up his calf.

He tore his mouth from hers. "Eliza." He saw the hurt that flashed in her eyes, and he knew she once again thought she'd done something wrong. He cradled her face in his hands. "Every time you touch me I can't bear it. Do you understand that? Your touch sets me on fire."

Her eyes widened, and her lips parted. "It…does?" The hesitancy in her voice broke his heart, and he dipped his head, capturing her lips once more.

"Let me show you."

He found her still wet, and adjusting ever so much, he slid inside of her. He closed his eyes against the sensation, gritted his teeth until he was in danger of breaking a tooth.

"God, Eliza. You torment me."

When he opened his eyes again, he found that mischievous smile once more on her face.

"You're enjoying this," he accused her, and of all possible miracles, she laughed, the sound soft and wholesome, and he could not for the life of him think of another time in which he'd laughed while making love to a woman.

But he'd never before made love to a woman like his wife.

He growled and kissed her again as he began to move. Like before, she arched against him, and it took all his strength not to come immediately. He wanted her to enjoy this. He wanted her to know what love really was.

The thought sent shivers down his spine, but all too quickly, they dissipated, leaving him with only the sheer knowing that he wanted this more than anything.

He couldn't hold on. She was so tight and clung to him in undulating caresses. He reached a hand between them and found her sensitive nub. He flicked it, and when she cried out against his mouth, he soothed it with a gentle stroke.

This time she broke the kiss.

"Dax." His name was a question and a declaration all at once.

He stroked her again as he quickened his pace. Her body coiled around him, and it was as if he could feel the anticipation of her release, and it was too much.

"Eliza." The word carried with it the last of his restraint, and he let go.

When she came, it was too much, and he lost himself in the waves of pleasure that washed through her and thus through him.

He tried not to crush her when he collapsed, but her arms had tightened around him and pulled him closer. He shifted, falling to the pillow beside her and dragging her into the crook of his arm to keep from breaking her hold on him.

He didn't know why, but he wanted to hold her now. Never before had he lingered after the sexual act, but he was coming to understand things would be different with Eliza, and right then, the county militia couldn't have ordered him from the bed.

"Dax." Her voice was tentative, and alarm coursed through him.

"Yes?"

"Dax, is it always…" In the pause, he filled the sentence with any number of things he feared she may end it with, but then she said, "Is it always like that?"

He smiled against the top of her head.

"No." He spoke the word with an assurance he didn't realize until he felt it escape him. "Only with you," he said.

He could feel her smile against his neck, and she snuggled closer to him, sending his heart into a spiral dive.

"Then I'm very glad you removed your trousers."

He couldn't help it. He laughed.

CHAPTER 10

*W*hen she woke, the bed was empty beside her, and she allowed a terrifying moment of insecurity to swamp her. She sucked in a breath and pushed the hair from her eyes, scanning the empty room around her.

Completely empty.

Henry was gone as well.

Insecurity was replaced with curiosity.

She turned to the bank of windows on her left and saw the edges of the drapes outlined in yellowy sunshine. She scrambled out of the bed only to realize she was utterly naked when her bare feet hit the floor. She spun around, trying to find her dressing gown while also trying to shield her more private bits. Whom she was shielding herself from she wasn't sure, but an inordinate surge of modesty suddenly overcame her.

Finding her dressing gown, she slipped inside of it and tightened the belt more than was necessary. She wanted to discover what lay behind those drapes, but she knew there were other necessities. Making her way to the corner, she pulled the corded bell pull to summon her maid, unsure where anyone was in the house nor what time it was. Only then would she allow herself to tug at the heavy drapes and pull one aside.

She wasn't sure what she'd been expecting, but what greeted her took her breath away. The ocean was a magnificent beast that roared its majestic head into cresting waves against the rugged coast that fell away behind the manor. The landscape was rough and ragged, so unlike the gently turned gardens of London and the carefully manicured grounds of country houses. This was something else. This was ethereal and confounding, terrifying and beautiful all at once.

The sound of the door opening behind her cut her perusal short, but she was pleased to see Lucy sweep into the room with a tray of tea.

"Good morning, Your Grace." Lucy was ever chirper no matter the situation, and she presented Eliza with a steaming cup of tea and a bright smile. "I should say the kitchens are right organized here. I wouldn't be surprised if Cook had taken a turn in the local militia."

Eliza couldn't help but to return her smile. "Where's Henry?"

"He's in the gardens with His Grace." Lucy disappeared into the dressing room off of Eliza's bedchamber and returned with a freshly pressed muslin gown of lavender and pink sprigs. "Do you know I don't think the duke's ever had a dog? They've been out there for some time, and I would hazard to say he's almost acting like a schoolboy."

"Henry or the duke?" Eliza couldn't help herself.

Something about the possibilities of the day, the newness of everything around her, had her normally pithy tongue at an extreme advantage that morning.

Lucy laughed. "Both!"

Eliza dressed quickly in between sips of tea and before

long, she'd made her way back down to where she'd come in from the carriage the night before. From there, she had entirely no idea where to go.

A footman took pity on her. "His Grace is in the east garden." He gave a neat bow. "I'd be happy to escort you, Your Grace."

She smiled. "Thank you..." She waited for the footman to introduce himself as she could not at all recollect any of the names she'd been given the previous night, and it was curious to find him blushing.

"It's George, Your Grace. I'm here to serve in anything you might need."

She followed helplessly as George wound his way through endless corridors and vexing turns. For a moment, she feared she'd never learn her way about the manor house, but then they passed an exquisitely carved grandfather clock in one of the many drawing rooms they passed through.

"It is truly after ten?" She turned a worried gaze on George who halted abruptly at her outburst.

"It is, Your Grace."

She peered about them at the silent room and empty corridors.

"But where is everyone?"

George's smile was assuring. "His Grace asked that the house remain quiet until you were about. After your long journey, he wanted you to rest."

She warmed instantly at George's words and had to turn away to hide her blush. It wasn't the long journey that had exhausted her. Dax had kept her awake most of the night with his lovemaking.

She cleared her throat. "That was rather thoughtful. Thank you."

George bowed. "Of course, Your Grace."

He turned once more and continued their journey

through drawing rooms and corridors. Finally when she was sure at any moment they would topple directly into the ocean, George indicated a final door with a bow.

"It's straight through here, Your Grace. You shan't miss the doors leading into the gardens."

She thanked him and pressed on. She'd expected another drawing room but faltered when she came into a dark study with resplendent bookcases of warm wood and deep inviting furniture. Along the wall opposite were tall doors of glass panes, thrown wide to the morning sunshine. Salty air spilled in and shook the curtains into a whirl of soft fabric.

This was Dax's study. She didn't know how she knew, but she could sense it. The rest of the rooms had been so impersonal, but not this one. The furnishings were carefully chosen with an eye toward comfort rather than appearance. The morning papers lay scattered about the ponderous desk set to one side, and a half-finished game of chess lay abandoned on a table before the dormant fireplace.

Carefully, she proceeded, suddenly feeling as though she were invading Dax's privacy. She'd traversed half of the room before coming upon a basket tucked against the side of a chair. It was filled with toys. Curiosity had her bending ever so slightly to take in the worn blocks and carved horses, scarred with age and use. She touched a single block with only her fingertips and realized how much she did not know about her husband, and yet she had never been more intimate with another in her life.

She straightened at a sound so familiar she moved toward it without hesitation. Parting the curtains, she stepped through to find Henry at full gallop through the gardens that greeted her.

And Dax, standing with his back to her as he watched Henry run. Her husband wore only trousers and a shirt, rolled to the elbows, and her chest tightened at the sight of him.

How had so much changed in a matter of days?

Last night had been a revelation. She had heard whispers that the sexual act could be pleasurable for women if the man was attentive, but she'd never thought she would experience such pleasure. She knew last night had been a fulfillment of her bargain with Dax, but she couldn't help but think maybe it was something more. The way he'd touched her had been so deliberate, so invoking. Surely he hadn't been simply playing along.

A finger of doubt scratched at the back of her neck even as she thought it. After all, he'd wanted an ugly wife. How did one inspire desire when one found the object of such so disappointing?

She squared her shoulders. He had asked for the chance to regain her trust, and she was going to do all she could to keep an open mind. That was the least she owed him.

She stepped up behind him, afraid to startle him, but he must have heard her because he turned, a boyish smile on his face.

"Did you know if you simply toss the bit of morsel into the grass he can find it from the mere scent?"

She couldn't help but laugh at his enthusiasm.

"Have you never had a dog of your own?"

He scoffed and toyed with a piece of what might have been sausage between his fingers.

"My father had hunting hounds back when he did that sort of thing, but never something as extraordinary as Henry." He held up a single finger of the hand without the sausage. "One does not dally with hunting dogs."

She laughed again and meant to say more, but Henry had heard her at that point and zipped around to career to a stop at her feet. She bent and scratched his shaggy head.

"And did you know," she said, "that Henry is actually a failure at what he was bred to do?"

She looked up to meet Dax's astonished gaze.

"Don't call my dog a failure."

Something dangerously warm flickered to life inside of her at his words, and she swallowed against it.

"Henry is a herder. The man I got him from had bred Henry to herd his sheep." She straightened, keeping one hand on the dog's head. "Unfortunately, it appears Henry is afraid of sheep."

Dax's expression grew serious as he studied Henry.

"It's all right, chum. I'm afraid of cats. They always look at you like they're planning your funeral. It's rather unsettling."

She laughed again. "Surely you can't dislike a good barn cat. They're rather useful at their work."

His look was skeptical, and she laughed while Henry barked for more sausage. Dax tossed the last of the sausage over his shoulder, and Henry took off like a spring suddenly let loose. She watched him go so that's why she didn't see her husband move toward her. He pulled her into his arms before she was prepared, and his kiss was warm and spicy from his breakfast.

"Good morning, wife," he murmured against her lips.

She couldn't help it. The last of her defenses were overrun in that moment, standing in the gardens awash with the scent of the sea, her husband's arms firmly around her. He pulled away reluctantly, lingering on her lips a moment longer.

"You must eat," he said promptly and moved away so she could see the table laid out behind him.

There were all manner of dishes from eggs and sausages to kidneys and tomatoes. Uncharacteristically, her stomach growled, and she pressed a hand to it.

He smirked as he said, "Did you sleep well?"

"When you let me."

She didn't miss the shock that registered on his face as she took a seat at the table, and she felt a measure of pride at her witty rejoinder.

He took the seat he'd obviously been using before tossing bits of sausage to Henry and picked up the teapot to fill her cup.

She helped herself to some eggs and sausages.

"Well, perhaps if my wife were less demanding in her requirements, she would get more sleep."

Her face warmed, but she couldn't help a smile.

"I shall keep that in mind."

He handed her the teacup, and she knew he deliberately brushed her fingers with his.

"Now, you'll want to eat up. We have a long day ahead of us."

She raised both eyebrows as she swallowed a bite of egg. "We do?"

He nodded seriously. "Today you meet the ocean. I should think you'd want your strength for that."

At just his words, a thrill shot through her. "You're taking me down to the ocean?"

Something passed over his eyes at her eagerness, but she couldn't have said what.

He smiled softly and said, "Of course. Weren't you looking forward to it?"

She nodded, poking at a sausage patty. "Yes, absolutely, but don't you have estate affairs to tend to? I'd assume the steward would wish to speak to you after your absence."

His expression was pained as he said, "He's already stepped in. He wants to discuss the results of the new breeding tactics we instituted this spring."

She paused with her eggs halfway to her mouth.

"Breeding tactics?"

He picked up his own teacup with a nod. "Yes, Sheridan is very particular about his breeding methods." He gestured with the cup. "I can't fault the man. His results are exemplary."

"But what are you breeding?"

He swallowed his tea. "Cattle."

She set down her fork. "You have livestock on your estate?"

He paused, a slow smile coming to his lips, and she realized she'd given herself away.

"Would you like to see them in our travels today, Your Grace? We have pigs and lambs as well." He cast a glance at Henry who was now gleefully rolling in the grass just off the stone steps leading down into the garden. "Perhaps we'll save the lambs for another day when Henry may be inclined to other activities."

Only too late did she realize just quite how excited she was to discover her new home. It wouldn't do to forget she was still disappointed in Ashbourne. But that could wait. She set aside her napkin.

"Shall we begin?"

* * *

HE DIDN'T RECALL the cliff being this precarious and potentially lethal. How many times had he run down the length of the rutted path leading to the water's edge without a thought to his safety? He'd even traversed it barefoot and carrying his various fishing poles and bait.

But in every turn he saw catastrophic danger to his wife. With every step, he ensured his foot was solid before allowing her to step down, even while firmly keeping her hand in his. She'd tried to bat away his assistance, but once they'd turned onto the path in the cliff face, she'd gladly taken his hand.

Henry, however, was already at the bottom. He could see the dog spraying sand as he sprinted from one edge of the beach to the other.

If he were honest, Eliza was more than sturdy in her descent, and even though she had taken his hand, he was sure before long she would be taking this path all by herself.

Perhaps with one or two of their little ones in tow.

He wasn't sure where the thought had come from, but after last night, he wasn't surprised it had. He studied her face as the sun dappled it through the sparse shrubs that clung to the cliffside. Had he never before noticed the way her attention was so precise, so genuine? Had he never before noticed the way her hair changed color in the sunlight? One might have thought it a mousy brown, but it wasn't at all. When the sun struck it he saw weaves of reds and chestnut.

Not that he could see much. The bonnet she wore was ridiculous by any length, but he knew it was likely demanded by propriety, and it would keep the sun out of her eyes. So he would manage with his disappointment in not seeing all of her glorious hair.

For it was as glorious as he thought it would be.

He had been selfish enough during the night to fulfill every detail he'd been imagining since he'd first taken in the thickness of her mane. The way it fell down her back, darkness against the pearl of her bare back. How he could wrap it in his hands as he cradled her face for another exquisite kiss.

God, he couldn't think of that right now. He was still trying to get them to the bottom without killing them both.

The path leveled out near the end, dropping gracefully to the beach below, but even when the danger had abated, she did not release his hand, and he tried to ignore the flare of pleasure it caused him.

Once their feet touched sand, he paused, giving her a moment to soak in what he knew was a spectacular sight.

Along this stretch of cliff, the land turned slightly inward, tucking the Ashbourne beach into a natural cove, shielded from the most turbulent of the ocean waves. Cliffs rose up on either side of the cerulean water as if marking the space for display like a painting in a museum. Specks of jagged rock dotted the surface of the water in places as the cove stretched out to the ocean proper, and waves crashed against them with a brilliant force of foaming whites and greens and blues. Seagulls screeched overhead as they searched for their next meal, and Henry barked gloriously at them.

Eliza said nothing.

He studied her face, drank in her expression as she stared out at the cove before them.

"Is it to your liking?" He didn't know why he asked the question. It wasn't as if he could control the movement of the ocean, but right then it was vitally important that she like it. Alarm coursed through him, and he knew he was treading dangerously close to the very thing he had meant to avoid.

He scanned the beach around them, a lifetime of memories flooding back to him without permission.

As a child he'd played on this very beach with Ronald and Bethany. It was hard to believe how different things were now.

"It's beautiful."

Her voice brought his attention back to her, and with it, the memories receded.

Her pleasure showed in her slightly parted lips and wide eyes.

Her attention shifted from the water to him. "May I touch it?"

He realized she spoke of the water.

He shook his head gravely. "No."

Her face fell for an instant.

"Not with your boots on. It's a known rule that boots are not allowed on beaches. Only bare feet."

She let go of his hand to place a fist against one hip. "Your boots are touching the beach, Your Grace."

He looked down as if surprised to find boots on his feet.

"Well, aren't I the idiot?"

He dropped to the beach without ceremony, landing with a thud in the soft sand as he wrenched his boots off, one after the other, tossing them unseen behind him.

Her laughter rivaled with the screech of gulls and Henry's barking.

She sobered and gathering her skirts in her hands, extended a single foot.

"While you are down there, would you mind?"

He set to work untying her boots, and soon he'd cast both of them aside, but he couldn't help but stare at her ankles. While he'd seen all of her the previous night, it didn't detract from the pleasure he took in seeing parts of her others were not privileged to see.

"Madame, I'm afraid we've encountered a problem." He looked up to meet her eyes even as his fingers began to wander up her leg. "Stockings are not permitted either."

He watched her eyes darken as his fingers traveled farther up her leg. He found the tie that held them in place on each leg, and he knew with a simple tug he'd have them freed. Except he didn't wish to let her go so soon. He let his fingers linger, brushing the bare skin of her inner thighs. He was rewarded when he heard the quickly indrawn hush of breath, and he smiled, allowing her a reprieve as he tugged loose each bow.

Her stockings slithered down her legs, and he steadied

her as she stepped free of them. He tossed them on her boots before standing and taking her hand once more.

She shrieked when the water rushed up to meet her toes, and she jumped back into his arms, her own going around him as she held herself up against him.

"It's a great deal colder than I'd imagined." Her voice was light with laughter. "Do you really swim in this?"

He couldn't have answered if the queen herself demanded it. The joy that surged through him at having her so carelessly throw herself into his embrace had him teetering on an invisible brink. He already knew he was falling in love with her, but with every moment, it grew more and more real. Soon it would be inevitable. God help him.

Eliza was not Bethany, but the idea of making himself so vulnerable once again scared him. He was older now with far greater responsibilities, and the idea that he could expose himself like that was ridiculous.

Eliza stilled against him when he didn't answer, and she tipped her head up to peer at him.

"Are you all right?" Her tone lacked the warmth it had moments earlier, and he regretted doing that to her.

He meant to reassure her that all was well, but seeing her face turned up to him like that struck him directly in the chest.

"You're beautiful," he whispered.

Her face closed at his words, and she tried to tug herself from his embrace, but he held her tight.

"You mustn't say such falsehoods," she said to his chest.

He used a single finger under her chin to raise her face to his. "It isn't a falsehood when I know the truth of it."

Her eyes darkened at his words, and he bent his head for a soft kiss.

When he straightened, he let her go, slipping his hand down to hers.

"The water will get warmer as the summer lingers on, I promise you. Hold up your skirts."

He didn't wait for a reply as he ran them both into the water with a great splash. Henry caught on to the fun and chased after them, sand and water spraying all about them.

Eliza shrieked again, her delight cascading into laughter as Henry soaked them both.

They waded until the cold had her teeth chattering, and he pulled her reluctantly from the water to dry on the warmth of the sand. He tugged her down beside him, and she collapsed with a final laugh.

"I never knew the ocean was such fun. I'd always heard such dreadful stories about it."

He eyed her. "Dreadful stories about the ocean?"

Her smile was mischievous. "Ships sinking and wild monsters that emerge from its murky depths." Her tone matched her smile, and something stirred inside of him.

"You invented these stories, didn't you?"

A shadow crossed her face, and he realized he'd just made her uncomfortable, as if he'd unknowingly poked a secret. He would remember that for later, but right now, he wanted her happy and smiling, the sun on their shoulders and their toes in the sand.

"I can just see the terrifying stories you would tell your little sisters to give them nightmares. You were a devious child, weren't you?"

This had her expression clearing, and he was grateful for that.

She pursed her lips and raised her chin. "I know not of what you speak." She gave him a side eye. "Besides, I'm sure a boy like yourself must have been up to his own dastardly deeds in a place like this." She gestured at the beach around them.

It was his turn to lose the laughter.

She quickly reached out a hand to place it on his leg.

"I'm so sorry," she said softly. "I had heard somewhere that…that they were your friends."

She didn't need to explain as he already felt the burning in his chest he always felt when he thought of them. Only now, the burning was a little less than it had been. He looked at his wife, wondering why it was the humiliation he had carried for so long seemed to be dimming.

"They were," he found himself saying when he most assured he would not speak of it. "Their estates bordered either side of Ashbourne, and we became close friends as children, spending summers here at the shore."

That was more than he'd said on the subject in the seven years since it had happened.

Her hand curved on his thigh, comforting in its pressure.

"Have you ever spoken of what happened? It must be painful to carry such betrayal with you."

He'd never thought of it like that. Her eyes searched his face, and he knew he'd once more give her an answer he'd never given anyone.

"I have not." He swallowed. "It was one thing to suffer the betrayal of a woman. It was another to watch your friend turn his back on you."

"The Marquess of Isley?"

He nodded, his eyes drifting back out to the hypnotic waves of the ocean.

"Ronald and I were friends at an early age. His mother would visit my mother, and we'd hide away in the nursery until he had to leave." The wind picked up, driving a blast of salty air in his face. He squinted against the sun. "Bethany we found later when we were old enough to explore the grounds on our own. She was dangling from a tree when we stumbled upon her. Scared her so much she let go of the branch. We were only lucky she didn't break her arm, or we'd never have been allowed to play together again."

He toyed with the sand at his fingertips.

"It must have been hard being an only child." He looked at her sharply, and she went on. "When your friends betrayed you, you had no one to turn to." She smiled softly as if seeing something he couldn't. "I will always have my sisters, and they will always have me. No matter what happens."

A sharp pain tightened his chest, and he realized it was because she hadn't included him in her statement. He knew it was too soon to have regained her trust, but it still hurt him.

He laced his fingers through hers as her hand still rested on his thigh. It would take time, but he knew there was hope.

"Are you ready for your first swimming lesson?"

She didn't answer, and he turned to take in her expression, which was one of absolute shock.

She pointed to the water. "In there? But it's so cold. My dress will be utterly ruined."

He leaned in, nuzzling the part of her neck left exposed at the edge of her bonnet before sliding his lips up to her ear to whisper, "But you won't be wearing your dress."

CHAPTER 11

*T*here was absolutely no way she was getting into that water without her clothes on. It was utterly freezing for one, but more, she would not undress in outdoors as they were.

She backed away from her husband's teasing lips, but when she saw his face, she realized he was serious.

"You really swim naked?"

He gave a firm nod. "Have since I was a boy."

"But it's so cold and…wet."

He stood, brushing the sand from his trousers.

"You'll get used to the cold, and there isn't a better day than this to give it your first try." He shielded his eyes from the sun as he looked up. "The sun will dry you once we're finished."

Without another word, he tugged his shirt over his head. Her lips parted, and she drank in the sight of him shirtless, the sun gleaming off his taut muscles.

For a bewildering moment, she couldn't for the life of her think how she'd gotten here. A confirmed wallflower of the most superb quality, she was now sitting on a beach in

159

Sussex staring at her ducal husband's bare chest. What a magnificent chest it was if she were honest. And yet, she was still sore from their lovemaking the previous night. This was not at all how she'd envisioned her summer unfolding, but she was not disappointed.

Until she peered at the water again.

"You really go in unclothed?" She scanned the cove around them. "And you're not concerned someone might see you?"

He peered at the top of the cliffs that cocooned them.

"There isn't another house for several kilometers on either side of us." His fingers went to the buttons of his trousers. "We are in greater danger of having our toes nibbled by those sea monsters of yours than we are of being seen by another human."

She envied how carefree he was with his body, his fingers undoing the buttons with careless precision. He stopped before he shucked them and motioned her to stand.

"Let me help you with your dress."

He pulled her to her feet and undid the buttons along her back with much the same carelessness with which he'd done his own. He gave her his arm to step free of the dress, corset, and petticoats, but he took pity on her and allowed her to keep her chemise and drawers. The wind was startlingly warm against her calves and her arms, and she shivered.

"Cold already?" His voice held a note of concern.

She shook her head. "No, it isn't that." She studied her bare arms, the way the flesh prickled at the sensation of the wind. "I've never felt the wind like this. On quite so much of me, I mean."

He touched her cheek, and she started, still not used to him touching her so unexpectedly.

"Can you see without your spectacles? I should hate to see them lost in the ocean if a wave catches you unawares."

She took them off and handed them with her bonnet to him. He studied her head strangely for a moment. He seemed to realize he'd been caught and looked away with a satisfied smile as he bent to place her things next to their pile of shed clothes. She patted her head lightly to see if something were amiss.

When he straightened, he shed his trousers, and she forgot entirely about how he'd stared at her head.

He caught her hand and pulled her to the water before she had adjusted to his nakedness. Even though she had already seen him undressed, it was a shock to see him in the clarity of daylight.

They reached the water, and the cold distracted her. When she thought they would stop, he pulled her farther, her feet digging into the sandy bottom to push against the oncoming waves. Finally, when he was about waist deep in the water, he stopped, pulling her in front of him.

The water had soaked her drawers, and she knew they would do her little good when she emerged as they were surely transparent. She pressed her hand to her bosom, but it would do no good. The water lapped at her frame, and soon she knew her small breasts would be visible as well.

"The first thing you must learn is how to let the water carry you."

"Carry me?" She looked up sharply. "Wouldn't I sink?"

"You can but not if you learn how to float." He skimmed his hand along the surface of the water. "Just as a ship will float along the surface of the ocean, so too can your body. You only need to learn how to displace the water to give you buoyancy."

He sank into the water until he had both of his arms locked around her torso, and they were nearly face to face.

She frowned. "I hardly think this is necessary."

He stole a quick kiss before tipping her backwards. "I assure you I am being the most proper tutor."

She doubted that very much, but as she pitched backward, her feet slipped from the sandy bottom, and she caught his shoulders to keep from falling.

"Are you certain I shan't sink?"

"I promise I've got you."

Her stomach clenched at his words, and she forced herself to focus. That wasn't what he'd meant. He was simply addressing the physics of their current situation. Still, her heart beat a little faster knowing he wouldn't let her sink.

When she was fully on her back, she kicked to keep her feet under her, but he stilled her with a hand to her abdomen.

"Let your feet float up so you're lying on the water."

"Are you mad? I certainly will sink then."

His smile wobbled with laughter.

"You will not sink. I told you I will not allow it. Just let your feet float up."

She did as he bid, which was a great deal easier than fighting the natural instinct to keep her feet down, and soon she was lying completely still on the surface of the water, her husband's arms securely around her torso, holding her up. She feared she may be too heavy for him, a burden to hold so exquisitely, but he didn't seem to mind. And furthermore, she couldn't help but sense the lightness that surrounded her.

He shifted, slipping one hand from underneath her. She panicked, her hands flapping against him to gain a hold. He laughed softly and calmed her fluttering with his free hand.

"Let the water take you."

The words didn't make sense to her, but he spoke them earnestly. She found she rather liked the way his voice calmed her, and she focused on his face, the sun flaring out around him as if he were an angelic creature.

He shifted, sinking into the water beside her almost as if he intended to float beside her. His one hand still pressed firmly to her back, and the panic did not return. Now, however, she found herself focusing on his words.

"Why should I let the water take me?"

It seemed like an unwise notion. Wouldn't she drown?

"The thing about swimming is to learn how to move with the water and not fight it." He turned and indeed, he did float up beside her.

She turned her head to keep him in focus, but the move only served to bring saltwater into her mouth and nose. She coughed and righted herself with a gentle pressure to her back from his hand.

"Move with the water?"

"Those sea monsters you've conjured? Have you ever wondered how they may make their way through the ocean? It's rather beautiful actually. The way they part the water to allow themselves to become a part of it."

"Become a part of the water?"

"Precisely."

She'd been so focused on his words she didn't realize he'd removed his other hand until it was far too late. But when she did realize his hand no longer held her up, she panicked, fluttering in the water, and just as she anticipated, she sank like a stone.

Water rushed into her nose and mouth, and on instinct, she swallowed and gagged. The entire ordeal lasted less than five seconds, but it might as well have been a lifetime. Dax plucked her from the water as if it were nothing at all and vaguely she understood his murmured words, and she obeyed, putting her feet down to find the bottom and stand surely on her feet.

His hands wiped madly at her face, pushing away the last

rivulets of ocean water, and she reached, grabbing his wrists to still his hands.

She blinked against the water until she could open her eyes properly and grin at him.

"That was absolutely glorious. May we try it again?"

His face had been tight with concern when she'd first opened her eyes, but at her words, his expression relaxed.

"You want to try it again?"

She nodded, droplets of water flying from her sodden hair.

"Oh, but I must. I had no inkling that one could float atop the water. It's absolutely breathtaking. Please. I promise to do better this time."

She wasn't sure how one's capabilities in terms of floating were judged, so she couldn't accurately determine how she had done. She could only presume that sinking and sucking in saltwater were two things one must not do when attempting to float. However, it had been her first time. The fact that she had achieved the endeavor at all should speak in her favor.

She poured all of her earnestness into her gaze, hoping Dax would take pity on her. It was almost certain he had other matters to attend to. Hadn't he said his steward had already come to speak to him about the matter of livestock on the estate? It was rather selfish of her to consume so much of his time.

Something passed over his eyes as he peered down at her, and for a moment, she thought he'd refuse her. Her stomach stilled at the thought, but quiet resolution overtook her. What else could she expect? She was being rather demanding of his attention. He'd spent all of the previous night with her as well.

She released his wrists and tried to take a step back, but

the sand caved under her feet, and she faltered. Only Dax's steady hands on her shoulders kept her upright.

"I'm so sorry. You must have other matters demanding your attention. I shouldn't have pushed so hard." She plastered on a smile. "Thank you so very much for bringing me down to the shore this morning. Henry and I both enjoyed it quite a lot."

A line appeared between his eyebrows as he said, "But can't you see you're the most important thing demanding my attention?"

Her chest squeezed at his words, and breath fled from her lungs. She had so much more to say in apology, but the air had left her.

It needn't have mattered because he kissed her.

Blast the man. He kept taking her unawares, which was something far too dangerous for her delicate confidence.

Just when she was certain she'd upset him, he did something to prove her utterly in the wrong.

This kiss was different than their other kisses, and she leaned into him, hoping to discover what it was. While she had tasted desire and want on his lips before, she hadn't tasted this. There was something giddy in the pressure he applied, happy in the tilt of his head.

When he broke apart on a laugh, she realized with a jolt she'd done something to amuse him.

She studied his jubilant expression. "What is it?"

He shook his head. "I believe I can safely say I've never met a woman quite like you before, Eliza."

She stilled at his statement, doubt rushing through her. "Is that a good or a bad thing?"

He kissed her again, softly this time, and now she tasted the longing she was coming to find he kept hidden away, as if he were afraid someone would find it. And as he pulled away, she knew it was Dax himself he was most afraid would discover the longing he tried so hard to keep tapped down. Her heart squeezed at the thought. She had been so worried he couldn't love her, she hadn't thought Dax couldn't love at all after what had happened.

"It is most certainly a good thing." He leaned back, adjusting his hold on her so she could drop back once more into the water. "Are you ready to try this again?"

She wanted to say something else. He'd told her so much earlier on the beach when she'd inadvertently plowed into his past. Perhaps if she could get him to talk of it, she could chase the shadows away from his eyes.

But she hadn't seen him this happy since she'd met him, and she wasn't about to shatter his happiness. Not now.

She let him lay her back on the water, its salty arms holding her up as somewhere in the distance Henry barked, happily snapping at the cresting waves.

* * *

RAIN DECIDED to make its appearance on their second day in Glenhaven, which meant Dax had the unfortunate circumstance of being trapped inside with his own thoughts.

The thought which plagued him the most was how true it was that Eliza should be the most important thing to him just then.

After their swimming lesson, they'd returned to the manor house for dry clothes and to take luncheon before he took her with him on his inspection of the estate. He learned she sat a horse well, and Henry had no problems keeping up, his long collie legs driving him ever faster than they'd let their horses go.

They met Sheridan at the cattle barns, and he wasn't sure who was more impressed with the size of the beef stock, Henry or Eliza. Both peered rapturously over the stockades.

When he finally went to collect her to bring her to the next paddock, he found her sitting atop the stockade fence, her riding habit giving her enough leverage to make it atop apparently.

She gazed down at him. "They're utterly beautiful."

It took him a moment to realize she did not speak of herself. He took advantage of the positioning to help her down, not for a single moment feeling shame at stealing yet another opportunity to touch his new wife.

He even managed to steal a kiss or two throughout the day.

Her favorite of all the animals turned out to be the pigs, which had surprised him.

"I took you for a sheep person," he noted.

She eyed him scandalously with a pained look in Henry's direction. Henry whined and ducked his head into Eliza's skirts.

"I stand corrected." He straightened his jacket and ensured they did not pass the sheep pens.

As promised, he came to her rooms after the household had gone to bed, and he found the awkwardness he had encountered when he'd first arrived the previous night had fled. She sat at her dressing table, brushing out her riotous hair instead of cowering beneath the bed clothes. Henry no longer required a morsel to allow him audience with Eliza, but Dax brought one anyway. The dog had earned it after his rigorous efforts of the day.

While he enjoyed every moment of making love to his wife, he could not ignore the warmth of contentment that blanketed him when he held her in his arms afterward. She fell asleep with her head on his shoulder, and he lay awake for some time afterward, staring into the darkness and wondering how he'd let himself get in this situation.

He welcomed a day of distraction in the village, but when

he awoke to the sound of rain beating against the windows, he knew it would not be wise.

While a typical bout of rain in London would do little more than dampen the hem of a lady's skirts, it was not so along the coast. Rains such as this whipped up in a frenzy when they struck the obstacle of the shore. Winds gusted, bringing with them all the refuse they could collect on their tumultuous journey up over the cliffs. The rain slashed at an angle, driving beneath greatcoats and umbrellas.

No, it would never do to introduce his bride to the village in this.

Although he should not have been surprised how captivating she found the sea storm. She rushed from the bed only moments after waking, pulling one of the blankets with her to cover her naked body as she thrust back the drapes and breathed in the sight of the angered ocean. He thought she would only study it for a moment and return to bed, disappointed in the sight, but instead, she'd curled up on the window seat, her hands pressed to the glass like a child.

He'd gone to her, settling on the seat behind her so he could pull her into his arms and let her rest against his chest. They'd sat that way until Henry had finally stirred, demanding attention for his needs.

He had taken Henry down to the gardens to allow Eliza time to bath and dress, and the domesticity of it threatened to suffocate him.

He stood just inside the opened doors of his study, watching Henry investigate the shrubs he had so enthusiastically discovered just the day before as if they were entirely new to him.

Dax had vowed not to enter into a situation that would threaten his heart so, but here he was, watching his wife's dog through the pouring rain and knowing he would run after the dog in the utter downpour should he so much as whine of an ailment or danger.

He scrubbed a hand over his face. Sebastian had been right. That was becoming clearer now.

Henry dove into what must have been a promising bush with a yelp of excitement.

Would it be so bad if he did let himself love her?

The thought had him straightening, his hands dropping to his sides.

It was a dangerous thought, one that had his guard going up, but at the same time, a quiet voice assured him it was safe to at least think it over.

Eliza was not Bethany.

If he knew anything of a person, it was that how one treated animals was a true reflection of a person's quality, and as Henry erupted from a different bush than the one he'd entered, Dax knew Eliza's soul was pure and true.

But could he trust her?

Could he ever trust again?

Henry splashed his way back inside, seemingly done with the wetness of the day and trotted over to the carpet where he promptly rolled as if to get the rain off of his coat.

"I'm afraid it will do no good, mate." Dax gestured to the door. "Best to find comfort in front of a fire on a day like this. What say we break our fast?"

Mrs. Donnelly had had a fire lit in the breakfast room as he'd suspected, and Henry found his way over to it, collapsing in a huff of air as if he'd not just slept the better part of twelve hours.

He'd just filled a plate with eggs when Eliza appeared in the doorway, turned out in another hideous gown that did nothing for her figure. Even as a man he could see that. He wondered what modiste she frequented in London and vowed to go with her the next she went to acquire something more appropriate for her.

The thought was ridiculous and rather unmanly, but he couldn't help the image of her wet through and in nothing but her underthings to tell him her gowns were all wrong.

"How would you feel about visiting the seamstress in the village for some summer frocks?"

She straightened from where she'd been giving Henry some scratches to eye him suspiciously.

"I brought summer frocks with me. There's no need—"

"You have a rather stunning figure that is not at all show-cased in your gowns, do you know that?"

He hadn't meant to startle her, but at the redness that appeared at her cheeks, he knew he had.

"I'm not so sure it's the gowns—"

He set down his plate harder than he'd meant to. "It is the gowns. You forget I've seen you with far less clothing." He gestured to her figure. "These garments practically hang off of you. That can't be very comfortable when you're trying to work with Henry."

She blinked. "How did you know that?"

He went to get a second plate to fill for her. "It would be the same if I wore a riding habit that was over large. Hardly the proper thing for a good ride."

The redness was already fading from her cheeks when he turned back.

"I suppose you might be right." She bit her lower lip. "Is there someone in the village who could assist me?"

"Mrs. Fletcher. She'll be able to help you."

She took a seat next to his at the table. "That will be splendid then." She picked up a fork, her eyes drifting to the window where rain still lashed. "Surely we won't go today, will we?"

He laughed softly as he took his seat. "No. I'm afraid a sea storm is not something to trifle with. We'll go as soon as it passes." A dismal thought suddenly struck him. "Eh, I know you will be shut in doors today, and I—"

"There's no need to entertain me. I'm not a small child." She took a bite of toast and swallowed. "I should wonder though if there is a small room somewhere that I may have for my affairs. Returning correspondence and such."

He looked up at the timid pitch of her voice, but she resolutely studied her eggs.

"There are more than enough rooms in the manor. You should have your pick."

"Any room?" She lifted only her eyes, and even then, her voice held a note of caution.

He gave a nod as he swallowed his sausage. "I recommend finding one in the south corridor. You'll have the most light throughout the day there."

Her eyes sparked at his suggestion, and he paused in his careful chewing.

Eliza had a secret.

He'd known all along there was something more to her than she let on, but he had suspected it had something to do with a matter of more tangible quality. But the way her eyes had lit at his suggestion of a light-filled room had him questioning his conclusion.

After all, what tangible thing could allow a woman to remain so involved in a marriage the husband had declared a farce?

He swallowed at the memory of his own carelessness.

"I have some letters to return, but I'm sure Mrs. Donnelly would be happy to show you the south corridor so you can choose which room suits you."

Her face relaxed into a genuine smile. "That would be lovely."

He thought that would be the end of it.

He rang for Mrs. Donnelly after they'd finished their meal and had lingered for some moments over tea and coffee, but he could sense Eliza's urgency. She really did seek a room with good light. How odd.

He truly thought he'd be rid of the notion of his wife hiding things from him when he made his way to his study and immersed himself in the two days of post that had piled up on his desk. Sheridan had left some reports on the calving the spring had seen and what they planned for the following year. He needed to read over the harvest expectations as the farm was largely self-sufficient and needed to produce enough feed to manage the livestock it held.

But no matter how tricky the figures or engrossing the topic, he could not let the thought of Eliza's expression stray.

Somewhere along the south corridor Eliza hid something from him.

He should let it go.

But the notion had nagged at him for weeks, and now he had something more on which to work, actual physical proof of her deception.

He set down his pen, appalled at his own thinking.

His wife was not capable of deception. It was his own storied past that had him even thinking it.

But it was his past that had him standing moments later, striding toward the door to see just what his wife was about.

He made it to the south corridor in moments, but he was met with absolute silence. The rain continued to beat along the roof of the manor house, and somewhere a clock ticked, but otherwise, the corridor carried nothing more than the ethereal quiet of a stately home.

He made his way down the hallway, peering into each room, finding each as empty as the last until he'd almost reached the end. It was a room his mother had used for music although his mother was the least musically talented woman in all of Britain, but she liked to have a place for her guests to retire to should they be stuck indoors on a day like it was then. She decorated the rooms in soft shades of violet, and the rear wall like all the rooms on this floor was a panel of windows casting out over a section of the cliffs.

The room was sparse of furniture now, the piano having long been removed, but there was still a long table set against the windows that had once been used for refreshments. He remembered as a boy hiding under the table with Ronald while some debutante droned on at the piano.

He faltered in the doorway as the memory washed over him, but soon his attention was caught by his wife.

A fire had been lit and candles brought in as the storm muted the light through the windows. His wife leaned over that same long table, a forgotten chair discarded behind her. She was examining something on the tabletop, her attention rapt, her fingers moving with delicate precision.

He didn't hesitate. He stormed into the room and snatched at the paper she held in her hand. She gasped, stifling a scream, but he didn't take a moment to either apologize or take in her face as he did not want to see or hear her excuses.

He didn't know what he expected to find, perhaps a letter to a lover she'd left in London, but had he been in his right mind, he would know the absurdity of such a notion. He'd crushed the paper slightly with his hasty grab, and now regret and guilt washed over him.

It was a watercolor of a small bunny.

His lips parted, and he raised his eyes reluctantly to Eliza, who cowered beside him, her eyes beseeching, her fingers hesitantly reaching for the paper he still held.

"Oh, please. I didn't mean to get in the way. Mrs. Donnelly said no one uses this room now." Her fingers reached tentatively for the paper in his hand. "Please, Ashbourne. May I have it back?"

He was back to Ashbourne. Horror at what he'd done seized his throat, and he could only relinquish the paper to her.

She set it carefully on the table and attempted to press the creases he'd made from it. But it was no use. He'd ruined the little bunny and the careful rendition of grasses that surrounded him.

"Eliza, I must beg your forgiveness. I—" But the rest of the words were lost to him.

His eyes moved, taking in the rest of the table. It was covered in watercolors. There must have been dozens of them. All small sheets of paper with a single scene of a bunny or a fawn, sometimes a turtle or a bird. Some contained just the watercolor, but others contained writing. He shifted, afraid to step closer, but needing to see what was written on them. At first it didn't make sense. The writing was nonsensical until he'd read several of them.

"You're writing a story with illustrations." The words came out as hardly more than a whisper.

Eliza didn't answer, and he shifted his gaze to find her. She still huddled against the table, her back bent as she tried futilely to remove the creases he'd caused in the paper he'd snatched. She wouldn't meet his gaze, instead focusing on the watercolor in front of her as she shifted ever so slightly.

Had he not been watching her so closely he would have missed it, as it was nothing more than the shift of her shoulder, but it effectively hid her face from him.

His stomach clenched, and he thought he might be sick.

"Eliza, I'm so sorry. I didn't know you wished to be an author. I had no idea—"

She whirled on him, straightening to her full height.

While he had expected to see the tears in her eyes, he hadn't expected such fury.

"I have no such wish, Ashbourne." Her words were steely and absolute.

He faltered, gesturing weakly to the scattered watercolors.

"But all of these drawings, the script on them, surely you mean to publish these one day."

That defiant chin went up, and her shoulders went back.

"These are not for publication, Ashbourne. These are for my children."

All at once it struck him.

The deal she had bargained for with him was not the result of hurt pride and a determination to see her duty fulfilled. Had he been wiser, he would have understood that society had taught Eliza to think very little of her own feelings, and she would never broker such a bargain.

No, this was something that ran deeper, truer.

He whispered the words even as they formed in his mind, "You want to be a mother."

CHAPTER 12

$\mathcal{D}$uring her first season, she'd stumbled upon a group of debutantes in the retiring room. Stumbled literally, for the door had a faulty latch. When she'd burst into the room, she discovered they were discussing the wallflowers present at the evening's ball and namely her. They were detailing just how precisely her face resembled that of her favored canines.

Even then she had been less mortified than she was now.

She looked everywhere but at Ashbourne, wanting so much to step back in time only a few seconds to keep him from figuring out what it was she truly sought from their bargain.

Never had she revealed her deepest desire, her yearning to be a mother, because in all reality, it had been so terribly unlikely until she'd met Ashbourne. Even now her life seemed like a dream, and she feared at any moment she would awaken.

"I don't see anything remiss in my natural desire to be a mother. Many women become mothers every day. It's not so unthinkable."

When he touched her, she jumped and reflexively tried to push him away.

He shushed her with soothing noises as he drew her into his arms.

"Eliza, darling, calm yourself. I wasn't thinking anything of the sort. I think it's wonderful that you wish to be a mother. I'm just saddened that you didn't feel comfortable telling me."

She stared resolutely at his chest, her body rigid as she refused to give into his warmth and assurances even for one inch. She knew that way lay danger. It would be all too easy to let his warm words and soft touch sway her, but she couldn't forget the words she'd overheard. They sliced through her even now when they were just a memory. She had to keep her wits about her.

"You know we mustn't stop at an heir and a spare. I believe those were the terms of the deal?"

He had her attention now, and she couldn't help but look up, meet his gaze.

"Yes." The single word cost her greatly, but she simply needed to hear what he would say.

"As an only child, I missed having the companionship of brothers and sisters. I shouldn't like our own babes to lack the benefits of a big family." His brow creased. "You do enjoy being part of a large family, do you not?"

"Oh, very much so." She hadn't meant to answer him. She hadn't meant to engage in this conversation at all, but once again, he lured her in with his gentle tone and promising words.

Like the first night they'd arrived, his honest tone alone had set her at ease, and now with his arms around her, it was all too easy to fall.

"Then why shouldn't our children enjoy the same comfort?"

He eased her away before she was ready to lose his touch, and she stumbled ever so slightly on the carpet.

"What is it exactly that you're doing here? I understand it's a story, but what is it about?"

Words were utterly foreign to her then.

No one had ever asked her about her watercolors.

Her first few attempts at speech fell hopelessly on the carpet at her feet, but she tried again, forcing her lips to form actual sounds.

"It's a simple story, and it's really not about the story at all. It's about the colors and shapes and the animals." She shifted the watercolors about on the surface of the table so he could see them properly. "When Jo was a babe—" She stopped, licked her lips, and straightened her shoulders.

Really, Eliza, this is not overly difficult.

"Johanna, my youngest sister, we call her Jo. When she was a wee thing, she had trouble with shapes and colors and animals and such. She would call pigs, dogs and cows, elephants." She licked her lips again and pressed a hand to her stomach. "My mother was gone by then, you see. Johanna's birth had been difficult, and Mother hadn't recovered when the influenza came. Poor Jo never really knew our mother."

She didn't realize Dax watched her until he reached up and pushed a lock of her wayward hair behind her ear. The gesture was so intimate, pain flashed in her chest.

"Mother was the one to always teach us things. Poor Jo didn't have anyone, and Viv and I tried to help. Viv being Viviana, of course. But there was Louisa, too. Only a year older than Jo."

Dax's expression grew serious. "Did you not have a nanny or a governess?"

"It's entirely possible our nanny had witnessed the building of Stonehenge, and our father didn't remember to

178

call for a governess until Viv was practically out for her debut. We're lucky we are naturally resourceful."

A smile played at the corners of his lips. "Indeed. So why these watercolors?"

She returned her gaze to them, pride filling her as it always did. "I couldn't find suitable material to help Jo with some of the more basic understandings, so I made them up."

"You made them up?" His baffled tone drew her gaze.

"Of course, I did. I couldn't let her continue thinking a pig was called dog. Imagine how offended Henry would be now."

As if understanding they were talking about him, Henry made a noise of agreement from where he lay sprawled in front of the fire.

"How did you make them exactly? You cannot be much older than your younger sisters."

She crossed her arms over her stomach. "I'm actually a good deal older. We believe our mother suffered two still births between myself and Louisa although no one speaks of it. I'm six years older than Johanna because of it. I was eight when I began making drawings for her. Just simple ones with some chalk and a slate. Eventually my father brought me some lovely charcoals from one of his trips to London."

At some point, he'd settled against the table, and with a start, she wondered if he intended to stay. When Mrs. Donnelly had shown her this room, she'd been elated at the prospect of having a little bit of the manor to call all her own. She thought the desk in her rooms would have been adequate, but curiosity had pushed her to ask for more... well, space. Not that she hadn't been enjoying Dax's company. It was just that after living with so many siblings, she was looking forward to having a little bit of quiet if only temporarily.

But the way Dax lounged against the table made it almost

seem as though the room weren't quite finished until he'd arrived.

"You speak fondly of your father."

She paused at his words, her mind faltering over their meaning.

"Should I not?"

He gave a casual shrug. "It could be said many members of the *ton* do not have such a relationship with their father."

Her shoulders sagged. "Did you have a poor relationship with your father?"

He gave a bark of laughter that startled her. "My father was thirty years older than my mother when they wed. It was like having a doting grandfather instead of a strict parent, instilling virtue and morals. My father never expected to have a child and so he showered me with gifts and attention. It was everything a child could have dreamed of."

"You don't seem to believe your own words."

He studied the carpet before answering. "Because he was so grateful for me, I always felt like a grand prize instead of his son. As if I were placed on a pedestal for the simple happenstance of my birth."

"I don't find you spoiled in any manner as your upbringing would suggest."

His laugh was rich now. "I will tell my mother you said so. She worked hard to counter the duke's attention, so I came up with a reasonably level head."

"Your parents did not wish to have a large family then?"

The shake of his head was precise. "The duke was happy to have me. He spoiled both myself and my mother and let us to our own devices. It was all merriment and laughter."

"That's not really what families are about."

He studied her for several moments before answering. "I'm beginning to understand as much." He gestured to the watercolors. "But you've carefully avoided telling me about your own father."

She followed the direction of his gesture and gave a small shrug.

"There really isn't anything to tell. Poor Father was left with the five of us, not knowing what on earth was to be done." She adjusted one of the watercolors, this one a rendition of a fawn amongst the reeds of a creek. "He was kind but distant, never really sure what to make of all of us." She fingered the edge of the paper. "I miss him terribly. Andrew is lovely and takes very good care of us, but there's something about having a parent. They're the ones you're always supposed to turn to, aren't they?"

He didn't answer her. Instead, he allowed his gaze to linger overlong on her face, and when heat flooded her cheeks, she looked away.

"It's strange not having anyone like that any longer." She traced the outline of a tree on the watercolor before her. "It's like you're suddenly all alone in the world."

She started again when he laid a hand atop hers. When she looked up, his gaze was piercing.

"But you're not alone." The words burned, destroying some of the shadow that had always lain across her world.

She wanted to believe he spoke of himself, but doubt still lingered in her mind. How much of this was real and how much a falsehood? The farce he wanted to make of his marriage?

She swallowed and broke away from his gaze.

"No, I'm not." The words were strong, but she spoke them to her watercolors and not to anyone that mattered. She forced a smile and backed away from the table, shattering the intimate cocoon that had enveloped them.

"I feel as though I interrupted you from something." She

gestured toward his person. "You were wearing a jacket this morning. I hope I did not upset you overmuch."

He stared at his shirt sleeves as if just realizing his state of undress.

"You've upset me not at all, Eliza." He crossed his arms once more. "I was going over the calving reports from Sheridan. It seems the herd had a good spring."

She couldn't help but brighten at this. "Truly? That's marvelous news. It seems your breeding experiment is off with a good flourish."

The embarrassment was quick this time, flooding her cheeks with color as she resolutely looked away. Dax was ever the gentleman though and did not make a comment on her blunder. He only straightened.

"It would appear so." He stood before her within seconds and tipped up her chin with a bent finger. "I shan't disturb you any longer if you promise I'll see you at luncheon."

Their position was intimate, but his words held even greater emotion. An understanding for the future. A wish to see her again.

She swallowed. "Of course. That is if you should like to have luncheon with me. I know I kept you away from your work yesterday."

His soft kiss stifled her words, but it was fleeting. By the time she got her eyes open, he was to the door.

"Eliza, there's one thing you should understand."

She blinked, expectantly, and his gaze was dark and brooding as it traveled over her, making her squirm as if he still touched her.

"I always want you with me."

He left before she could reply, which was probably best.

* * *

It was all too easy to fall into a routine after that.

They spent their mornings at their respective tasks. He at his desk or in the fields with Sheridan, addressing estate business. She in the former music room with her watercolors.

They would meet again for luncheon. Sometimes on the terrace but more often, they would take a basket down to the shore where they would luxuriate in the sun-drenched hours of the afternoon. She would tell him about her work, what went well and what didn't. She was hoping to begin an entirely new storyline about a fairy princess. She'd never done anything whimsical, but she thought the storyline would appeal to a more creative child.

He would update her on the development of the calves that had been born that spring and the health of the herd. Although should he be going out to the paddocks, she often accompanied him. Her love of animals was effusive, and he felt himself being pulled by her joy. He eyed the herd in a new way, finding new outlets to allow them greater health and more enjoyment. The herds flourished, but his wife's happiness overflowed.

He realized too late she was suited to manor life here at the shore. Henry took to running beside her horse on their early morning rides and evening walks through the fields. The wind pulled her hair from its riotous knot within moments, and she'd taken to braiding it instead. The bonnet was replaced with a sagging, wide brimmed hat that kept the bright sun from her eyes, but regardless of such care, soon her skin turned a delectable tan dotted with freckles.

Much to his delight, the tan reached everywhere thanks to their swimming lessons, and he enjoyed every stretch of it.

Her swimming improved as well, and soon she was challenging him to a race through the cove. When he allowed his mind to linger, he remembered the last time he'd experienced such fun along the water's edge, and he decidedly pushed the thoughts away. He didn't want the past intruding on his future.

Days melted into weeks, and one morning he realized with a jolt it was nearing the end of July. While he'd kept a keen eye on estate business, there were other matters he'd let slip, wishing to give his focus to his afternoons with Eliza.

It was only luck that his wife should appear in the breakfast room one morning rather overwrought, or as nearly overwrought as Eliza could get, that allowed him to broach the subject he'd let slip in his enjoyment of their quiet summer.

She pulled at her gown as she entered, attempting to sit the waist just so, only to have it ride up again.

"It's the strangest thing," she said by way of greeting, although it needn't matter as he'd only left her minutes before to allow her to dress while he brought Henry out to the gardens. "This gown simply will not cooperate today."

He eyed the garment she wrestled with, noting how her bosom filled out the neckline more than it once had, and the sleeves pulled at her wrists.

"It's probably the salty air and the moisture." He gestured for her to sit while he got her a plate. "It can wreak havoc on clothing if one is not careful." The grin he gave her was devilish. "And it's not as if we've been avoiding the shore."

She frowned. "I suppose not."

"It's rather convenient, however, that you should be in need of the seamstress in town as there's a matter I appear to have neglected these past few weeks."

She eyed him as he placed her plate in front of her.

"The Ashbourne summer ball."

If it were possible, her tan faded in an instant.

"I beg your pardon?"

He poked at his eggs. "The Ashbourne summer ball. It's a tradition each Ashbourne duke has held since time immemorial." He raised his gaze carefully from his plate to find she still stared at him as if he'd told her she could have no more dogs. He swallowed. "The Ashbourne summer ball is a fete for the county. All the gentry in Sussex attend if able. Mrs. Donnelly has been handling the arrangements for years now, and I am sure she will be able to assist you in its management."

"All of Sussex?"

He nodded and pressed a sheepish smile to his features. "Something like that."

She put down her fork before eating a morsel.

"Well, I suppose I had better get started on it. I shall see Mrs. Donnelly immediately."

He raised a hand. "But you haven't broken your fast."

She considered her plate. "With how my gowns are fitting, I should think one missed meal will hardly matter."

He sat up. "You must eat. We're going into the village today, and you'll want your strength."

Her eyes widened at this. "We are? Whatever for?"

"For a gown for the ball for starters." He waved his fork carelessly. "You'll want to pick up some more gowns you can wear down to the shore as well. I'm sure Mrs. Fletcher likely has something more suited to the shore life."

She blinked as if he'd told her they were moving to France.

"Mrs. Fletcher?"

He gave a short nod. "Yes. The seamstress in the village, remember? You still have not eaten."

She pressed a hand to her stomach. "And I don't know that I can. I've never planned a ball before."

"Mrs. Donnelly is here to assist you. It's really the same thing every year. In fact, I'm sure Mrs. Donnelly has already arranged most of what is needed. You'll simply need to address the guest list and the invitations."

Only too late did he remember her wallflower status when she melted from a healthy tan to a sickly green.

"Eliza." He set down his fork and gave her his full attention. "Would you rather your first ball be under the nose of every haughty matron of the *ton* or here on the shore where the rules are relaxed, if not entirely forgotten?"

She seemed to consider this, her mouth screwing up on one side.

"I suppose there is merit to your thinking."

"That was very difficult for you to say, wasn't it?"

She picked up her cup finally and filled it with tea.

"I do not know what you speak of, Your Grace."

Her tone had him smiling.

As it was a short, uneventful drive into the village, he had the gig brought round so he could drive them himself. The air was fine with a slight breeze coming in off the water, and he knew Eliza would enjoy the chance such a ride offered.

It took much pleading and not a small amount of bribery with some leftover hen to get Henry to stay at the house with George, the nice, young footman. For an odd reason, Henry seemed taken with him.

"I am certain I have something suitable to wear for this ball. There is no need for the expense—"

He cut her off with a kiss as it was one of his favorite ways of getting her to stop speaking. Over the past several weeks, he'd watched her confidence grow, but the erosion of twenty-six years to her confidence could not be undone in one summer by the shore. So whenever she would spiral into a dither of self-loathing, he would effectively end it with a kiss. It was a form of treatment he could wholeheartedly endorse.

He set her up in the gig without further statement and climbed in beside her.

"You'll like the village, I think. You may even find some scenes to add to your illustrations."

This caught her attention, and he hoped the conversation about the gown had ended.

"Do you really think?"

He gave a nod as he set the gig in motion.

"Most certainly. Village life along the shore is ripe with interesting things to teach young ones. We should even have time to go down to the docks so you can see the fishing boats."

She'd switched back into that damn bonnet again, likely because she would actually be seen, and when she turned with interest on the subject of fishing boats, he could only see part of her face.

"I should love that. Will it truly not be a bother for you? I know you wanted to go over the figures for feed for the piglets with Sheridan."

He guided the horse around the end of the drive and directed it toward the road that led down into the village.

"You've been paying attention." He slid a glance to find she'd turned her face to the road again.

"It's hard not to pay attention when piglets by nature are so adorable in countenance."

"Piglets are adorable?"

Now she did turn to him, and even the edges of her bonnet could not hide her smile.

"Of course, they are. Please don't tell me you're immune to their charm."

At the word, his mind flashed back to the first conversation he'd had with Sebastian on just the very topic. He turned to find her still smiling at him, and he couldn't help but return it.

"No, I am not immune to their charm," he said, even as he realized he spoke of something entirely different.

Her smile grew soft as he continued to gaze at her, and it was as if some unspoken message passed between them. He was only lucky she broke it off or he may have driven them off of the cliff beside the road.

He kept his eyes firmly affixed between the horse's ears for the remainder of the journey, and they arrived in Glenhaven proper without incident. He helped Eliza alight before taking her arm and tossing a coin to a village boy to watch the gig until he came back.

Mrs. Fletcher's shop was not far into the village, and they strolled past only a few shop fronts before he drew Eliza up onto the porch of a small shop set into the cliffside. A bell rang above the door as they entered, and a woman emerged from the back of the shop. Gray touched each temple and lines bracketed her eyes, and it startled him to find Mrs. Fletcher had aged.

How long had it been since he'd been in her shop?

"Your Grace!" Mrs. Fletcher exclaimed, sweeping from behind the counter that lined the back of the shop. "We'd had rumors you were up at the manor house." She didn't pause to give him greeting but instead turned with a curtsy to Eliza. "And with your bride, no less. Welcome, Your Grace."

Eliza let go of his arm to return the curtsy. "Thank you, Mrs. Fletcher."

The seamstress waved her hands. "Oh, I'm just so delighted you're here." Her face cleared, and finally she addressed him. "But why are you here?"

She reached out a hand and without hesitation, pinched his cheek just as she'd done when he was a boy. Eliza stared, and he shuffled his feet.

"My wife requires a gown for the Ashbourne ball, Mrs. Fletcher."

The older woman pressed her hands together in obvious delight.

"Oh, the ball!" She wiped a hand over her forehead. "Of course. How could I forget?" She turned to Eliza, narrowing her eyes as she studied her but without spending more than a couple of seconds, she waved at Dax. "Leave us if you will, Your Grace. I have much to discuss with your wife about her attire."

He turned to Eliza. "I'll just be along the shops should you have need of me."

Eliza's smile was quick. "No need to worry. I shall be just fine."

He bid them goodbye and disappeared through the shop door but not before Mrs. Fletcher called for reinforcements from the back of the shop.

CHAPTER 13

"What an honor it is to have you in my shop, Your Grace."

Mrs. Fletcher had led Eliza to a small dressing room off of the main shop floor and now she found herself standing atop a dais, her arms outstretched as Mrs. Fletcher took measurements, her fingers deft and sure.

As soon as Dax had left, Mrs. Fletcher called on her daughter for assistance, a Mrs. Longbottom, who was an exact replica of her mother if only several years younger. They shared the same soft smile and alert eyes, moving with precision to drink in a person and all there was to know about them.

The effect should have been disconcerting, but no one had ever taken such interest in Eliza before then. She found the treatment rather endearing.

Until Mrs. Fletcher straightened with hands to her hips.

"Well, Your Grace, I should like to speak frankly if I may. As I tell all my clients, it's really in your best interest."

Eliza stilled, her hands going to her stomach as tension boiled there.

"What is it, Mrs. Fletcher?"

The older seamstress raised her eyes to meet Eliza's gaze as Mrs. Longbottom shook her head silently behind her mother.

"I assume it was a London modiste who dressed you in yellow, was it not?"

Eliza looked down as if just realizing she wore such a shade of sunshine.

"I was told it's this season's particular color."

Mrs. Fletcher gave a soft snort. "I thought as much. The London modistes have only a concern for fashion as it is what keeps them in business. They must dress their clients to whatever the rage is that season even if it does nothing for the woman's figure or coloring." The seamstress pointed a finger at Eliza's gown as if she were indicating a dead fish. "Are you at all attached to this particular style and color?"

Eliza had very little concern for dress at all, only in so much as it hindered her from working with Henry.

She gave a shrug. "I have no feelings on it whatsoever."

Mrs. Fletcher's smile was quick. "I was hoping you would say as much." She gestured to her daughter. "Let's help her out of it then."

Eliza's hands reflexively dug into her skirts.

"Take me out of it?"

Mrs. Fletcher wrinkled her nose. "You don't wish to wear that out of here, do you?" She waved a hand at the back of the shop. "I have some designs that are nearly finished that will work well on you. They should keep you in fashion until I can get the rest of the gowns to you."

"Rest of the gowns?" Eliza dropped her hands. "Mrs. Fletcher, that's really unnecessary. It's only the one gown—"

But Mrs. Fletcher was already moving away as Mrs. Longbottom came forward with a soft smile and began to undo the buttons that ran down the back of Eliza's gown.

Before she knew it, she was swathed in a dressing gown of the most luxurious silk she'd ever felt, her feet up on a cushioned stool, a teacup in hand, and a plate of delectable treats at her elbow. She had never been fawned over quite so much in all her life. Trips to the modiste in London were always painful affairs with seamstresses poking her with pins and telling her to stand up straight. The problem wasn't that she failed to stand erect. It was that standing up straight did little to address the problem of having nothing with which to fill out the gowns.

Mrs. Fletcher seemed to not have a care about the matter, and once Eliza was safely settled in a comfortable seat, Mrs. Longbottom and Mrs. Fletcher brought out their work as if they planned to do it directly in front of her. Eliza couldn't help but stare. She'd never seen two women tackle an endeavor with such precision and focus.

"Now then," Mrs. Fletcher said as she gathered a gown of such deep green, Eliza imagined a forest would spring from it at any moment. "Tell us about yourself then, Your Grace. We were so pleased to hear of your arrival at the manor house."

Eliza wrapped both of her hands around the cup of tea, unaware until she'd put her feet up as to how tired she seemed to be that morning. Perhaps it was all the walking and swimming she'd been doing the last few weeks. Viv would be appalled if she saw the number of freckles that had appeared along her checks, to say nothing of the tan that had crept over her skin. It was probably best that no one knew just how much of her it covered.

"I wasn't aware that my arrival had caused such a flutter in Glenhaven."

Mrs. Longbottom laughed. "Oh, of course it did, Your Grace. There isn't much that happens here in the village, and it's such a wonderful reprieve when news comes down from the manor house."

"Are you from a family in London then?" Mrs. Fletcher adjusted the gown on her lap, picking up a needle with careful dexterity.

"My family is the Darbys, and my brother is the Duke of Ravenwood."

Mrs. Fletcher nodded politely as Mrs. Longbottom gave her a hopeful smile as if whatever Eliza had to say would be the most interesting thing she would hear that day.

Eliza continued as it seemed she would be the one doing the talking that morning while the seamstresses applied their needles to the gowns in their laps.

"I have three sisters as well. I'm about in the middle of the lot of them."

Mrs. Longbottom looked up expectantly. "How lovely. Will your sisters be coming to visit this summer, or are they already wed with families of their own?"

Eliza couldn't help the way her heart squeezed at the thought of Viv and the family she should have had by now.

"I hadn't thought of it, if I'm honest. There wasn't much time to discuss it before we left London."

She thought back to the anguish and tears that had been her departure from London, and while she could say things had gotten better, there was still a finger of doubt that needled at her. It was clear Dax had no intention of a love match, but after his reaction to her desire for a room for her watercolors, she wondered if it weren't something more. If she hadn't known better, she would have said Dax were jealous or perhaps fearful of her keeping something from him. It was a preposterous idea, but she just couldn't seem to shake it.

She sipped her tea, determined to enjoy the company of the mother and daughter seamstresses.

"I do hope they can make it. The shore is such a lovely spot to be in the heat of summer. Although I must say, the winters can be quite trying." Mrs. Fletcher's smile suggested she knew too well just how trying.

"Have you lived here your whole life?" Eliza eyed the tray of sweets Mrs. Fletcher had placed next to her. She'd never been one for biscuits and such, but her stomach was feeling a bit growly that morning. Dax was correct in trying to get her to eat more for her breakfast, and she would do well to remember that in future. Life at the shore meant a great deal of activity more than she was used to.

"Oh yes. We grew up at the manor house actually. My father was the steward there, you see. We had the cottage just off the main drive by the livestock paddocks."

Eliza pushed herself up in her chair at this bit of news. "Truly? So you must have known Ashbourne when he was small."

Mrs. Fletcher shook her head ruefully. "As you probably know, His Grace came to the manor late in the previous duke's life. I was already married to Mr. Fletcher and setting up shop here when His Grace arrived at the manor." She stopped in her precise stitches to flutter a hand as if remembering the moment as clearly as when it happened. "Oh, it caused such a stir. A young lad up at the manor house. We were all so happy for the duke. He had always been kind to his staff and generous to the village. It was so wonderful to see him granted such happiness." She set down her fluttering hand. "And the duchess. Such a lovely lady. It was something out of a fairy tale."

Eliza could picture it, a young Dax whose arrival had been heralded with such grandeur and happiness.

"Was he an adventurous child?" She wasn't sure why she asked the question, but something about the wildness of the cliffs and the untamed nature of the ocean had her wondering what a young duke-in-training would do with such an environment.

Mrs. Fletcher and Mrs. Longbottom shared a laugh.

"His poor nanny. There was nothing she could do to keep him from trouble. He was always a spirited one." Her eyes dimmed slightly at the end of her sentence, and she quickly picked up her needle to resume sewing.

Eliza's grip on her teacup tightened at the sudden change of mood.

"I can imagine how lovely it would be to grow up here. I'm so glad he brought me here for the summer."

The smile returned to Mrs. Fletcher's face. "Oh, as are we. We were oh so worried His Grace would never find love after what happened."

The biscuits and tea turned to a lump in her stomach, and Eliza had to set down her teacup to prevent herself from spilling it.

"Do you speak of the humiliation he suffered?"

Mrs. Fletcher let out a breath. "It was so much more than the humiliation. His heart suffered so. We never thought he would love again."

Her smile was over bright, and Eliza had to look away, anxious fingers clawing at her throat, threatening her breath.

"Oh?"

Mrs. Longbottom was the one to shake her head now.

"He was just so in love with Lady Bethany. We never thought he would recover from it."

And there it was.

The doubt she had sensed lurking solidified and suddenly she could touch it, taste, feel it.

It wasn't that Dax didn't want to fall in love. It was that he couldn't. The damage Bethany had wrought was lasting and true, and he'd never recovered from it. He had thought Eliza capable of betrayal because he knew nothing different. She swallowed against the realization.

Mrs. Fletcher was right. She just didn't know the truth of it, but Eliza did.

She folded her hands across her stomach, refusing to let her realization show.

After all, did it truly matter?

Dax was kind to her. He showered her with attention and showed great affection for Henry. Did it matter that he would never love her?

She didn't know.

Mrs. Fletcher cut the last of the thread on the gown in her lap and stood, shaking it loose. It fell to the floor in a cascade of deep forest green with carefully placed cuffs and a generous curve to the torso.

Eliza shook her head, both at the beauty of the simple gown and its unrealistic proportions.

"It's lovely, Mrs. Fletcher, but it's much too large. I should never hope to fill it out."

Mrs. Fletcher and Mrs. Longbottom shared a laugh and a knowing glance.

"I think you will be surprised, Your Grace. You are sure to swell more than you ever expect. It's like that with all new mothers though. You just don't know what to anticipate."

Eliza had been about to stand, but she stopped dead at Mrs. Fletcher's words.

"What is that?" she asked, her mind racing ahead of her, sorting through the seamstress's words.

"I grew ever so much with Nancy here. I was just a little sprite of a thing before." She laughed. "I was quite the sight."

"It was the same for me." Mrs. Longbottom stood and shook out her own gown, a near replicate of the green one but this one was in a deep shade of lilac with a gorgeous row of flowers trimmed along the hem and cuffs. "I was a little wraith of a thing carrying my two big boys. I never thought I'd be capable of it. But somehow our bodies just know what to do."

Eliza finished standing, putting her hands firmly across her flat stomach.

"I think there's been a mistake, Mrs. Fletcher. I'm only here for the ball gown."

Mrs. Fletcher laughed and laid a hand on Eliza's arm.

"I know that, dear. But even I can tell just by looking at you, a babe will soon be on the way, and you'll be needing to let your gowns out." She waved carelessly as she bustled her way through the shop toward a row of ribbons. "Just be sure to come by before heading back to London this fall. We'll alter these gowns and any others you need for the growing babe."

* * *

ELIZA WAS SUSPICIOUSLY quiet on the ride back to the manor house.

She wasn't very talkative when they had supper on the terrace or walked Henry in the gardens before retiring for the evening. It was as though she were not quite present, but somewhere deep in her mind where something made her both happy and sad at the same time. He wondered just what had gone on in Mrs. Fletcher's shop.

That night when they made love there was an earnestness to it that hadn't been there before, as if Eliza had taken her inner struggle and brought it out as if it were something she could physically wrestle with. Her kisses were ardent, her caresses deliberate. And when they finally fell asleep, her arms were locked tight around his torso.

She was like that for several days following, and every time he chanced a glimpse of her walking in the fields with

Henry or striding along the beach, her feet awash with the waves, he thought for the briefest of moments she was someone else entirely.

It didn't help that Mrs. Fletcher's gowns had transformed her. When he'd gone to fetch her that day at the shop, he hadn't expected she'd be outfitted with a new gown immediately, but there she had been, resplendent in a forest green gown that lit up her complexion. It also fit properly, and for the first time, he didn't fear she would fold in half in a strong breeze.

Now she roamed Ashbourne Manor like the mistress he knew she was always meant to be. Henry trailed at her feet, and her wild hair commanded the wind as if it were made for such things. He wasn't sure what had happened to the wallflower he had married, but he suspected she hadn't changed at all. It was simply how he viewed her that had changed.

The ocean and the shore had cast a light on her that had never before had opportunity to let her shine. She did here, brighter than she ever would in London. Here she was mistress of all the wind and sea spray she touched. Here she was home.

The thought sent shivers down his spine. He had long given up trying to refute Sebastian's warning for he knew now that it was Eliza herself that could slay him. Beauty was such a flimsy weapon. He should have realized.

The realization only drove him to be more diligent when it came to his emotions. While he enjoyed her company, craved her kisses, and genuinely took interest in her pursuits, he steeled his heart against it. He kept his focus on the livestock and the breeding plans. He met regularly with Sheridan to ensure the health of the crop that would be needed to meet their feeding requirements, and he made routine inspections of the entire estate to ensure any necessary repairs were made immediately.

But his nights were still for Eliza.

He had made a bargain with her after all, and he was a man of his word.

As much as he wished to remain aloof, he could not when he held Eliza in his arms. They were beginning to learn each other's nuances, manners, and thoughts. Their lovemaking grew richer, deeper, more poignant. It was after they had made love though that he was truly in danger, when Eliza would lay her head on his chest and tell him of her childhood, the antics of her sisters and brother, and the time spent getting the family dog to sit at the table like a human.

It made it difficult to concentrate as he sat at his desk that morning going over the wheat yields from the previous years as they projected what should be planted in rotations for the following year. His wife had taken Henry off in search of a place to work on her watercolors as the morning had proved a bright and considerably pleasant one. He'd watched her disappear over the fields, her wide brimmed hat flopping as the wind played with her braid.

The sweep of domesticity that overcame him at the sight made him want to wretch, but at the same time, it was as though he'd been given a prize he couldn't quite believe he'd won.

A knock at the door shook him from his thoughts, and he looked up just as Stephens entered bearing a silver tray with a card atop. The clock hadn't even chimed ten yet, and it was terribly unfashionable for calling hours. At the sight of the card, his stomach churned, knowing whomever it belonged to was not here for a social purpose.

Stephens bowed and extended the tray. As soon as Dax fixed eyes on the name scrawled across it, the blood drained from his head.

. . .

Lady Bethany Danvers, the Marchioness of Isley

"Lady Isley has requested an audience. Shall I tell her you are in?"

Dax stared at the card, years of hurt and betrayal crashing through him.

He stood with resolution.

"Please show the lady to the front drawing room."

Stephens bowed in departure and slipped out the door. Dax took a few moments to collect himself before starting the trek to the front of the manor house. He had several minutes to gather his thoughts. He'd had seven years to think about what he would say to Bethany should he ever see her again, and his mind rattled with the possibilities.

Words of accusation tripped over his tongue, and his hands shook with the pent up anger he'd carried for so long.

But even as all of this simmered inside of him, a single thought stilled his progress, and he stood silent in the corridor.

Why had she come now?

She'd had seven years to make amends. Why was she suddenly here today?

He knew word of his marriage had likely spread throughout the *ton*, and he knew from personal account it had spread through the village. But Isley had not occupied the adjoining estate in nearly a decade, preferring instead the title's main country seat in Derby.

There could only be one reason Bethany was here now, and it left a sour taste in his mouth.

She stood facing the windows opposite the door when he entered. Her gown was simple but exquisitely cut. His body reacted to the silhouette of her figure as he knew she had expected it would. Her golden hair was pulled up under a small hat and hung in sweeps of curls about her face.

And God, her face.

He hadn't forgotten a single detail of it.

When she turned to him, her chin was tilted slightly up, giving her a woeful expression anyone would find endearing.

But not him.

"Bethany." He spoke the single word as if he were sighting a rat.

"Dax." The word was breathless and coaxing, but he stood his ground.

"What are you doing here?"

"Oh, Dax." Her voice was suddenly filled with tears, and his suspicions grated along the back of his neck like nails. "It's too terrible."

He thought for a moment something had happened to Isley. The man may have betrayed him, but once upon a time, they had been friends, childhood friends, and those were always the most precious.

"Why are you here, Bethany?" He asked again, putting more ice into his voice.

She took a step toward him and faltered as if sensing he was dangerous. "Oh, Dax, I heard about your marriage, and I had to come. It's just too awful."

He flexed his fingers. "Bethany, I'm sorry if you feel my marriage was a slight against you—"

Now she did come closer, sweeping forward in a rush of bows and flounces, her beribboned reticule bouncing against her arm.

"Oh, Dax, it isn't that at all. It's just that—" Her words were cut off by a sudden flow of tears.

He didn't want to succumb to her machinations, but her cheeks were wet, her breath hitching. Bethany was a good liar, but she was not a good actress.

He took a hesitant step forward. "Bethany, what is it?"

She studied him through her tears. "I didn't want to marry Ronald, Dax. I didn't want to. My father—"

The last of her sentence was lost in a rush of tears, and something inside of Dax broke. Seven years of pent up rage evaporated, and he stepped forward, taking Bethany by the shoulders.

"Bethany, what are you saying?"

When she looked up, her lower lip trembled, and her chest hitched on another sob. "Isley made a better offer for my hand, and my father accepted it. I didn't know until it was too late. I refused, Dax, and he forced me to go to Gretna Green to have the thing done."

She dissolved in another fit of tears, and without thinking, he pulled her into his arms, pressing her head to his chest.

Her father had accepted another offer for her hand?

His mind reeled, scrambling to find purchase on a reality that no longer existed. One question still lingered though, and he eased her away from him.

"But why are you here now?"

He thought she would crumble into another fit of tears, but oddly, she seemed to gather herself.

"I had always thought—" She shook her head. "It's sounds so silly when I say it. But I had always thought there was still a chance for us as long as you remained unwed."

He looked into her eyes, shimmering with yet more tears, and he searched the lines of her face, the set of her chin, the focus of her gaze. He found nothing. Nothing there that warned him. Nothing there that suggested what she told him was not the truth.

A yearning buried so deep beneath the hurt of betrayal bubbled up inside of him. Once he would have done anything for this woman. Once his body had ached for her.

There had been a time when he couldn't have imagined a future without her.

Bethany.

She had always been there, and she still was there, in the most golden memories he had of his summers in Glenhaven.

Bethany.

He didn't see the kiss coming because his thoughts had run away with his consciousness, but when her lips touched his, memory exploded through him. His eyes drifted shut of their own accord as he tried to reassemble the flashes of memory her touch sparked within him.

He had been so young, so in love. The future had been a vast openness of possibilities.

She gathered the lapels of his jacket in her hands and pulled herself up on her toes to deepen the kiss.

This was all he'd ever wanted. Bethany. His Bethany. Coming back to him. This was redemption. This was everything.

At least it might have been once. But not anymore. Because now he had Eliza.

Only too late did he register the sound of Henry's growl.

He shoved Bethany away from him, violently severing their kiss, and his gaze flew to the door.

Eliza stood there, her braid unraveling across one shoulder, her wide brimmed hat limp. Henry stood by her side, his ears back, his teeth showing beneath a snarling lip.

"Eliza." He stepped forward, which was a mistake.

Henry lunged but didn't come after him. Instead the dog shifted, putting himself between Eliza and them.

"Eliza." He didn't know what to say. He didn't know where to begin, how to explain what she'd seen.

But his throat closed when he saw the look in her eyes.

Gone was the mistress of the fields and the commander of the sea wind.

The Eliza who stood before him was the wallflower from the Sudsbury ball, impervious to any hurt because society had taught her to expect it at every turn and she'd grown immune.

"Eliza." It was the only word he could say, but she never acknowledged he'd even spoken.

Instead she said, "Come, Henry. This is no concern of ours."

The dog obediently backed up, but he kept his gaze on Dax as they returned to the corridor. The click of the dog's nails against the marble the only sound as it faded away.

He didn't remember untangling himself from Bethany. He didn't remember if he'd bid her good day or seen her to her carriage. He'd only gone after Eliza to find her sheltered in her rooms.

But he couldn't reach her because it was the first time he had found her door locked to him since arriving at Ashbourne Manor.

CHAPTER 14

*S*he hadn't cried.

What would have been the point?

He had agreed to get her with child, not to love her. He'd held up his end of the bargain. She knew that with certainty now and not just from the wisdom of a seasoned seamstress. Her monthly was very late, and she could only hope what that meant.

Especially now as she sat all alone in the room she'd taken over for her watercolors.

Rain marked the windows before her, and the sea wind was feisty as it played with the windowpanes, shaking and rattling them. She heard and saw none of it as she held her hands over her stomach, hoping for a flutter of movement to assure her of the life within.

Her watercolors lay untouched behind her. She hadn't painted a single one since that day she'd happened upon Dax and Bethany in the drawing room. She didn't need an introduction to know who the beautiful woman was. The tension in Dax's shoulders as he held her, the way he tilted his head to accept her kiss, it told Eliza enough to know the truth.

Dax had never stopped loving Bethany, and it never mattered if Eliza were a wallflower or not. There was no room in his heart for another so long as he still held feelings for the woman who had betrayed him.

The horrible truth was Eliza wanted Dax to love her. Of course, she did. She was being a rather irrational wallflower if she denied wanting to be loved. Didn't everyone want the same thing?

These last few weeks in Glenhaven had been like an awakening, and for the first time, she believed herself deserving of a man's love.

Fate had a funny way of reminding one of her place.

Henry bumped her hand, and she started. He looked up at her with imploring eyes, bored from being banished inside because of the rain. She smiled, studying his deep eyes.

"Perhaps we can do some work while we wait for the carriage to arrive."

Henry wagged his tail, and she liked to think he was responding to her words even though she knew it was only the sound of her voice he enjoyed.

She'd only just broken up a bit of ham from the uneaten lunch Mrs. Donnelly had brought her on a tray when a sharp knock at the door proceeded Stephens.

Eliza had no concern that it would be Dax coming to see her. He only came to the connecting door between their rooms at night, and every night she dismissed him. His side of the bargain was already done. He needn't be bothered until the outcome of this pregnancy were known.

She smiled and pressed her hands to her stomach. "Are they here?"

Stephens gave a bow. "Yes, Your Grace. I offered to put them in the east drawing room, but they seemed rather enchanted with the vestibule."

She couldn't stop a laugh. "It is rather imposing. I'll go down just now and see to them. Thank you, Stephens."

He gave a bow and left.

She turned to Henry who sat expectantly beside her.

"Henry, are your aunties here? Should you go find them?"

At the command to find, Henry was off with a bark. She usually provided him with a scent to seek out, but she was fairly confident in his interpretation of the word *aunties*.

She was more sedate in her journey down to the main floor and across to the vestibule as she took a shortcut Henry didn't have access to, and she was fairly certain she would arrive ahead of him. However, she was stalled when she came upon more voices than she'd expected.

Namely a male voice interspersed with the female ones.

She hesitated, trailing a hand along the wall as she bent her head to listen.

Realization dawned, and she couldn't help a smile as she pushed forward into the foyer to find Johanna sparring with the Duke of Waverly.

"One would think when ladies were present a gentleman would give way to the ladies' carriage in such conditions."

Sebastian looked carelessly out the windows that flanked the massive front door.

"It's only some rain. As Englishwomen, I would expect you're used to such conditions, as you call it."

Louisa shook her head, her lips slightly parted as if astonished. "You are rather like my sister, Eliza. Did you know that?"

Sebastian might have blanched, but the lighting was too muted for Eliza to be certain.

"I have never had the circumstance to be compared to one's sister."

Louisa openly stared, her head shaking thoughtfully.

"How fascinating. Do you know they call you the Beastly Duke?"

"Do you know it's rude to point out the gossip of others in the presence of the one being gossiped about?"

"That can hardly be true." Louisa snorted her disbelief. "How am I to learn what you understand of what's said about you if I cannot ask it of you yourself? You are the afflicted party here."

Sebastian crossed his arms. "I would hardly call myself an afflicted party."

Louisa opened her mouth to say something, but she stopped and seemed to changed her mind.

"What *are* you doing here?" she asked instead of what she'd meant to say.

Sebastian dropped his arms and peered around him as if looking for salvation.

"Ashbourne invited me for some leisure by the sea. Why are you here?" He spoke the last question as if asking Louisa how she might have contracted a particularly nasty tropical disease.

Louisa was not at all affected by it. She only smiled her unending smile, and her eyes grew ever wider in earnest.

"Eliza, of course. She sent for us. We've never spent a summer at the shore even though our sister's married to the Duke of Margate and his seat is directly on the ocean. The duke is a bit of a wanker as I'm sure you heard."

Sebastian did blanch now, and it was all Eliza could do to keep from laughing and give herself away.

"I had heard something of the sort, but I would say it's quite common for dukes of the peerage."

Louisa tilted her head in consideration. "But I don't think it's true of you, is it, Your Grace?"

Eliza took pity on Sebastian as he searched the corners of the vestibule for someone to save him. She stepped in with a louder than necessary click of her heel just as Henry finally made his way down the main staircase at a barking run.

Johanna jumped behind Louisa, never the fondest of Henry, but Louisa bent and put her hands to her knees to brace herself for Henry's impending collision.

Eliza took the opportunity to approach Sebastian quietly. "I must apologize for my sisters. They have the unfortunate circumstance of having been raised by a rather direct woman."

"Your mother?" Sebastian raised an eyebrow.

"No. Me." She flashed her teeth at him. "It's rather good to see you, Your Grace, although I must admit I didn't know you were expected."

A shadow passed over Sebastian's eyes, and not for the first time, she doubted the truth of the rumors about him. Sebastian was rather cold in his manner, but she thought there was a robust beating heart under that austere exterior.

"I am not surprised to hear that." His look was knowing, and she had to turn her gaze away.

Either Dax had written to Sebastian of their situation or a summons from Dax was reason enough to believe trouble was afoot at the manor house. Either situation was not to her liking, and she cast her attention on her sisters whom Henry had finished greeting.

Louisa had her arms wrapped around Henry. "Oh, I did miss this boy." She looked to Eliza. "Are we to have lunch? We haven't a thing since we left this morning."

"I'll ring for a tray while you get settled. Come along, and I'll show you the way. Ashbourne Manor is a particularly vexing labyrinth."

Her gaze traveled hesitantly to Sebastian, who still stood at the door, his hands behind his back as if he had all the time in the world to stand motionless in a vestibule. She thought perhaps she should invite him to take luncheon, but as he'd not been expected, she wasn't sure there was anything arranged for a formal meal.

Sebastian, ever the gentleman in disguise, saved her with a simple nod of his head. He'd wait for Dax to come fetch him then.

"We shall see you for supper?" While the question was the one propriety demanded, she hoped with all her might that the guests may choose to dine separately this evening as she had not laid eyes on Dax since that fateful afternoon in the drawing room, and she had no wish to do so now.

"That would be lovely, Your Grace, but I believe the duke had some sort of hunting expedition in mind when he sent for me." Sebastian's smile was comforting.

She drew a deep breath and smiled. "How lovely. I shall see you upon your return then."

Sebastian gave a deep bow, and she couldn't help but notice the way his gaze slid cautiously to Louisa before she herded her sisters up the main stairs in the direction of the guest quarters, Henry adoringly in tow.

"What an interesting man," Louisa said when they'd gained the upper floors and were alone in the vast corridors of the east wing. "I had thought the Beastly Duke would be something more of a disagreeable creature, but really I think it's just that he's in a foul mood." She turned a thoughtful gaze on Eliza. "He does rather remind me of you. Not that you're in a foul mood. Although I can't imagine why you would wish to have your sisters underfoot during the summer of your first year of marriage."

Thankfully they had entered the guest suite just at the moment, and Eliza drew a deep breath. "I stumbled upon Ashbourne in the front drawing room. He was kissing Bethany Danvers, the Marchioness of Isley."

Johanna was the first to whirl about, her jaw slack, her

eyes wide. Louisa—dear, sweet Louisa—let out nothing more than a soft, "Oh."

"Harlot," Johanna seethed.

Eliza tilted her head. "Actually, I'm not entirely sure it's her fault. Ashbourne seemed to be the instigator in the affair."

She recalled all too clearly the way his strong hands had gripped the marchioness's shoulders, the way he'd pulled her so close.

Eliza swallowed and went to the windows to draw back the drapes.

"Isn't the view magnificent? Even through the rain you can tell just how spectacular it is."

She felt her sisters' gazes on her, and she turned.

"It's not as if I expected a love match. What an entirely unnecessary notion." She gestured around her. "Look at all that I've gained in the union. You should see the watercolors I've done since we arrived. And Henry is getting more exercise than ever, and—"

She'd been about to say she'd learned how to swim, but the words stuck in her throat as her memory burned with the echo of Dax's touch as he laid her back in the water, the feeling of his arms around her, so safe, so sure that nothing could ever hurt her.

She raised her chin and plastered on a smile. "There's a ball to be arranged as well. Apparently it's a family tradition." She stepped forward and took a hand from each of her sisters even though neither had spoken since her pronouncement. "And both of you are here to help me plan it." She frowned. "Although I had wished Viv would come along too. Is it really true she went to Margate for the summer?"

Louisa blinked several times but finally answered, "Yes. She wanted to spend the summer alone apparently, recuperating by the sea."

"But isn't she concerned she'll see...well, Margate?"

Louisa shook her head. "He's racing curricles in the Lake District this summer. Apparently he stands to win a great sum if he carries off the races he's committed to."

Eliza could only nod at this, imagining what it must be like for her sister to be alone in her husband's country seat. As she turned her gaze to the windows though, she began to understand what it might mean.

Eliza knew she would never spend another summer away from the ocean. No matter what was to come. She'd always make sure to return to the manor on the cliffs. Her hand drifted to her stomach at the thought. Perhaps with her children in tow.

She blinked as if to clear her thoughts and forced another smile before turning back to her sisters.

"Now then, let's get you unpacked and settled, and we'll catch up."

Louisa and Johanna both simply stared at her, ready for her to sprout an extra limb at any moment.

She smiled harder. "I'm fine. Really."

But she knew she was only trying to convince herself.

* * *

"I WISHED to inform you that you were right regarding the matter of beauty over charm."

Dax eyed his friend over his glass of whiskey, but Sebastian did not so much as smile in response. They'd fled to the hunting cottage his father had kept at the outskirts of the Ashbourne estate. There wasn't much hunting to be done along the seashore, mostly grouse and pheasant, and Dax suspected the cottage was more a means of escape for his father than actual sport.

Regardless, it suited Dax's needs at the moment, and he

relished the sound of the fire crackling before him and the rain striking the roof. The only thing that would make it better was if Eliza were with him, curled up on his lap while Henry snoozed by the fire.

He took a bigger swallow of whiskey.

"I can't say that I derive any pleasure from being correct." Sebastian toyed with the rim of his glass as it sat perched on the arm of his chair. "I can hardly see how this would warrant my immediate departure from London where I was quite enjoying the absence of, well, everyone as the city has emptied for the summer."

"Eliza caught me kissing Bethany."

Sebastian's fingers stilled on the glass.

"Bethany of the great betrayal?"

"That would be the one." Admitting it felt like chewing glass.

Sebastian made a noise of acknowledgment, but it was tinged with sarcastic disappointment.

"She said she needed to tell me the truth of what happened." He didn't know why he felt so compelled to defend himself.

Likely it was the fact he'd doubted the truth of Bethany's revelation from the moment he'd realized Eliza had seen the kiss. It had felt all too…contrived. He wouldn't put it past Bethany to plan such an occurrence, but how was she to know Eliza was even in residence or where she would be?

He gave himself a mental shake. No, it wasn't possible for Bethany to have so much information to orchestrate such a plan.

"And what, pray tell, did she say was the truth?" Sebastian's disbelief was obvious in his tone, and it rankled.

"That her father had accepted Isley's offer for her hand without her knowledge."

Sebastian's finger stilled on the rim of the glass. "And you believed her?"

Dax thought back to that afternoon. Bethany had seemed so earnest. Her eyes told him nothing but truth, and the way she had clung to him...well, it had felt all too real.

But he had been fooled by her once before.

"If it weren't the truth, then what cause would she have to seek me out?"

Sebastian set his glass on the table between them.

"I struggle with the moniker Beastly Duke when I am clearly more astute at affairs of the heart than most others." He broke his gaze away from the fire to stare at Dax. "Bethany hurt you once to great public humiliation. Would she not be so inclined to humiliate you privately and ruin any chance you had at a happy union with your bride?"

"That would seem rather petty, and Bethany has never bothered with something she views as beneath her."

"But that was seven years ago when she had you in her clutches. Now something that was once beneath her may be her last hope."

Even considering that he may have been the pawn in Bethany's malicious game had his teeth grinding, but he couldn't help but see the sense in Sebastian's words. After all, the man had been right about Eliza's charm.

Oh, God, Eliza.

"Be that as it may, it still leaves me in a terrible situation with Eliza."

"And which situation would that be?" Sebastian asked. "The one in which you were caught in the act or the one in which you realize you have true feelings for your wife and have now put yourself in an irreparable state?"

"Irreparable?" He tasted bile just speaking the word. "Surely the situation doesn't call for such a hopeless word."

Sebastian's gaze was direct. "Some situations are unfortunately hopeless, my friend. I pray you have not gotten yourself into one."

Dax swallowed and looked away, unable to hold his friend's gaze.

It was several seconds before he spoke.

"The second one." The words were soft, hardly a whisper, but he may as well have dropped an anvil directly between them.

"So the Jilted Duke has fallen in love with his wife. What a terrible outcome." Sebastian picked up his glass again. "You are in a rather hopeless situation then."

Dax pushed to his feet and went in search of more whiskey. "I'm beginning to dislike your use of that word."

"It's vexing, I should say, but it's the only word that's appropriate at the moment."

Dax turned to study his friend. "Appropriate?"

Sebastian did not look at him as he replied and not for the first time Dax thought his friend to be addressing his own past more than the current question.

"Sometimes one must view a situation as hopeless to have any hope of acquiring the motivation to get out of it."

Dax sat down without refilling his glass.

"You're saying I must think the situation hopeless."

"Yes, that's exactly what I'm saying. How are you to win her back if you think a weak apology will do the trick?"

Dax thought of the locked door he found every night, even now when nearly a week had passed.

"I don't think an apology is what she seeks."

"Of course, it's not. She believes you willingly kissed Lady Isley. An apology will not convince her otherwise. An apology is nothing more than words, and she's already learned not to trust words."

"Then what can be done?" Desperation flared inside of

him so unexpectedly, he had to grip the arm of the chair to keep from slipping to the floor.

Sebastian uncrossed his legs and sat forward, elbows to knees.

"The first thing I must ask you is this. Did you kiss Lady Isley or did she kiss you?"

Dax straightened at the question. "I hardly think that's relevant."

Sebastian helped up his hands and sat back. "If you are not interested in winning back your lady love—"

"Bethany kissed me," Dax said quickly, pursing his lips in a frown.

"Did you return the kiss?"

"Y—" He had automatically turned to the affirmative, but now that the question was asked, he couldn't really remember. He had been so overcome by the nostalgia of it that by the time he realized it was something he no longer wanted it had been too late. He shook his head. "No, I didn't, but it took me too long to realize I didn't want her kiss."

"Too long because Eliza discovered you?"

"And it may have given Bethany the wrong impression."

Bethany hadn't returned to Ashbourne Manor since that day, but he still couldn't quite recall what he'd said to her as he'd ushered her out to go in search of Eliza.

Sebastian's expression darkened. "Do you think Bethany may return?"

"No, she wouldn't." Dax was quick to shake his head, but even he didn't believe his words.

He didn't know what Bethany could be capable of, but he knew with sudden clarity that he would keep her away from Eliza no matter what it took.

He sat forward in his seat.

"You must tell me what I can do to win Eliza back."

A very dark part of him worried it was too late. He'd

already shattered her trust in him once, and now he'd done it again. Only this time, it was the ultimate betrayal. He'd not only betrayed her trust, he'd broken their wedding vows.

The words shouldn't have mattered, and any number of gentlemen broke them every day. But Dax was a man of honor, and he had sworn he would keep those vows no matter what it took. Except he hadn't anticipated Bethany returning to his life.

"You must show Eliza that you mean it."

Dax stared at his friend, worried the man may have drunken too much.

"Show her what?"

Sebastian sat forward again, his urgency palpable.

"You must show her that you mean your apology. You must show her you are contrite, that you are sincere in wishing forgiveness, that you will do anything to win her back, and then do it."

Dax had never before heard his friend speak with such feeling, and once again, he wasn't so sure about the role society had cast him in. His friend may have experienced something that had driven him to be so crass, but underneath it all, Sebastian was still the boy who fought the bullies alongside Dax at Eton.

"But what is it I can do?"

Sebastian sat back, crossing an ankle over the opposite knee. "That is something you will need to figure out."

Dax's shoulders sank as if he'd just been deflated by Sebastian's words.

"You make it sound so simple, Sebastian."

His friend shrugged and steepled his fingers. "Love never is easy. I don't know who thought it was, but he needs to stop spreading lies about it."

Dax sank back into his chair, his empty whiskey glass resting on his knee.

It was several minutes later when Sebastian spoke again. "You know I wasn't the only one summoned here."

Dax slid him a glance. "What do you mean?"

"Upon my arrival I was greeted by two rather spritely young women, one of whom came bearing a sharp tongue."

Dax raised an eyebrow. "I can only assume they are sisters to my wife, and the sharp tongued one was likely to be Johanna." He could readily recall her parting words of warning after the wedding.

Sebastian's brow furrowed. "No, I do believe this one was called Louisa."

Dax struggled to recall the quiet, nearly cherubic sister as she had been nothing but sunshine and flowers at the wedding, spouting happiness like a fairy trailing twinkling lights.

"Louisa? Are you sure?"

Sebastian shifted uncomfortably. "Quite sure."

Dax could only shake his head. "If she's asked her sisters to come, it doesn't bode well for me."

"How is that?"

Dax remembered what Eliza had said of her family. That no matter what happened she always had her sisters and her brother. For the first time, Dax understood and may have even envied her that.

He considered Sebastian and knew that at least he was not all alone in this. "Do you think I shouldn't still apologize?"

Sebastian moved only his eyes as if what Dax had said was preposterous.

"Oh, you will most certainly still need to apologize, but it will not be enough. Haven't you already apologized for the matter of calling your marriage a farce?"

Dax cringed. "I was thinking the same thing. Why should she believe me again when I continue to betray her trust?"

"Because this time you will show her you mean it with a gesture that says as much." Sebastian grew quiet as if collecting his thoughts. "You do mean it, don't you?" he finally asked.

Dax studied his friend as the rain continued to pound the roof above them. There in the quiet of the hunting cottage he knew he was safe to admit any truth, and Sebastian would take it no further. So Dax admitted the thing that could hurt him most.

"I do mean it. I love her, and I must find a way to prove it to her."

This seemed to satisfy Sebastian as the tension melted from the man's shoulders.

"Then you'd best come up with something astounding because your wife will have reinforcements in the way of her sisters."

Dax recalled the formidable Darby sisters, and he couldn't help a smile.

"I shall do well to remember that."

Sebastian stood. "Now then, did you actually bring me here to hunt or are we going to sit here talking about our feelings?"

It was at that moment the sky unleashed another torrent, and rain pelted the cottage, the windows shuttering with the beating.

"I believe there are some playing cards to be found around here," Dax said, standing.

"Those should be just fine," Sebastian replied and went in search of more whiskey.

CHAPTER 15

*S*he hadn't expected how much joy she would find in sharing the seashore with her sisters.

It only hurt a little to walk along this stretch of beach without Dax beside her, but she resolutely shut the thought away. Her sisters were here, and Henry galloped along the water's edge, snapping playfully at the retreating waves. The warm sun and gentle breeze were all she needed to make the day utterly perfect.

She wasn't at all surprised at how taken her sisters were with Ashbourne Manor. It had been three days since their arrival, and they'd slipped into the rhythm of the manor as if they belonged.

They'd started planning the Ashbourne ball. Louisa had taken over flowers and Johanna had started on decorations. Mrs. Donnelly had provided Eliza with the guest list from previous years, and she was going through it now. Cook was preparing a menu for them to review, and they thought they might make a visit to Mrs. Fletcher's shop to see if it were possible for Louisa and Johanna to get new gowns as well in time for the ball.

Planning the ball was a welcomed distraction even if she couldn't help but feel like the farce Dax had called their marriage. It had been easy to avoid him the past few days as he and Sebastian left the house in the early morning only to return once they'd retired for the evening.

Only the past two nights he hadn't come to her door.

She didn't want to feel anxious at the thought or wonder why he hadn't tried her door. It wasn't that she wished for him to visit her. Not anymore. She just couldn't stop thinking about what Viv had said.

A man doesn't care about a woman he doesn't chase.

So why had Dax stopped coming to her door?

She knew eventually he would give up. Why wouldn't he? There was nothing to keep him drawn to her now that Bethany had returned. Still, there was that pitiful part of her that continued to hope.

Henry splashed Louisa as he bounded out of the water, and she screamed with delight, much like a small child, and it shook Eliza from her thoughts. She watched her sister pick up her skirts and chase after the dog through the retreating waves. Henry loved every minute of it and chased her back.

"Do you think she will ever grow up?" Johanna asked beside her.

"Oh, I certainly hope not." Eliza shielded her eyes from the sun and watched as Louisa followed Henry in his crusade down the beach.

They were some distance away when Eliza spotted another figure approaching from the opposite end of the cove. Her heart gave a flutter at the thought it could Dax, but the figure was slight and even from this distance, Eliza could tell it was a woman.

Fear gripped her, and Johanna must have sensed it because without hesitation, her sister stepped in front of her.

Eliza held up a hand, stopping her sister.

"It's all right," she said, even though she felt anything but. "If she's come to speak to me, let her. She is no concern of mine."

Johanna eyed her warily, and while she didn't continue to shield her sister, she didn't retreat either. Absently, Eliza realized Henry had stopped barking, and she caught sight of Louisa holding the dog at bay farther down the beach. Both watched with marked anticipation.

Bethany Danvers, the Marchioness of Isley, cut a stunning figure even as she attempted to make her way through the clinging sand. She was not at all dressed for such an outing, but she presented a dashing figure in dark purple with black highlights. Even her bonnet was gorgeous with an array of purple feathers and a small bird perched at the brim.

The marchioness's smile was cold when she reached Eliza.

"I think we have no need to bother with introductions," she said.

"No, I should think not. You're trespassing." The words came out before Eliza could stop them, and she knew she'd surprised the marchioness when the woman's eyes widened.

"Is that so? I'm sure Dax would think differently."

"Ashbourne can think whatever he likes. Right now, I am occupying the beach, and you are not welcome here. The standard rules of trespass apply."

Eliza wasn't sure if it were her disregard of Dax's feelings on the subject that surprised Lady Isley or her utter lack of response to the woman's obviously threatening demeanor. It didn't matter. Eliza really had not a fig left to give this woman.

"Well, then I shall be quick in getting to the reason for my visit."

Johanna scoffed. "It's hardly a visit. Invasion is more like."

Lady Isley tossed Johanna a glare but wisely did not respond. She returned her focus to Eliza.

"Ashbourne is mine. I think it would be best if we were to have an understanding between us about the matter. I shan't get in your way if you shan't get in mine."

Eliza tilted her head. "And what exactly is your way?"

Lady Isley stuttered at the question. "What?" she asked awkwardly.

Eliza crossed her arms. "What exactly is it you want with my husband? You seem to have certain designs in mind, but as Ashbourne has only spoken ill of you, I can't imagine what you think they might be."

The barb had struck home as Lady Isley's mouth opened without sound emerging. She snapped it shut and rolled back her shoulders.

"Dax loves me, and you must stay out of the way. We can all get along if we mind our own business."

"And what business is that of yours?" Johanna asked.

Lady Isley slid her glance to Johanna, color rising up her cheeks. "Who *are* you?"

"She's my sister," Eliza answered promptly. "Answer the question."

Lady Isley snorted. "I should ask you the same question. You had no right marrying Dax."

"I had no right marrying Ashbourne?" Eliza eyed Johanna. "Did you hear that? This harlot says I had no right in marrying my husband."

At the word *harlot*, Lady Isley let out a muttered curse and stepped closer, poking Eliza in the chest. Henry's growl could be heard down the beach, and Eliza could only hope Louisa's grip on his collar was strong.

"You listen, you ugly wart. I should have been the one to marry Dax, not you. I should be the one sitting in luxury in Ashbourne Manor." She paused here and with stunning speed, reached out and yanked loose the sleeve of Eliza's gown. It tore with a sickening rip and collapsed limp at her wrist.

Eliza didn't move. Lady Isley's chest heaved now, her anger flaring.

"I should be the one with new gowns and pretty hats. I should be the one with servants to dote on me. I should be the Duchess of Ashbourne." She finished her speech with a flourish of spittle raining from her mouth. Sensing her gaff, she swiped a hand roughly over her mouth before leaning ever closer. "Stay out of this, spinster. Or you'll regret it."

Eliza studied the woman, despair and curiosity warring with the irate figure the woman presented. There was no way to refute the woman's ardent claim, so Eliza settled for the only thing to be said.

"The hem of your cuff has gone off. You'll need someone to fix that."

Lady Isley's whispered curse was more of a guttural moan this time, and without another word, the marchioness turned and marched off. Only it was more of a stumble and hobble as the woman was not at all dressed for sand.

Louisa appeared between them in seconds, Henry collapsing against his mistress's side. Eliza bent to scratch his head reassuringly.

"It's all right, boy. She's just a bully. No real threat."

"Whatever did she mean telling you to stay away from your husband? What an odd woman." Louisa straightened her bonnet.

"Did you hear what she said?" Johanna asked, still studying the place where Lady Isley had disappeared up the cliff.

Eliza straightened, following her gaze.

"That she was the one to deserve new gowns and

baubles?" Eliza asked, moving her gaze to study the damage Lady Isley had done to her own gown.

Louisa looked between them. "Why would she say that? Isn't she wed to the Marquess of Isley? Surely he can buy her new gowns."

Johanna and Eliza shared a look.

"Perhaps he cannot," Johanna said quietly. "Did you see how her cuff had come undone?"

Eliza nodded. "It looks as though it had been folded under to hide the wear, but it had not been properly pinned."

Louisa sucked in a breath. "Oh. How unfortunate."

Eliza felt both of their gazes on her.

"What are you going to do?" Johanna hardly whispered the question.

Eliza straightened her shoulders and pushed her spectacles up her nose.

"I'm going to do the practical thing, of course."

"Fling mud at her?" Johanna offered with raised eyebrows and a wide smile.

"Spread vicious rumors that she smells of pig dung?" Louisa asked.

Eliza couldn't help the smile her sisters always brought to her face.

"No, of course, not. I'm going to write Andrew."

Johanna's smile melted into a frown. "How is that the practical thing to do?"

Eliza crossed her arms, unknowingly protecting the babe that grew in her stomach.

"Why would a woman I've never met make the effort to climb down that cliff and threaten me to stay away from my own husband? What an odd thing to do."

"She's crazed with love," Louisa breathed, her eyes wide as if imaging the entire sordid affair.

"She's loony off her block," Johanna suggested.

"Love or madness would not drive one to do something such as that," Eliza said gesturing to the cliff.

Louisa frowned, and even that expression was endearing on her fresh face. "Then what is?"

Eliza shook her head. "Only money would make someone that irrational. I intend to write Andrew to find out the state of the Marquess of Isley's affairs."

* * *

ONCE WHILE AT Eton he had been dared to walk the parapet of the rector's home in a slicing rainstorm. In the nude, of course.

And even then, Dax was less scared than he was now, and all he must do was knock on his wife's door.

The night was quiet, the house having gone to bed hours before, but the light beneath the connecting door gave him hope his wife was still awake. He'd only seen her and her sisters in passing over the past several days as they went in and out of the manor house, Henry in tow. They'd usually been bubbly with chatter, but his wife had always appeared somewhat removed, as if their chatter hadn't reached her quite yet.

It pained him to see it. While he knew he was the cause of it, it hurt even more to see her so distanced from her sisters' company. He didn't know why he hadn't thought of telling her to extend an invitation to her sisters earlier in the summer. They were close after all and until their nuptials, Eliza had always lived under the same roof as them. It must have been quite an adjustment to leave them.

But earlier in the summer, he'd been too consumed by Eliza's attentions to realize anything beyond them.

The pain burned hotter in his chest, and he absently rubbed a hand against it to quell it. He knew he was in the wrong here, and worse, he feared the power Bethany had over him. It wasn't that she was physically irresistible nor did he find her particularly alluring. It was their shared history that had her pulling him in. It was as if by conquering her physically, he could right the wrongs of the past, which had been done to him.

He knew he'd been wrong as soon as his lips had touched hers. By the time he'd thought to push her away, a sour taste had already developed in his mouth, and he was left wanting for his wife.

He had absolutely ruined everything, and the first thing he needed to do was apologize.

Raising a single hand, he gave a sharp knock at the door.

"Eliza, I must speak with you," he said before she could raise an objection.

"Come in." The two words were spoken crisply and without hesitation, so much like his practical Eliza it nearly caused him physical pain.

He had the beef he'd squandered from dinner at the ready when he entered and tossed it to Henry before the dog could elicit more than a warning growl. Placated, he laid his head back down as he lounged on the window seat, the night ocean breeze ruffling his fur from the open window.

It would serve him right to find Eliza abed, tucked under the covers with her virginal nightdress buttoned up to her throat, much as she'd been on their wedding night. His body clenched at the sight of her, desire racing through him, and he had to clear his throat several times in order to calm his nerves.

"Hello." He hadn't meant to say that, but upon seeing her, more rational thought simply fled.

He was starved for her. It really hadn't occurred to him until he laid his eyes upon her, until her gaze was focused on him, but even as he yearned toward her, he stopped.

This was not the Eliza he had come to know over the past few months. This was the Eliza he had found on the ballroom floor. Her gaze was cold and alert, her jaw tight as if wary of an ambush. He swallowed again, knowing he'd done this as well. He'd made her climb back into the shell society had made for her.

"Hello," she said in reply, her voice soft and neutral.

There was a book open on her lap, one hand relaxed against the page as if holding her place. He wanted to sweep the book away and pull her into his arms. He wanted to spend the night pressed up against her, entangled in her heat as he'd spent so many nights that summer.

"I've come to apologize."

She did not react. "Is there cause for an apology?"

He recalled what she had said when she'd left them standing in the drawing room that day. That it was none of her concern. He wondered if she truly believed that.

He took a step closer. "There is. I behaved poorly, and I hurt you."

"You did no such thing." She tilted her head as if confused.

While he had anticipated the apology would be difficult to deliver as remorse and regret swamped him, he had not expected how it would irritate him when she so blatantly disregarded her own feelings.

He opened his mouth ready to press on but shut it. Her gaze was so sterile, her jaw tight, as if she were doing all she could to hold back her feelings.

He hated it.

Without further hesitation, he strode forward and sat on the edge of the bed, pulling the damn book away so he could take her hands into his. She gave a small gasp of surprise, and now her eyes were wide, her gaze anticipating.

"Don't pretend what I did meant nothing to you." This was not a planned part of the apology, but he couldn't stand for her to be so aloof. "I kissed another woman, Eliza. I betrayed your trust, and I broke the vow I gave you on our wedding day. You have a right to be upset."

He wanted her to rage. He wanted her to yell. He wanted to know she felt something for him in return.

Instead, she only frowned. "That isn't part of our bargain, Your Grace."

He stilled. The words were spoken with cool abandon, and her use of his formal address was quite effective in wedging a distance between them. But he wouldn't let it. He gripped her hands, turning them so his thumb stroked her palms. He saw the moment it affected her as her gaze dulled, her lower lip loosening.

"I don't care what our bargain was. This is no longer about our bargain, Eliza. This is about me hurting you when I swore I would never do it again."

"You don't need to apologize, Dax." The words were spoken so softly, so earnestly, they rendered him speechless. He stared at her, his argument dying on his lips as the real Eliza surfaced, her eyes sharpening as she drank him in. "What you did has nothing to do with me, and it has everything to do with your past, with Lady Isley. I know that."

"It doesn't make it right. I should—"

"Dax, I cannot expect anything from your future if you haven't settled with the events of your past. It doesn't matter if I'm beautiful or a wallflower, if I'm outgoing or sullen. None of it matters if you aren't willing to take the risk of loving someone else again. And if that is how it stands, I will not let what you do determine how I feel."

The words struck him directly in the center of his chest, and he was left without air, his lips parted and yet unable to draw breath. He studied her, her words echoing in his ears.

"Do you really believe that?" He didn't know why it was

important to him, but her words were having a clearing effect on him he hadn't anticipated.

He thought he would simply come in and apologize to her for betraying her trust. He had not expected to have his understanding sent into such upheaval.

She tugged her hands from his, and while he didn't want to let her go, he realized she was changing their positions. She cradled one of his hands in both of hers.

"I believe it because it's true. Why did you kiss her, Dax?"

He sat back, her question leaving him unstable.

"Why are you asking that?"

"Because I know you didn't kiss her out of desire, did you?"

He pushed to his feet, wrenching his hand away. How did she understand so much without him explaining how he felt?

"I did not kiss her because I wished it." He paced away from her, unable to speak the words while looking at her.

"Then why did you do so?"

He opened his mouth ready to say it was Bethany who had kissed him, but he realized what a weak excuse that was. He could have stopped her. He knew what she was about even as she leaned in. There was no reason he couldn't have prevented it all from happening.

So why hadn't he?

He turned so he could look at her.

"I don't know why." The words were the truth even if they felt like he was making excuses.

"Would it help if you told me what happened?"

He considered her. The candle she had been using to read by dappled her with soft light, and he wanted nothing more than to crawl into bed with her, pull her against him, and let the warmth of her comfort him. He collapsed in the chair he had occupied their first night at Ashbourne Manor when he'd sat across from Eliza and begged her to give him a second chance. So much had changed since then, and yet, they seemed to be back at the very beginning. Each stepping carefully as they figured out how to navigate around each other.

"I don't know what happened," he muttered, scrubbing his hands over his face. "Stephens came to fetch me when she arrived, and when I got to the drawing room, she was... desperate." He tried to recall the first image of her he had glimpsed upon walking into the room, but now the entire afternoon was muddled.

"Why was she desperate?"

He looked up when he heard the sound of the bed clothes being pushed back. Eliza slipped from the bed, and even the sight of her bare feet had his heart rate picking up.

"She said her father had arranged her marriage to Isley without her knowledge, and she had always hoped that as long as I remained free, there might have been a chance for us to be together one day." He said the words in a trance as Eliza made her way over to him and took the chair opposite his, tucking her feet underneath the chair as she sat.

She looked so prim sitting there in her nightdress, her braid over one shoulder. She'd removed her spectacles for reading, and her face took on a softness that called to him.

He licked his lips and had to try twice to get his next words out. "I don't know now why I believed her. She sounded so earnest." He shrugged. "I still don't know if what she said is true."

"But at the moment you believed her?"

"I had to." The words were whispered, and he may as well have taken a knife and sliced through what was left of his marriage.

Eliza didn't move. She gave no indication that his words had hurt her the way they did him to merely speak them. But he knew. He could feel it in the way she kept herself so still, in the way her hands fisted into the lengths of her nightdress, in the way her mouth remained so tight.

With each word he spoke, he tore her down a little more, and yet he couldn't stop.

"I had to believe that what she said was true because then I wouldn't have suffered such humiliation. I wouldn't have been so betrayed. And I could—"

He would be free to love Eliza.

The realization washed over him with such ferocity it was as if he were caught in an ocean wave in December. His eyes flew to Eliza's face, but her expression remained cold. He couldn't blame her. This was the second heartfelt apology in the course of their mere months-long marriage, and he had no right to expect it would do anything other than convince her not to trust him.

He stood suddenly, propelled by a need to make it right.

"Eliza, I love you. I know you don't believe that, and I know I've given you no reason to. But I do, and I'm going to make this right."

The only sign that she'd heard was a slight softening of her mouth.

"Dax, you mustn't—"

He closed the distance between them, pulled her to her feet, and kissed her soundly. She gave no resistance. In seconds, her arms were around his shoulders, her fingers digging into his back as she held on.

He released her just as quickly and took a step back. She rocked slightly on her feet, but he daren't touch her.

"I love you, Eliza," he said when he thought she'd regained her senses. "I love you, and I'm going to do everything in my power to show you."

He didn't wait for a response, but he didn't miss the way her hand trembled as she touched her lips as he left the room.

CHAPTER 16

*S*he took to replaying that kiss in her mind over the next few days.

They were sitting on the terrace nearly a week later, the ocean breeze toying with their luncheon none of them had been eager to consume as all three Darby sisters were preoccupied. Louisa and Johanna were both mired in a deep discussion of whether the invitations for the Ashbourne ball should have yellow ribbons or blue ribbons, and Eliza could think of nothing but the kiss her husband had unexpectedly delivered her the previous week.

She wanted to forget about it. She wanted to let her anger at him for hurting her continue to boil, but the truth of the matter was it did not. Instead, she hung suspended in some sort of odd in-between state where she wasn't quite sure where she stood. Was she Eliza Darby or was she the Duchess of Ashbourne? She wasn't sure anymore.

The only thing she could be sure of was the babe growing in her womb. It was beginning to make itself known with its occasional morning upset and bouts of nausea throughout the day. She tired easily now and found herself sitting absently about the manor.

To say nothing of her gowns.

Mrs. Fletcher had been right. She did need the extra room in her gowns as her body had already begun to change. Her reflection in the mirror showed a woman not only full of the color of the sun but also one with dewy cheeks and perky lips. Most surprising of all was how she filled out all those bits of her gowns that had never once before even touched her body.

She felt resplendent, which in itself was such an oddity it only added to her unease.

That night Dax had come to her room realization had crashed into her with the suddenness of a sea storm, and she knew she had been right. It left her aching and uncertain, but Dax had seemed so determined to make things right.

But what was right?

He'd started their marriage off by calling it a farce, and now she'd found him with another woman in his arms. She wanted to hide away in her rooms with Henry and her watercolors at the thought of it, but she just wasn't so quick to succumb to the wary nonsense her wallflower days had taught her.

She no longer wanted to hide. She no longer wanted to feel the sorrow of always being found lacking.

She wanted to walk along the beach, feel the sun on her face and the wind in her hair. She wanted to watch Henry bite at the waves and chase sea gulls. She wanted to trek along the fields of Ashbourne Manor from livestock paddock to livestock paddock, watching the herds grow and thrive.

She wanted everything.

And if Dax didn't want her...

It hurt. It hurt deeply. Her life would be a little less full without him, but as she settled her hands on her stomach, she knew she would be all right.

"You will have to tell him, you realize."

Eliza started from her thoughts and met Johanna's gaze. "Tell him what?"

Louisa set down the sample of ribbons she'd been sorting through. "Why, that you're carrying his child, of course. You can't expect him not to notice."

Johanna snorted. "I'm not so sure when it comes to men. He may, in fact, be left utterly in the dark until the young one's arrival."

Eliza looked between them sharply. "How did you know?"

"Because you're always doing that." Johanna laughed and pointed to where Eliza cradled her stomach. "Did you expect us not to notice?"

"I'm quite frightened Ashbourne will find out the truth from someone else, you know," Louisa supplied. "You really must tell him. Tonight after supper perhaps."

Dax and Sebastian had taken to joining them for the evening meal. It wasn't a formal affair by town standards, and Eliza found she enjoyed the relaxed atmosphere.

Dax was polite if distant, but it was not as if he were keeping himself from her. It was more that he was distracted by something. She watched them as they took wine and brandy in the drawing room at supper, and while he joined in the sharing of childhood stories and outlandish tales, he was somehow removed from it all. As if whatever it was that occupied his mind was so important as to consume him entirely.

A very secret part of her wished it had something to do with her.

He hadn't returned to her rooms since that night. Every night after supper, he escorted her to her door and bid her goodnight. Again, he wasn't rude. He was simply distracted, and she couldn't help but wonder if it had to do with his vow to show her he loved her.

"No, I don't think right now would be ideal."

"Perhaps on the child's first birthday then," Johanna suggested.

"You're rather acerbic today," Louisa said.

Johanna shook her head. "Is that so? If that's the case, I should like to say another thing. It's rather curious how you find yourself with Waverly."

Louisa's face went an instant shade of tomato. "I don't know of what you're speaking."

Eliza sat up. She'd wondered the same thing after watching her sister carry on with Sebastian. Her sister was always determined to be the bright spot in the room, but with Sebastian, it was almost as if she'd accepted it as a personal challenge, an affront to the duke's naturally cool demeanor.

"Hardly. I can't tell if you wish to challenge the man to a duel or propose marriage. Which is it?"

Louisa picked up her ribbons again. "I haven't decided actually."

This made Johanna laugh.

"Would you truly consider marriage to the Duke of Waverly?" Eliza had to ask the question because she'd never considered Louisa marrying. She supposed if Viv had her way, they would all be married off. But Louisa was dear somehow. In Eliza's mind, she'd always be her little sister in need of just a touch more help than the rest.

Louisa shrugged. "As I said, I haven't decided."

Johanna took a sip of lemonade before saying, "Please do inform us when you have it sorted. I would love to be there for either occasion."

Louisa's smile was blinding. "I shall."

Mrs. Donnelly appeared then, rolling a cart of sweets and

a fresh pitcher of lemonade onto the terrace with her. She paused in replacing the lemonade.

"Oh, Your Grace, I do beg your pardon." The housekeeper's eyes raced across the tableau of invitation carcasses strewn across the table. "His Grace has already seen to the invitations for the ball. Had he not informed you?"

Eliza stilled. "No, he did not."

Mrs. Donnelly folded her hands along her stomach. "I'm so very sorry, Your Grace. It must be my mistake. George took them to be posted last week. Should you like to see one of them?"

"Yes, I would like that very much."

Mrs. Donnelly slipped back into the house.

"Whatever does that mean?" Louisa said, setting down the ribbons with enough of a thump to articulate her disappointment.

"I don't know," Eliza whispered.

"Does this have something to do with that Isley woman?" Johanna asked.

Eliza shook her head. "I don't know. Andrew hasn't returned my letter yet."

But even as she said the words, her mind spun. Was this what had Dax distracted? Did it have something to do with the ball? He said he would make things right, but how did the ball's invitations do that?

Mrs. Donnelly returned within moments and handed Eliza a silver tray containing a single invitation.

"Thank you," she said to the housekeeper.

Mrs. Donnelly bowed. "Please let me know if there will be anything else." She slipped back into the house without a sound.

Eliza picked up the cream paper and set the tray down on the table nearly upsetting her glass of lemonade as she wasn't looking. Louisa and Johanna vacated their chairs and hurried to lean over Eliza's shoulder and read the invitation.

The invitation was simple in design, drawing the viewer's attention to the script, for the script was the true masterpiece.

The Duke of Ashbourne requests your presence at the traditional Ashbourne summer ball where he is proud to introduce his new wife, the Duchess of Ashbourne.

Your reply is appreciated.

THE WORDS WERE direct and simple, the remainder of the invitation detailing the specifics of the ball, but Eliza could see none of it.

Where he is proud to introduce his wife.

"Dear God, he's recreated the ball where he was humiliated." Johanna pressed a hand to her mouth as if surprised she had uttered the words.

Eliza blinked and read the invitation again, but the words remained the same.

"Surely, he can't think—" Louisa choked on the words, swallowed, and tried again. "He doesn't think you won't show because of what he did. Does he?"

"More importantly, will you?"

Eliza shook her head and raised a hand, silencing them both. "One at a time. What did you say?"

It took a physical effort to pull herself from the words of the invitation, and she hadn't understood either sister.

"Would you truly not show to the ball because he kissed Lady Isley?" Louisa's eyes were wider than usual.

"Of course, I wouldn't. It's my duty to—" She stopped, the words catching in her throat.

"He thought Lady Isley showing to her proposal ball was a given as well," Johanna whispered the very thing racing through Eliza's mind.

"And she humiliated him." Louisa took the invitation and held it closer, studying it. "He's made the ball about you now instead of a mere tradition. The guests will be satisfied with nothing but you. No food, drink, or music will suffice as a substitute."

Johanna released a breath. "He's given you all the power."

Eliza's hands strayed to her stomach again, and she realized her sisters were right. Somehow in the past few weeks, cradling the baby she held within her had started to bring her comfort. It was a wonder Dax didn't already suspect.

And now this.

"Power?" Eliza questioned, although she feared she already knew what her sister meant.

Johanna crouched in front of her, meeting her gaze. "He's letting you decide, Eliza. He's telling you he wants to trust someone again, and he's leaving it up to you."

Eliza licked her lips. "But I would never neglect my duty."

"This isn't about duty." Johanna stood and took the invitation from Louisa. "This is about love."

"What am I supposed to do about that then?" She blinked up at the pair of them as they hovered over her.

Louisa's smile was quick. "We must ensure Mrs. Fletcher's gown for you is spectacular."

* * *

THE GOWN WAS INDEED SPECTACULAR, far more beautiful than anything Eliza had acquired at a modiste in London.

It was constructed of the finest sapphire silk that showcased her complexion the way it was always meant to be with her dark hair appearing alluring and lush, her creamy skin kissed by the sun until she simply glowed. The generous neckline would once have done nothing more than amplify her shortcomings, but now she filled it out quite nicely, and dare she say, she had actual womanly bits.

It was a marvel of some proportion, but she was too distracted by the rest of the gown. Mrs. Fletcher had done a clever fold of the fabric across her midriff, concealing the soft roundness that had developed there in the past week. The skirts flared in a tantalizing bell. There was nothing to be said except the silhouette of the gown made Eliza appear voluptuous for the first time in her life.

She cradled the babe within her, speaking softly. "I suppose motherhood suits me."

"It certainly does."

She started at the sound of Louisa's voice behind her as she'd been studying her reflection in her dressing room mirror.

Louisa looked exquisite as always, but her eyes were just a bit damp with unshed tears. Johanna gawked from behind her.

"You look beautiful." Johanna's tone was one of disbelief.

Eliza turned back to the mirror. "Do you really think so?"

Johanna stepped into the room and joined her in front of the mirror. "All this time, this is what you truly look like and none of us knew."

"I think Ashbourne knew." Louisa spoke the words from behind them, and they turned to her. Her smile was soft as she said, "It's time for you to join your husband in the receiving line."

Eliza's stomach clenched at the words.

The day of the ball had dawned with rain striking the windows, a storm pushing in off the sea. It had cleared quickly though, leaving a refreshing coolness about that beckoned the coming arrival of fall. She wasn't sure how the summer had passed so quickly or how it could have been such a whirlwind of emotions. She couldn't have guessed what would have happened when Viv had returned to see her sisters safely wed.

Eliza certainly hadn't expected Dax.

She drew a fortifying breath and gathered her skirts.

"What must be done must be done." She kissed each of them of the cheek with a promise to meet up with them later and went out in the hall to make her way to the vestibule where they were to receive their guests.

She was nearly to the front hall when the rumble of carriages reached her, and she peeked out the nearest window. She blinked, unsure if she'd seen correctly. There was already a line snaking its way down the drive of the finest carriages she'd ever witnessed. Each one was more dazzling than the first.

She turned her attention to the clock standing guard at the top of the stairs and was shocked to find it was hardly the hour when the ball was to begin. Lud, to think of the crush that awaited them already.

She hastened her step, making her way down to the vestibule without pausing, wanting nothing more than to get this over with. It was why she wasn't thinking when she stepped down onto the marble floor and nearly collided with Dax.

"Oh." The sound was light and breathless in the cavernous space, and she drew back involuntarily, picking up her skirts as she did so.

Dax was as she'd expected him to be, but still, it took her

breath away. Gorgeous was the word her sisters had used, and Eliza knew it to be fitting. He was dressed all in black with only the white of his cravat to offset it, and it only served to make him appear more intimidating.

But the way he looked at her stopped her heart.

His gaze was intense, but it was the shock of his parted lips that drew her attention. She'd surprised him. It was writ across his face, and for one silly moment, pride and triumph surged through her.

How silly. Such things were so terribly superficial, and yet, she'd never felt pretty. When Dax looked at her then, she did though, and it felt so, so terribly good.

"Hello, Dax," she said with a soft smile.

He opened his mouth, but he said nothing, his lips closing on air as he continued to stare.

It was as if she stood at the top of a waterfall, and the energy of the falling water pulsed beneath her feet. Anticipation thrummed through her, and her breath quickened. Something was about to happen. She didn't know what or how she could possibly know that, but she did. She could feel it. It was in the intensity of her husband's gaze, the way her hands shook ever so slightly against her skirts, in the way she couldn't quite seem to draw a full breath.

She knew he had meant to recreate the ball where he'd suffered his humiliation, but there was something else unsaid.

He held out a hand to her, a smile coming to his lips.

He wasn't going to tell her what more there was. It seemed he was going to show her.

He drew her hand through his elbow, bringing her closer to him than she'd been since that night he'd kissed her so abruptly. Her heart raced, and she had to swallow to regain her composure.

"Hello, Eliza." The way he spoke her name was deep and inviting, and it sent a thrill racing down her spine.

She knew that voice, but she'd never heard it outside of their bedroom walls. She shivered and tightened her grip on his arm.

"Guests have already begun to arrive." She barely got the words out, and then, she didn't know why she spoke them. Were they a warning for him or for her?

He leaned closer, his smile going up on one side. "Unfortunately."

He spoke only the single word, and it was enough to leave her raw. Before she could find out what he meant or what it was he planned, he swept her down the hall to where they would stand to receive their guests and gave Stephens the nod to open the door.

Peeling each layer of clothing from her body would not have left her wanting more than she did then.

What had he meant when he said it was unfortunate the guests had arrived? What was it he had planned? What did he mean to show her?

It was all she could do to maintain her composure as he introduced her to dukes and duchesses, earls and countesses, barons and viscounts. It seemed no one wanted to miss an opportunity to see just who had caught the Jilted Duke.

She couldn't blame them. She was just as surprised as they were, likely more even.

Here she was, once the most common wallflower, now standing beside Daxton Kane, the Duke of Ashbourne, as his wife. Nothing could have surprised her more.

At least, she thought there wasn't until after an interminable time later, the receiving line had dwindled, and the first strands of music filtered through the air. Without a word, Dax took her arm again, and she squared her shoulders preparing to enter the ballroom and join the rest of their guests.

Propriety would have Dax selecting someone of appropriate standing with whom to partner for the first dance, and she turned, hoping to find Sebastian. If she were to start the dancing, she would at least have someone with whom she could converse.

Only Dax never released her arm.

Instead he drew her out on the dance floor with him, sweeping her into his arms as he prepared them for a waltz.

Her breath froze in her lungs, and she felt the hundreds of gazes of a crowded ballroom upon her. The whispers started almost immediately, and even over the notes of the violin and the thrum of a cello she could hear them.

A husband never danced with his wife unless he were showing her undue attention. By dancing with her now at the start of their ball, Dax was showing everyone just how important Eliza was.

If she had felt beautiful before, she felt invincible now. Heads turned, whispers died away, and the entire attention of the crowd was on her.

So she raised her chin and smiled.

He returned her smile as he swept her into the first turn of the waltz as the orchestra soared to life. Soon others melted onto the dance floor, but she didn't notice them. She saw only her husband and the way he watched her as he carried them across the floor.

One dance became another and another, and soon she was handed off from one partner to the next. A duke here and an earl there and then a marquess. Never before had she been so popular a partner as she was that night, but even as she moved from gentleman to gentleman, something wasn't quite right.

Her eyes searched for Dax among the crowd, and only

once in a while did she catch sight of him. He did his duties as host, dancing with all of the appropriate partners and conversing with the men in the card room.

Never one to ignore a suspicion, she couldn't help but notice the lingering unease that sat on her shoulders. Finally, Sebastian took pity on her and stepped in to partner her in a quadrille, which upon finishing, he escorted her directly to the refreshment table where she was swallowed up by her sisters.

They handed her a glass of lemonade and pushed her into a chair, her feet sobbing with the relief of sitting.

It was Sebastian who spoke. "You're a lot like a pair of oxen I know."

She blinked up at him but couldn't stop the smile when both of her sisters gasped.

"That's rather rude," Johanna exclaimed.

Eliza raised her glass. "There is a magnificent pair of oxen on the estate that I would quite enjoy being compared to."

Louisa only shook her head, making a tsking noise as she studied Sebastian with rapt attention.

"Still, it's rather not done." Johanna put her hands to her hips as if to emphasize her point.

Sebastian waved a hand carelessly. "Have you seen the work a pair of oxen can accomplish? I'm not sure there's a higher compliment than being compared to one."

As riveting as this line of conversation was, the unease began to prickle its way up her arms once more, and she interjected, "Has anyone seen Ashbourne?"

"He was at the whist table with the Earl of Westin last I saw. Shall I fetch him?" Louisa offered.

Eliza shook her head and stood, giving her empty lemonade glass to her sister.

"No, I shouldn't have you fret yourself. It will be nice to have a turn about the place after so much dancing." She tossed a smile in Sebastian's direction, which he returned with a slight nod of acknowledgment.

She made her way across the room to where the ballroom spilled into a suite of drawing rooms that had been set up with gaming tables. The room was hazy with the smoke of men's cheroots and pipes, and the din of voices was even greater than the ballroom proper.

She took only a couple of hesitant steps within, sure Dax couldn't be found inside, when motion to her left caught her eye. There was a corridor just off the card rooms that led to the retiring rooms, and there she saw Dax, standing with his back to the gaming tables as Stephens handed him a tray with a folded piece of paper atop it.

The prickle of unease exploded into a roar as she saw Dax take the paper, open it, and read it as if it contained a message. He nodded in the affirmative to Stephens, who gave a bow and departed. Dax turned, tucking the paper into his pocket and slipped out into the corridor.

She followed, of course. Dax didn't know about the day Bethany had confronted her on the beach as there hadn't been an occasion to tell him. She was alert to the undercurrents, and feeling the sway of betrayal, she slipped into the corridor just moments after her husband.

His footsteps were silent as he made his way from the ballroom, moving ever deeper into the house, silence growing around them. She realized with a jolt he was going to his study. She hung back, letting the space between them grow as she knew which way to go. When he did, indeed, enter his study, she paused.

Perhaps she had been wrong.

It could have been a message of urgent business, and Sheridan had requested his presence.

She moved to take a step back when her heel caught on a bit of fabric. She bent and picked up the white, starched bit of linen. It was a handkerchief. Her first inclination was to hold it to her nose to discover the telltale scent of perfume, but she paused. The handkerchief was plain and unadorned, not that of a lady's at all.

It was at that moment that footsteps behind her had her swinging about. She pressed a hand to her jumping heart when she found George the footman coming down the corridor with a metal bucket used for cleaning the hearths.

"Your Grace," he said upon seeing her.

She smiled. "George, would you please go let Henry out of my room? He'll be able to find me, and I believe I shall need him. Do hurry please."

George set down the bucket where he stood and with a wave took off in the direction of their personal quarters.

Clutching the handkerchief in her palm, she strode down the corridor and without hesitation entered her husband's study.

CHAPTER 17

*H*e had prepared for a backhanded attempt such as this, and so he wasn't at all surprised when Stephens had appeared with the note from Bethany.

He'd read it quickly, even less surprised to find its contents rather appalling, and without hesitation had gone to put an end to the nonsense. He wasn't sure how, as he was quite certain Bethany would not see reason or fact, but he had to stop her from meddling in his life.

It no longer mattered if she had hoped for a future that saw them together. It no longer mattered if her father had accepted another offer for her hand. It only mattered that he loved his wife. Eliza was right. He had had to let Bethany go if he were ever to love again, and he had. Only it had taken betraying the trust of his wife to realize it.

He was righting that wrong now, and he wanted nothing more to do with Bethany when he strode into his study.

He didn't bother with a greeting as he shut the door behind him.

"Using threats of violence to get my attention," he said, holding up the note she had sent him.

"It is only a threat against myself." She was crying already, and her voice was wet with tears.

"I don't believe you," he said calmly. "You've never been one for expending unnecessary effort. What is it you really want?"

At some point in his walk from the ballroom, he'd come to realize Bethany could very well be playing this game now because she wanted something else. Perhaps it was to humiliate Eliza for taking the place she saw as rightfully hers. Or perhaps it was for something far more sinister. He had to remember that and keep the space between them.

This was something better thought in practice than in reality because she launched herself at him the first chance she got. He stood just inside the door with the clutter of the study between them. She took no notice, knocking into a side table and spilling the basket of odds and ends beneath it as she made her way over to him.

"Dax, you must listen to me. I can't live like this. You must do something."

He raised an eyebrow and took a step back. "I must do something? You married a marquess. Your life could not be all that miserable."

She balked at his words, reeling back against the sofa.

"Ronald is not the man he once was." Her voice had sobered somewhat and when she spoke Ronald's name it took on an edge.

He crossed his arms. "You would have me believe that Ronald is mistreating you."

He didn't miss how her eyes slipped away from his and lingered on the carpet overlong.

"I never spoke such things, have I?" When she looked up at him, she moved only her eyes, keeping her chin down so as to give him a baleful look.

His suspicions raged hotter, and he dropped his arms,

sauntering over to the cabinet where he kept his store of whiskey.

"So it's just that you're unhappy then, is that it?"

He heard her straighten behind him, the rustle of skirts and the soft screech of the leather on the sofa warning him of her approach. He straightened and sidestepped behind his desk with his glass of whiskey before she could reach her target.

She faltered against a chair, her hands digging into the cushions.

"You don't know what it's like, Dax. You don't know what it's like to know such coldness. Have you ever been so alone that you crave the company of the staff just to know you're alive?"

He turned on her, the whiskey in his glass sloshing.

"I do actually. It was the night of the ball I had thrown in honor of our engagement, but you didn't show."

She paled at his words, and he knew he'd cut her.

"I already told you what happened—"

"Actually, you didn't," he cut her off. He swallowed the last of his drink and put his glass down with a hard thud on his desk. "You said your father accepted another offer for your hand, but you did not say where you were that night."

She opened her mouth once without speaking and shut it again as if to consider her words. She seemed to come to a decision, and when she lifted her eyes, he saw more tears there. Only he also noticed her cheeks were suddenly pink with color as if she had to put forth considerable effort for those tears.

He stilled, knowing something wasn't quite as it seemed.

"Oh Dax, it was just awful. I was on my way there when my father suddenly stopped me. He locked me in my rooms to keep me from going to you."

"That must have been terrible. Being locked in your

rooms on such a night. It was the end of the season after all, and as I recall the weather was particularly unbearable. It must have been stifling in your rooms."

Her eyes widened as tears speckled her eyelashes. "Oh, it was!" Her words rushed together as she seemed to pick up interest in her story. "It was so hot and stuffy I almost couldn't breathe. It was unimaginable, Dax. The suffering."

She had lunged toward him with her last words, but he sidestepped again, putting the sofa between them.

"Yes, the suffering," he said drolly. "Only it was April, in fact, and quite rainy and cold. Had you truly been locked in your rooms that night you would have remembered that."

Her face cleared suddenly, and the tears that still streaked her face seemed ridiculous.

"Where were you, Bethany?" It would be the final time he would ask it.

For the first time since seeing her again, he thought he saw real honesty on her face. Her features relaxed into a semblance of the woman he once knew, and the woman he thought he once loved.

But it lasted only moments, and he might as well have imagined it for she stepped forward in a rush before he had time to react and threw herself into his arms, her lips colliding with his.

* * *

ELIZA ENTERED the study at the precise moment Bethany Danvers, the Marchioness of Isley, kissed her husband.

Again.

"This sort of thing grows rather dull. Wouldn't you agree?" she asked.

At her first word, Dax shoved Lady Isley away from him, tripping over the low table behind him in the process. It sent him sprawling backwards at it propelled Lady Isley away and into a chair. Eliza didn't recall seeing Lady Isley's name on the guest list, and for just a second, a surge of trepidation spiked through her. Maybe she was wrong about all this. Maybe she was destined to be a wallflower forever, trapped in a loveless marriage.

She raised her chin and kicked the thought away. She was done being a wallflower and the coward it made her. She had been happy here at Ashbourne Manor, was still happy if only...

If only she had her husband back.

Dax righted himself against the sofa, his eyes flying to hers. "Eliza—"

She held up a hand to cut him off. It was her turn to ask the questions.

By that time, Lady Isley had shoved the hair that had fallen from her elaborate twistings away from her face and righted herself in the chair. When she met Eliza's gaze, her smile was feral.

"You," she hissed.

Eliza placed her fisted hands on her hips. "Yes, it is. I have a rather annoying habit of always being me, and you have a rather annoying habit of trying to steal my husband. Now why is that?"

Lady Isley gripped the chair with both hands as she levered herself up. It wasn't impressive as the woman could hardly be more than a meter and a half tall.

"He's mine, spinster, and it will do you well to remember that."

"Ah, I see where there's been a mistake. You see, I actually married Daxton Kane, the Duke of Ashbourne, while it was you who jilted him. I could see where this would cause confusion."

Eliza could not have imagined what Lady Isley expected,

but it was certain it wasn't Eliza's sharp tongue. Lady Isley's nostrils flared as her eyes grew wide. The marchioness took a threatening step forward.

"How dare you!" she seethed. "How dare you ruin the beautiful thing Dax and I have."

"Oh, but you're mistaken again. What you and Dax had was nothing but an illusion orchestrated by you. You never loved Dax, but you did wish to acquire the duchess title, is that not true?"

It had been entirely a stab in the dark, but when Lady Isley's eyes shifted quickly to the left, Eliza knew she had her.

Lady Isley recovered herself, straightening her shoulders. "I will not stand for such lies. How dare you impugn my person."

"How dare you try to extort money from my husband."

It was as if all the air in the room was sucked from it in but a moment. Eliza had been peripherally aware of Dax in the background, standing rather unkempt from his topple into the sofa, staring open mouthed at his wife, but at her pronouncement, his lips snapped shut and his eyes narrowed as he moved his gaze to Lady Isley.

Lady Isley went utterly pale. "What are you suggesting?"

Eliza took a moment to ponder the room, letting Lady Isley writhe for just a bit longer.

"I'm not sure actually. I'm operating on only enough information with which to build the scaffolding, but the structure of the thing is rather lost to me. I suppose it's because I'm not inclined to betrayal. I think that's why I prefer dogs to people most likely. They don't know how to be disloyal."

Lady Isley sucked in a breath. "I have never betrayed Dax."

Eliza snorted. "Oh, quite the contrary. You've been leading him around by training strings for quite some time now. I think it's time to end that. After all, at some point Ashbourne should start respecting himself, don't you think?"

She could feel Dax's hot gaze on her, and she knew she'd struck a nerve. It didn't matter. He needed to hear what she had to say. She might have cowed to every belle society had produced, but here in her home, she would not stand for it any longer.

"You manipulate Ashbourne's feelings to get what you want, isn't that true?"

Lady Isley's hands had fisted in the skirts of her gown. "How dare you," she repeated, her tone dropping dangerously low.

"And now you're in need of money, so you come to him again." Eliza held up a single finger. "What I can't figure out is how you plan to go about it. Perhaps you plan to be his mistress and hope he might support you financially? I've heard such an arrangement might be done."

Lady Isley's eyes widened, and her jaw threatened to snap clean off. "I will not respond to such scathing lies."

"The fact that you require funds is not a lie nor your attempt at getting the money from my husband. But I wonder. Why is it that you believed your plan to become his mistress might fail?"

Like a bolt of lightning splitting the night sky, Lady Isley's face suddenly cleared. "How do you know that?" she whispered.

Eliza's smile was slow, and she realized this must be how Henry felt when he knew he was on the scent.

"Because of this." She opened her palm and let the handkerchief she'd found in the corridor dangle between two fingers.

Lady Isley gasped a breath. "Where did you get that?"

"If you're going to attempt blackmail, you should really be

more careful." Eliza held the incriminating linen between both of her hands. "Now then. I'd like to know why."

Color had appeared in Lady Isley's cheeks, and Eliza wondered if she'd pushed the woman too far. The marchioness took another threatening step forward, but she was stopped by a sudden low growl coming from the door.

"Ah, Henry. Come here, boy. Keep the terrible woman away. I wouldn't want her ruining my pretty gown."

Henry trotted into the room and stood dutifully between her and Lady Isley. The marchioness eyed the dog as if he were nothing more than a common rat.

"Lady Isley?" Eliza prompted, and Henry gave another growl, choosing to show just one side of his fangs this time.

Lady Isley jumped back, her lip curling up, words spurting from her mouth as she tried to get behind the chair she had just vacated.

"It's you!" she spat. "You're the reason my plan wouldn't work, you wretched spinster."

Eliza tilted her head. "Me? Whatever have I done?"

Lady Isley threw out an accusing finger pointed directly at Dax. "He loves you. He actually loves you, you ugly cow."

For a moment, her confidence fled, and her gaze shifted to Dax, who still stood motionless beside the sofa. He loved her? But there was Lady Isley, what she had done to him, the way he—

"I knew the moment I kissed him my plan wouldn't work. He was already in love with you!" Lady Isley hurtled the words as if they were an insult.

Eliza couldn't look away from Dax, realization crashing through her until she nearly forgot entirely where they were. Only when Lady Isley spoke again did she come to her senses.

"He didn't want to kiss me!" Her tone had turned sullen and whining. "How dare you rob me of him!"

Eliza recalled the handkerchief in her hands. She held it up again. "So that's when you decided on blackmail?"

Lady Isley lunged, only to be driven back by Henry's growl. "I didn't want to get him involved. He's too stupid for such things, but you left me no choice."

"I see."

Finally, Dax took a step forward. "Would you care to enlighten the rest of us about what is going on here?"

Lady Isley snarled. "Ask your wife."

Eliza couldn't help the laugh. "Oh, there's no need to ask me. I'd be happy to show you."

Lady Isley froze, her eyes on the handkerchief. "What do you mean?" she nearly whispered, her anger quickly being replaced by fear.

"I believe your intent was to lure my husband into this room only to be caught in a compromising position by your husband at which point Lord Isley would demand money to keep the scandal quiet. Do I have it now?"

"You can't prove it." Lady Isley pushed back the hair from her face. "You can't prove anything."

Eliza smiled, enjoying every second of watching Lady Isley squirm.

"Oh, but I can," she whispered and then lowered the handkerchief in front of Henry. "Henry, dear," she said before leaning down until her lips almost touched the dog's ear. Finally, when the tension grew so great she thought Lady Isley might snap in two, she whispered, "Find it."

Henry sniffed at the handkerchief for but a second before he gave a cry of chase and was off like a shot. He tore through the study, nose to the ground, the chairs, the sofa, even Dax himself, as he throttled through the space. Lady Isley screamed and tried to climb the chair she'd been using as a barricade as Henry plunged through the room.

Eliza watched him, glorying in the beauty of Henry exercising his natural talents. It was a sight to behold, but it ended all too soon as she knew it would. Henry wasted no time in finding his prey.

The dog had reached the terrace doors, which were draped for the night, and dove within the folds. Within seconds, his baying cry turned to the snarls of a dog acquiring his target.

It also helped when the man began to scream curses.

"Blighted son of a whore! Get this mangy creature off of me!"

Henry erupted from the drapes, his teeth firmly clenched on the seat of Ronald Danvers, the Marquess of Isley. The marquess batted ineffectually behind him as he couldn't see the dog that pulled him from his hiding place.

Eliza allowed Henry a few more moments to have his fun. When Lady Isley's screaming grew to be too much, Eliza relented.

"Henry, release," she said calmly, and the dog immediately let go of the marquess and marched over to her, resuming his position in front of her. "Good boy," she said, giving him a hearty scratch between his ears.

She looked up to find her husband studying her, his lips slightly parted. His gaze drifted between his old friend and her, seemingly unable to form words.

Lady Isley's screams had melted to pitiful cries while Lord Isley held both hands to his behind in an apparent attempt to soothe the place where Henry had grabbed hold.

"Well, go on, man," Lord Isley mumbled, "have your say." He directed this to Dax, but Dax only studied the man before turning back to her.

"I'm still a bit lost on one point," he said.

She raised an eyebrow, and he continued.

"How did you know Lady Isley required money?"

Eliza gave a quick nod. "I wrote to my brother, of course.

He inquired into the affairs of the Isley estate, and it appears the title is…well, quite broke."

Lord Isley scoffed. "Damn your tongue!"

"Don't speak to my wife that way." Nothing could silence the room faster than the sound of murder in Dax's voice.

He considered the man who was once his childhood friend, and Eliza's heart squeezed with all Dax must be thinking. She wished none of this were true. She wished she had been wrong about Lady Isley. But more, she wanted to ensure her husband never suffered such betrayal again, not when she could prevent it.

"It's gambling debts, isn't it, Ronald?" Dax finally asked.

Lord Isley looked away without answering.

"I thought you had stopped such childish things when you left Eton."

Lord Isley gave him a scathing look but said nothing.

Dax turned his attention to Lady Isley. Eliza wasn't sure what she had been expecting. A small, petulant part of her wanted to see Dax rail at his former love for her duplicitousness, but the rational part of her knew that would do him no good.

But strangely enough, Dax said nothing at all. Instead, he walked to the terrace doors, and pulling a drape aside, unlatched a single door and pushed it open.

He turned back to Lord and Lady Isley and said, "Get out of my house."

Lady Isley squeaked a cry of repugnance. "Surely, you can't be serious. It's dark out there, and we're so close to the cliffs. We could—"

"You should have thought of that before you decided to blackmail me." Dax's voice never rose.

Lady Isley scrambled off her chair. "Dax, listen, aren't we old friends? Surely, you can see—"

"I said get out of my house, Isley. I've given you enough of

258

my attention for this lifetime. All of it belongs to my wife now. So get out."

Lord Isley, ashamed, beaten, and cowardly, scampered out the door and into the night without so much as meeting his old friend's gaze.

Lady Isley had more nerve, which she turned on Eliza.

"You—"

It was the only word she got out before Henry gave a ferocious bark and lunged. Lady Isley screamed and plunged into the cold night. Dax shut the door and snapped the latch with a thud of finality.

He stood like that for some time, his fingers still on the latch he had used to shut out his once precious childhood friends. Eliza's stomach churned with emotions. She wanted to go to him, to put her arms around him in some semblance of comfort. He'd just had his entire childhood unraveled in a single night. A childhood was a thing meant to be savored, a time when innocence kept the scary parts of the world at bay. That was a lie to him now.

But she couldn't move for another thought consumed her.

Dax loved her.

Had loved her even from before Lady Isley had tried to entrap him.

She licked her lips and cradled her stomach, only to drop her hands when she realized what she was doing.

Finally, Dax turned. She readied herself. He showed time and again that night that he did, in fact, love her. Lady Isley's confession was only the last nail to be driven into the truth. Eliza *knew* it now. She could feel it coursing through her as if Dax's love were a physical thing.

She hadn't expected her husband to love her, and she found it was far scarier than anything else she had faced yet.

Dax walked toward her slowly, and with each footstep,

her heart raced a little faster. Only he didn't come to her. When he reached Henry, he knelt, scooping up the dog's face in his hands and pressing his forehead to his.

"Thank you, my boy," he whispered, and Eliza's heart splintered into a million beautiful pieces.

Henry gave his face a lick, his tail thumping so hard it beat against Eliza's thigh. Finally, Dax stood and met her gaze.

Tension whirred between them so thick it threatened to suffocate her, and before she could stop herself, she blurted, "Do you really love me?"

His smile was slow and tempting as he closed the distance between them. This time he took her face into his hands and pressed his forehead to hers.

"Are you never going to let me have the last say?"

She swallowed. "I would if you were more efficient about it."

He smiled when he kissed her. "Yes, Eliza Darby, I do love you."

"It's Eliza Kane, actually."

He laughed as she returned his kiss.

When he finally pulled away, it was only to gather her against him.

"I'm sorry I didn't tell you sooner. I had only just realized it that night I came to apologize." He narrowed his gaze. "I'm sure you have something to say about that as well."

"I do," she said and wrapped her arms more tightly about him. "I love you, too."

His smile showed his surprise, and she knew he hadn't expected her to say it. She reveled in that smile until reality came crashing back.

"Speaking of realizing things, there's something I must tell you."

His smile wavered. "What is it?"

"Do you recall our bargain?" She licked her lips, suddenly nervous.

He gave a quick nod. "Ah, yes. The bargain. I apologize for being remiss on my part. I was momentarily befuddled."

She reached up a single finger to press into the cleft of his chin. "Well, about that…"

 *pril 1840*

"I THINK we should name him after your father."

Her husband's frown was swift. "We are not calling him Herbert. I would not do such a heinous thing to my son."

Eliza cradled the babe against her up-drawn knees, marveling at his tiny features and the way he cradled his hands just beneath his chin.

"Well, we're not naming him after my father. Clive works for some gentlemen, but this little one doesn't really seem like a Clive."

Dax adjusted the pillows behind them so he could draw his wife and child against his side.

"We could name him for your brother."

She wrinkled her nose. "Andrew would hate that. He doesn't care for such attention."

"A middle name then," Dax suggested.

She rested her head back against his shoulder. "I think that will do, but that still leaves us without a first name."

They were nestled in their bed at Ashbourne House as the rain pattered against the windows and a fire crackled in the hearth. Mrs. Fitzhugh had brought a cart of tea earlier, and while Dax had consumed nearly all the petite fours in a fit of new father nervousness, Eliza had downed nearly the entire pot of tea as she was finding motherhood particularly acute at producing thirst.

While she had wanted to have her baby along her beloved cliffs at Ashbourne Manor, Dax had insisted they come into London where they were nearer the doctors, but the birth had been uneventful, much as her pregnancy had been. She was finding pregnancy and motherhood suited her, which was pleasing as she'd never doubted it for a moment.

It was nice to have her sisters close though, and as the season had just commenced, Viv had insisted Johanna and Louisa remain in town so as to best position themselves for the marriage mart. Eliza felt an immense amount of relief at not having to join her sisters in the annually appalling ritual of acquiring a husband.

She quite liked the one she had caught last season, and she was happy to remain ensconced in their home with him and their newborn son.

She traced the delicate arch of her son's eyebrow, her mind rattling through names.

"What about George?" she said several minutes later.

"George is a fine name." Dax turned his head, and she could feel his gaze on her. "Where did you get the name George?"

She gave a small shrug. "Oh, nowhere in particular," she answered even as her eyes drifted to where Henry lay sprawled on the rug in front of the fire.

He had become even more attached as she'd grown with

pregnancy, and she was fairly sure he was never going to leave their son's side as he'd already been over to explore the new baby with heart-shattering earnestness.

Dax stroked their son's cheek with a solitary finger.

"George it is then," he said.

She smiled and nestled back into her husband's arm even more. He turned his head and pressed a kiss to her cheek.

"Thank you for my son," he whispered, and the words sent her heart galloping.

But then his lips began to explore, nuzzling her neck.

"Dax." She spoke the word as both question and reprimand.

He pulled back his head. "As I recall, our bargain was for the heir and the spare, was it not?"

She met his playful gaze. "I believe it was."

His smile turned to a smirk. "Well, I wouldn't want to be accused of inefficiency again, now would I?"

He kissed her even as she laughed.

Jessie decided to be a writer because the job of Indiana Jones was already filled.

Taking her history degree dangerously, Jessie tells the stories of courageous heroines, the men who dared to love them, and the world that tried to defeat them.

Jessie makes her home in New Hampshire where she lives with her husband and two very opinionated Basset hounds. For more, visit her website at jessieclever.com.

Printed in Great Britain
by Amazon

54250338R00161